IN THE MIDST OF IT ALL

IN THE MIDST
OF IT ALL

SHONDA CHEEKES

A
PUBLICATION

A STREBOR BOOKS INTERNATIONAL LLC PUBLICATION
DISTRIBUTED BY SIMON & SCHUSTER, INC.

Published by

SBI

Strebor Books International LLC
P.O. Box 6505
Largo, MD 20792

ISBN 0-7394-5765-9

Distributed by Simon & Schuster, Inc.
1230 Avenue of the Americas
New York, NY 10020
1-800-223-2336

Cover design: www.mariondesigns.com

Manufactured and Printed in the United States

**TO THE VICTIMS AND SURVIVORS OF 9/11
WE WILL NEVER FORGET**

*Most of us spend our lives
as if we have another one
in the bank*

Ben Irwin

CHAPTER 1

ASIA

Breathe, Asia! Breathe! Just open your mouth and breathe, damn it!

I sat straight up as I struggled to keep from choking to death on my own saliva. I could feel Johnny's weight shift in the bed as he jumped up to aid me. The feel of his hand making contact with my back was a welcomed one.

"Come on, baby! Get yourself together! That's it."

My eyes adjusted to the outside light shining through the open window.

"You're having a bad dream again. It's okay," he said as he continued to pat my back in hopes of helping to stop the choking.

I took a deep breath in between the coughing and gulping that produced little burps.

"That's it, baby." His voice was now a soothing tone.

It was the third time this month I'd had the "drowning dream" and I was glad Johnny was here this time. This time was worse than any other time. I was scared I would've drowned if he hadn't been with me. The coughing only came after I was able to pull the first gush of air into my lungs.

"You've got me scared to leave you alone," Johnny said as he continued to rub my back through a sleep-induced haze.

"I'm okay," I said in a breathless whisper. I was now sitting on the edge of the bed with my fists pressed deep into the mattress. "I need something to drink." A cold glass of water would help to put out the fire burning in my throat.

"You want me to get it for you?"

I shook my head side to side. "No, I've got it. You go back to sleep."

I searched the floor for my favorite nightshirt that had gotten discarded earlier. I slipped off the bed and padded my way down the hall toward the front of the apartment to the kitchen; pulling the oversized blue shirt over my head. I grabbed a glass from the cabinet and almost dropped it due to the violent shake dance my hands were doing. I leaned on the counter to catch myself.

What in the hell is wrong with me?

A moment later I heard the faint squeak of my bedroom door as Johnny opened it wider. The sound of his heavy footsteps followed. He had come looking for me. The clock on the microwave illuminated a green glow; it was well after two in the morning.

"Why are you standing in the dark?"

I looked up at him. A picture of manly perfection. All six-point-five and three quarter inches of him. Beautiful chocolate—not the watered-down version either. Mahogany skin covered every inch of him; except for his ass and my favorite part—the mighty dick. Both of those areas were at least one—maybe two—shades darker.

Johnny stood a few feet from me in all his glory. A smile crossed my face as I slowly took inventory of what I'd been getting for the past ten months. He was definitely packing. As Aunt Mae would say, "Cock Diesel, baby!" Most importantly, he knew what to do with it. Don't you hate it when a man has all the right equipment, but doesn't have a clue what to do with it? Hmm, not Johnny. He'd taken me to new heights sexually. The things he'd taught me had given me a newfound respect for not only my body, but the female body in general! That chant, *"Use what we got, to get what we want,"* has an entire new meaning now. To think, all this time I thought I was really doing something.

The burning sensation in my throat reminded me why I was standing in my kitchen leaning against the sink in the wee hours of the morning.

"You coming back to bed soon?"

I opened the fridge and grabbed the Brita water pitcher. With each swallow of the cold water the heat calmed and so did I. I placed the empty glass in the sink and held my head down for a second. I could feel Johnny as he moved closer to me. His hand was on my back, rubbing me.

"All better now?"

"I'm fine. Just needed something to drink."

I coughed and then turned to him. He grabbed my hand and led me back to the bedroom. Johnny climbed in on his side while I walked around to mine. He slid over after I got in, pulling me into his massive, muscular chest.

"Same dream?"

"Yeah. This time we were further out. The more I tried to breathe, the more water I swallowed." I coughed from the thought of it.

"I don't know, baby. Maybe you should go talk to someone. There's got to be a reason why you're having them; especially so suddenly."

I stared at the window again. Listened as the nothingness stirred around outside. No sound that would let on we were only forty-five or so minutes away from the city known for never sleeping.

What could this shit mean?

I could feel my eyelids grow heavy. As scared as I was to close them, I knew it was a losing battle. Johnny pulled me back far enough into him so my backside was up against his midsection. I could feel the onset of an erection.

"Do you see what time it is?"

"Umm, hmm," was his response.

"Then you know we have to be up in about three hours?"

He lifted my hair off my neck and kissed it. Kissed it softly over and over. Was hitting my spot and knew it. I pushed my backside deeper into him. I couldn't resist him when he did anything near my neck or back. Something about being rubbed ever so softly on those sections of my body turned me on in an unnatural kind of way.

I felt the proverbial poke. The poke that let me know he was ready to do bed battle.

"Umm," I moaned. The arch in my back got deeper. Gone were the thoughts of sleep and bad dreams.

"You know I'm trying to make up for lost time," he whispered into my ear.

"Oh, you've done that and more in the span of one night." I thought about how long and hard he'd loved me earlier that night.

"You want me to stop then?"

I rolled over so we were facing one another. I loved his athletic physique.

His thighs looked to have enough power to crush a man. His biceps resembled small mountains. And his dick… well, it was something to be admired. The first time I saw him with no clothes on I was damn near scared enough to back out. Get up and put my clothes back on and tell him it was nice knowing ya. I kept asking myself, *How in the hell am I going to be able to take all of that?!* And he wasn't even completely hard at the time! But once my juices began to flow; my pussy became a nice-fitting glove for him.

Hungrily, he savored my lips as if they were his life support system. "Umm, baby. I've been thinking about you all day," he moaned.

"I see. You wanted your pussy, huh?"

"Don't I always?"

He licked a circle around my nipple before submerging it into his mouth. He knew it was another move that drove me wild. Once he realized the nectar he sought was flowing from the well, he wasted no time in going to take a drink.

Johnny was a master with his tongue. He ate my pussy so good, I don't think I'll ever be able to let another man go down on me for fear they would never live up to him. Johnny could do tricks I'd never seen or felt a man do before. He would roll and twist his tongue around down there and drive me damn near wild. After a good five minutes I was begging him to fuck me before I exploded. But it was never quite done until he had my clit at attention.

"Without working the clit it's all a waste of time," he would say. And Johnny *never* liked to waste any of his time. Not one time did I ever get up dissatisfied.

When my left leg began to shake and the arch in my back pushed my chest as far as it would go, he knew I was good and prepared.

"Yeah, Baby. You're ready for me now."

He took his powerful thighs and opened my legs wide as he took the head of his dick and spread my juices around.

"You want it, don't you, Baby?" he asked, as he inserted the head slowly. "Tell me how much you want it, Baby."

"You know how bad I want it. Don't make me flip you over and take it," I said breathlessly.

"Oh no, Baby. I'm in control of things. I'm gonna give you exactly what you want. What you need." He scooped my legs over the crooks of his arms and brought my body up into position. With a long, hard thrust he entered me and pulled back out only to repeat it again, and again. Rocking me slowly until he got into the right groove. He picked up the tempo once my body had been repositioned into another fulfilling position. The sound of our skin making contact echoed throughout the room. Johnny leaned down and began to feed me his thick, luscious tongue.

I looked down at the contrasting colors of our skin. His deep chocolate against my a' latté. We would have a beautiful little brown baby if we were to mix the two.

Johnny took his finger and vigorously rubbed my clit. My left leg began to shake again. That all too familiar feeling began to creep in. The contracting of my vaginal wall muscles locked down hard on Johnny as he continued to do his part.

"Baby... baby... baby..."

"Yeah, Baby, that's it. I want you to come for me," he coaxed as he continued to rub my clit.

I couldn't get my mouth to work. The harder he pumped, the louder my moans got. Right when I thought I wouldn't be able to take anymore, my legs bucked tight and he knew he'd done his job once again. I thrust my middle toward him and wrapped my legs around him tightly as my pussy continued to skeet and contract around Johnny's shaft. The haze. The beautiful haze had come into my head and had me floating. You know you've been fucked good when you feel like you're having an out-of-body experience.

Still unable to talk, I threw my arms around Johnny's neck as he passionately kissed my neck down to my nipples. This caused me to come a little harder. I slowly let go of my many grips on his body and lay back on the bed. He pulled out of me and looked down at his work.

"Damn, Baby, you starting to skeet further than me." He smiled, then took two of his fingers and swirled them around in my cream and placed them in his mouth.

"Sweet as always." He got up and went to the bathroom and came back with a warm washcloth. As was our routine, he carefully cleaned me up and then went to the bathroom to wipe himself down afterward. He grabbed the open condom wrapper from the floor where it had been tossed and headed back to the bathroom.

Practicing safe sex was a must. We'd both been tested before our first encounter, but I still wasn't ready to go straight-up raw. While the primary safety precaution was catching a disease, catching a baby was running a close second. I had no intentions of being anyone's *baby mama* if I could help it.

Slowly, blissful sleep began to take over. Forgotten was the fearful dream. Good sex and contentment had replaced it. I would sleep soundly the remaining two hours and however many minutes I had left.

CHAPTER 2

ASIA

The buzz of people moving about and ringing phones had faded into silence in the office. Four-thirty was quitting time at Xposure. We liked to give our people a head start on the other commuters in the city. 2001 had turned out to be a very good year for us in all aspects. From our business to personal lives. Seven months into the new year and we were well ahead of where we were the year before. The ladies of Xposure PR & Event Planning had become the "*Go To*" girls in the industry. Being tied to Chance Productions had its perks, but we'd more than proved ourselves with the handling of the many events we'd been involved with since the premiere last year for Alex's company. For the record, the movie was a blockbuster hit, but the success was overshadowed by other things.

I was finishing up my last call of the day. A few last-minute details that needed to be taken care of for an event slated to happen the following weekend. This weekend was a free one. Johnny and I had made plans to hang out with Yani and Alex tomorrow night. But tonight was "Girl's Night Out." The one day in the week we all got together to talk shit and enjoy a few drinks while we caught up with each other.

After ending the call with my contact at the hotel, I punched in Johnny's number down at the precinct.

"Detective Johnson," he bellowed.

"Well hello, Detective Johnson. How's your day going?" I adjusted the hands-free headpiece so I could hear him better.

"Hello, Ms. Fenton. I'm having a good day, considering I spend my day looking for hardened criminals. How'd your meeting go?" He'd replaced his hard no-nonsense voice with the smooth baritone I'd grown fond of.

"We got the account."

"That sounds like an invitation for a celebration."

"I know. I was thinking we could go to Caroline's tomorrow night."

"Caroline's? What's going on there?"

"There's a comedian I really like and he's going to be there." I could hear Yani heading my way.

"So, what'd ya think?"

"I'm in. What's his name?"

"Whose name?"

"The comedian."

"Oh, Teddy Carpenter." I laughed about our brief Abbott and Costello moment.

"Teddy Carpenter? Is he new on the scene?"

Yani stuck her head in and pointed at her watch. I waved her off. Told her without opening my mouth I knew what time it was and I was coming.

"Now see, if you were a true *Def Comedy Jam* fan you wouldn't be asking me that question."

"I've watched more than my share of *Def Comedy Jam* and I think it's pretty hard to remember each and every comedian who was ever on there."

"Well he's the comedian from D.C. The one who said he lived in a black house, in a black neighborhood, and drove a black car?" I sat back deeper into the chair.

"Hmm, it's not clicking for me right now."

"You know. He would talk about how much he loved being with big girls."

"You mean the one who did the skit with the chick standing behind him? Where she had her arms hooked through his and did the hand movements for what he was saying? When it got to the end she grabbed his nuts?"

"That's him. I love him. He's so funny." I was laughing at the thought of the girl's hesitation to actually grab Teddy; until he said the line again. She was a good sport about it.

"Yeah, dude's mad funny. You're going to call and make sure we can get in? You know you're the bigshot with all the connections."

"Okay, Mr. Big Time Detective. You've got more pull in this town than me." We both laughed.

"Well, it's Friday. My sister's standing here with her hands on her hips and attitude on her face. I need to get going." I shut down my computer and put my Palm Pilot back in my purse.

"Am I going to see you tonight?"

"If you want to."

Yani stepped out. I figured she was going to grab her things from her office.

"Of course I want to. I'd love to walk through the door and into the bedroom and find you waiting for me in your birthday suit."

"Butt-booty-naked? Umm, that sounds tempting, but you know tonight is about the girls."

"I know. Just a wish."

"We could have a repeat of last night. Maybe pick up a can of whip cream." I let out a low moan.

"You better get going." I could hear the sound of papers rustling in the background. He had changed gears on me. His voice was back to a no-nonsense tone.

"What's going on? You rushing me off the phone now?"

"Remember, I'm at the office?"

"So am I."

"I'm not sitting in a plush ass office like you. The privacy factor doesn't exist here. I'm in a room full of other people with a simple cubicle wall dividing us. Even though I spend a lot time with them, I don't want them staring at me with a rock hard dick."

"I'll let you off the hook then. See you later?" I smiled as I visualized the bulge that was surely growing in his pants.

"That's a definite yes."

Our playful banter was always sprinkled with sexual undertones. I laughed and hung up the phone. I turned off the light in my office and walked down to Yani's. She was slipping into her shoes.

"Squared everything away with Mr. Lover Man?"

"What would I need to square away? Johnny knows the deal. Friday nights are for the girls."

"That's good to know. You ready?" She grabbed her purse off her desk.

"I'm only going to have a drink or two; then I'm out."

"All right now. You know what Mama used to say about making a man your world. When he leaves it you cease to exist. Don't learn the hard way like I did."

"Johnny's not the reason I'm leaving early."

"Asia, don't try and play me. I know getting home to Daddy Good Dick is all you can think about right now. It's only one night a week we all get together. Don't go changing things up 'cause you got a man now." She turned off the light in her office.

"It's been a really busy week and I'm tired." While I was tired, the thought of surprising Johnny was tempting.

"Let's get going then. Wouldn't want to make you hang out with me any longer than you want to." She grabbed her bag and walked out ahead of me.

"Whatever, Yani."

❖❖❖

"Hey, Linda!" We exchanged yuppie air kisses. Yani repeated the same motions when she moved on to her.

Linda looked cute and carefree in the sassy, pink, Baby Phat wife-beater and denim skirt with the lighter faded V piece in the front that fell right at her knees. The pink, sexy, wrap sandals with three-inch heels were the finishing touch to her outfit.

"How are things at the office? Still busy?"

"Things couldn't be better. How about you? People still traveling; even though the economy seems to be ready to take a nosedive?" Yani asked.

"Business is still booming," she said as she removed her heavy black plastic shades and slid them back onto the tight ponytail that fell just below her shoulders.

We tried to meet somewhere different every week. Last week it was Justin's, this week the Shark Bar. Tucked away on Amsterdam between 74th & 75th. Half a flight above street level. The hole-in-the-wall was known as a mecca for soul food cuisine.

We made our way through the throng of people. The expected crowd. Yani had called in for the reservations on Monday so we'd be able to walk in and avoid the inevitable wait.

Brina had been relentlessly talking about the place for the past two weeks. We knew we'd end up there when it became her week to pick the spot.

The bar was overflowing with the after-work crowd. A bunch of attractive, well-dressed people. A sea of black, navy blue, and charcoal gray suits. Male and female. They all seemed to be patiently waiting for the hostess to announce their names. Inviting them to come partake of the infamous soul roll—filled with chicken, black-eyed peas, and collards. The Louisiana deep-fried crab cakes were more my thing. With an order of BBQ grilled shrimp to accompany it, I was good to go. I never ordered food at restaurants that I could make at home. So if white people wanted to know if "Black people eat a lot of chicken" for real, they wouldn't be able to tell by examining my plate.

The intimate setting of the dining room held more bodies as we were escorted to our table. More than a few recognizable faces dotted the room. If you were into being seen and wanted to feel like you were somehow a part of the "Who's Who" crowd, this was the place you wanted to be. That's one of the main reasons Brina chose it. She'd been checking for a new Knicks player and they were well known for coming in here.

"Where's Brina?" Yani asked.

"She's on her way. She called me before I left the office." Linda slid into her seat.

"Tracey will be your server tonight," the hostess announced as she handed out menus. "You ladies have a good night." After a slight bow of the head she was off to seat the next group.

"What are you ladies drinking tonight?" Linda asked as she browsed the menu.

"I'd like a Cosmo. What about you, Asia? Maybe a Black Screw would do you some good," Yani jokingly said.

"You're so funny. I'm going to the bathroom. I need a break from the peanut gallery." I rolled my eyes at Yani as I stood up.

"I'll walk with you. I've been holding my water all the way here." Linda tucked her handbag underneath her arm and stood behind me.

"Don't worry, Asia, I'll have some more when you get back." Yani licked her tongue out at me playfully as she reached in her bag for her cell.

"Can't go an hour without calling to check in?"

"I'm not checking in. I need to talk to my husband about something important before I forget. Plus I need to check on the kids."

"That's checking in," Linda and I said in unison.

"Fine. I won't call then." She snapped her cell shut.

"Yani, don't mind us. Go ahead and make your call and we'll be right back." Linda pulled me off toward the direction of the bar.

"What's up with that?"

"Nothing."

"Nothing? Seemed like *something* to me."

"You can't help it, can you?"

"I sure can't. I'm nosey and proud of it. Stop being a bitch and tell me what's going on with you."

We pushed our way past the crowded bar.

"How do you know it's me with the problem? Why didn't you ask if something was going on with Yani?"

"Because I know you, Asia Fenton, and something isn't right. You're giving Yani much attitude. So talk." She spun around and stared into my face, with her hand on her hip in a defiant stance.

"I don't know, Linda. I was thinking about something that's been going on with me. Plus Yani was irking me with the lil' smart remarks about Johnny before we left the office."

"You're not having second thoughts about turning down his proposal again? He seems to be moving at an above normal pace, but Johnny's a good guy."

"No that's not it. I'm crazy about him."

"Then what's the problem?"

"We'll talk about it once we get back to the table. I'm not about to talk freely while we're surrounded by strangers. You never know who might be listening." I scanned the faces of the numerous females who had congregated in the ladies room.

Linda's head followed the same route. "Oh, okay."

We took our place in line. A few minutes later we were back at the table. Before my butt touched the leather of the seat, Linda was on me to spill it.

"It's nothing big. I've been having this crazy dream lately."

"About?"

"I fall into the water while I'm out on a boat. I struggle to get back to the boat and Johnny's staring down at me. His hand's stretched out for me, but I'm slowly starting to sink. The dream's so real, I can actually feel myself drowning; taking in water and all. I always wake up to difficult breathing. Coughing wildly. I always wake up right before I'm about to die. I don't know what to make of it."

I stopped playing with the corner of the napkin in my lap and looked up at them.

"How long has this been going on?"

I was about to answer Yani when the waitress came to the table. Yani had ordered our drinks during our trip to the ladies room.

"Who has the Apple Martini?"

I raised my hand and patted the space in front of me. The waitress sat the bright green liquid in front of me and handed off the other drinks—a Cosmo for Yani and Watermelon Martini for Linda.

"Whenever the last person in your party gets here, I'll come and get their drink order, Mrs. Chance."

"Thanks, Tracey."

"I'll be back with that soul roll and order of crab cakes in a few." The overly friendly waitress walked away.

While I'd heard the food was supreme, I'd been told the service at the Shark Bar always left a little to be desired. I guessed she'd just started working there.

"So, how long?" Yani looked at me and waited for me to continue.

I shrugged my shoulders and looked down into the fancy glass in front of me. "Not too long, but I've had it three times this month already."

"Is that the only time you have this dream?" Yani asked.

"When?" I took a sip.

"When Johnny's there? Does it seem like those are the nights when you have the dream?"

I shook my head and then took a nice slow sip before answering. "No, he was only there last night. He knows about them though."

"Umm," Yani said and took a sip from her drink.

"Umm? You say that like you know something."

"I'm not saying I know something; per se. I'm thinking it may have something to do with Johnny. Maybe it doesn't."

"Girl, don't be ridiculous." I waved her off.

"Wait a minute now. Hear me out."

I rolled my eyes and looked over at Linda who was all ears.

"Maybe you were looking for Johnny to be your savior after the mess with Hayden and he hasn't done that. You're still dealing with a man whose time is being dominated by something other than you. While Johnny's attentive, you only get his time when his job allows it."

Linda looked at me and then back at Yani.

"That's it? That's the best you could come up with?" she asked incredulously.

"What do you mean, the best I could come up with? Doesn't it make sense to you?" Yani took a long sip from her drink; draining the contents completely.

"You need to slow down with the drinks. That's what makes sense to me," I said.

Linda and I laughed. Yani threw her hand up to signal the waitress who was passing by.

"Can you get me another one?"

She grabbed the glass from Yani's hand.

"Another Cosmo coming right up."

"You do remember you have to drive home?"

"How many times do I have to remind you that I'm a grown ass woman? I know my limits. Tonight it's four; or five. Depends on how strong the drinks are." She turned her head and scanned the room.

"Here comes Brina." Yani threw up her hand and waved Brina in our direction.

"Hello, divas." She came around to each one of us and placed an air-cheek kiss on both sides of our faces.

"What took you so long to get here? You're the one who picked this place."

"Uh, excuse me. Unlike you, I happen to work for someone else." She rolled her eyes at me. Her attitude didn't reflect the prim and proper business attire—a pewter-colored A-line skirt with matching jacket—she was wearing. When she was with us you'd never guess she was a paralegal at a top law firm.

"That's not my fault. Sounds like you need to do something about it if you're that unhappy."

"No one said I was unhappy. I happen to love my career."

"Then stop complaining about our complaining."

I could see Yani trying to give her a signal.

"What's that about?" I asked Yani.

"What?"

I mimicked the hand movements she'd done to Brina. "That."

"Brina, your girlfriend here is in bitch mode today. So consider yourself warned. Better yet, ignore her." Yani and Linda laughed. Brina looked confused.

"You know what? I can take me and my bad mood and go home."

"If you're ready to leave, say you want to leave. Don't sit here trying to look for a good enough reason to go."

"I'm not looking for a reason to leave…"

Yani threw her hand up to silence me.

"Back to what I was saying." I reeled back a bit in my chair and looked at her. I couldn't believe she'd cut me off, as if I was unimportant. "Your ass is still losing out to a man and a situation."

The waitress returned with Yani's drink and took Brina's order.

"Whatever, Yani. I need to talk to your mother-in-law so she can help me out. Yvonna was right on the mark with that dream about you and…"

Yani took a huge gulp of her drink this time. I could've kicked myself for bringing it up. We'd done our best to treat it; almost as if it had never happened. It had taken two months for her to stop crying about it. The loss of Angel at the hands of Jarrin had almost crippled Yani with grief. While Alex had also gone through his own time of mourning, he had to put it behind him sooner; so he could help Yani. Between him, the kids, and the support of the women who loved her—Mama, Carmen, and me—she came out of it fine.

"Oh, I have some good news I wanted to share," Linda said, keeping the conversation moving. "There's another conference for travel agents coming up for Carnival. This time we can bring up to five guests with us at a fraction of the cost. Are you guys up to it?"

"Girl, tell me when to pack my bags," Brina replied.

We all laughed.

"We know you're not going to let an opportunity like this pass," I teased her.

"Who would? Hmph, you can act big money if you want, but a sistah like me is always looking for a hook-up."

"We know," we replied in unison.

My cell phone rang. I pulled it out of my purse and checked the caller ID. Johnny's name flashed across the screen. I hit the talk button.

"Hello?"

"Hey. I wanted to know if you're planning on coming over here tonight. Since you're already in the city, you can drive here instead of going all the way out to Canarsie."

"You don't have to make up excuses why I should come over. Say the word and I'm there." I smiled as I thought about seeing him.

"Bitch, get off the phone! He knows Fridays are ours!" Brina yelled loud enough for Johnny to hear her.

He chuckled. "Looks like I have to wait my turn."

"I'm just like, so popular," I said in my best Valley Girl impersonation.

"How much longer will you be?"

"I don't know. We haven't ordered our food." I glanced down at my watch. It was only a quarter to seven.

"I'll hit the video store on my way in. Anything you want to see?"

"Whatever you pick is fine."

"All right then. I'll let you get back to your girls before they curse me out."

"Bye, sweetie." I shook my head and hung up the phone; a slight smile on my face.

"Are you leaving?"

I glared at Yani like she'd grown another head. "No!"

"You've been in a funky mood most of the evening, then you get the call from DGD, and now you're smiling."

"DGD?" I asked. Linda and Brina were both as confused as me.

"Daddy Good Dick. Damn, get with the program, ladies." She took another sip from her glass.

"Girl, what movie did that come from?" Linda asked.

"None. She's been trying her hand at quirky acronyms. She thinks it's cute." I gave her a look of warning.

"Oh, please. You're the damn queen of acronyms, Ms. 'I know you're not taking DBPs.' Now you tell me, who would sit down and think of some shit like that." We all laughed at Yani. It was the question I'd asked when she was wasting time waiting for Jarrin.

"DBPs? What's that?" Brina looked over at me; confused.

"Dumb Bitch Pills," Linda responded before I had the chance.

"Oh. Okay."

Linda gave me that *knowing* look. Sometimes we wondered if Brina had her own special supplier of DBPs; especially when it came to the men she often dated. That's a whole 'nother story.

"For your information, Ms. Yani…"

"Remember, I'm the oldest, so watch what you say." She had her finger up as a warning.

"You're the one…" I thought about the smart remark she'd said. "What the hell does that have to do with anything?"

"Just thought you needed reminding. I know how forgetful you are when it comes to who's the oldest and the respect you *should* show me."

"For your information, Ms. Instigator, I wasn't about to say anything about leaving. Hell, I was checking my watch and wanted to know why he was calling me. Our night is just getting started. And being the oldest doesn't automatically entitle you to respect."

"Be honest with us. You know you can't keep your mind off dick for a couple of hours."

"You need to shut up, Yani. I know you're not talking."

"Yes, I am. I keep telling you, you better remember what Mama used to say."

"What are you talking about?" I asked.

"Girl, we're not stupid. We know your man is a cop…"

"Detective," I corrected her.

"Oooohh, detective. Excuse me for breathing." She rolled her eyes. "Anyway, like I said earlier, the *detective*'s job keeps him from being able to spend the time you want. He's off tonight and y'all want to spend some quality time together. But when he's not around you're hanging with us." Yani picked her drink up and finished it off.

"Wait a minute. I know this bitch here isn't putting us down for a man. As much as she loves to throw up in your face about not dropping your girls when you get a man. I know that's not what we're talking about here?" Brina asked. "Besides, we hang once a week. Is it really going to kill you to be away from him for a couple of hours at the most?"

"Look, I'm fine. Yani's the one trying to make it into something more." I rolled my eyes at Yani yet again.

"Don't try to blame this on me." She placed her empty glass on the table and waved her hand to signal the waitress on the other side of the room.

"Damn, you drank that like it was water."

"So, stop worrying about me. I'm…"

"Yeah, we know… you're grown." Linda and I laughed.

"Back to you wanting to run home to your man. We've already lost Cheryl from our circle. Got herself a man…"

"A piece of man at that," Yani blurted out.

"But a man," Linda pointed out.

"And now she's put us down completely. It's been three months since we last saw her on a Monday, let alone a Friday night." Brina turned her head as something caught her eye; distracting her attention from our conversation.

"Oh, my God. Look at that fine specimen of a man," Linda said as a Morris Chestnut lookalike walked by on the other side of the room.

"Umm, umm, umm. If I wasn't married, I'd try and get a taste of that chocolate." Yani licked her lips as she closely watched him walk by our table. Shocked the hell out of us when she stuck her hand out and pretended to palm his ass.

"Yani?!" we all said.

"What? I'm still a woman. Being married simply changes your options. Don't trip." She flung her hand in the air and waved us off, then turned to give Mr. Chocolate one last look before he disappeared into the crowd of people standing near the bar.

"You're really feeling those drinks. Maybe you need to chase it with some water." I pushed the water glass closer to her.

"And you don't have to remind us, you're the oldest. Everyone in here can tell you're the oldest by looking at you." I laughed.

"Cute, Asia."

"Can we cut the sibling rivalry act and get our night started? I'm starving and we haven't glanced at the menu yet." Linda picked up her menu and urged the rest of us to do so.

My cell phone rang again. I looked around the table.

"Don't look at us," Yani said as she kissed the rim of her glass and took a long sip.

The phone rang again.

"Aren't you going to answer it?"

"Not right now. I'll check it later."

"Don't sit up here trying to prove something to us," Linda threw in.

"I'm not trying to prove anything to anyone."

"Girl, I ain't mad at you. Hell, if I had that dark chocolate teddy bear waiting at home for me, I'd be trying to get home to him, too."

"Mind your business, Brina."

"Since we're all girls, I thought your business was also my business."

"It's only your business when it has to do with someone hurting me. Other than that, I can handle it."

A few hours later I was sitting in front of Johnny's building thinking about all that had been said that night. Was I losing myself in this man? Was I making him my life and my world as I vied for his full attention?

I thought about Yani's remark about having firsthand experience. Jarrin had been the Alpha and the Omega in her life. Nothing mattered but what *he* wanted. It seemed at one point, every sentence she spoke always started with Jarrin and ended with him. While I knew Johnny loved me and I him, I was conscious to be careful not to tread through that water.

I took a deep breath, then opened my car door. He'd given me a key three months ago which I used to open the lobby door. I stood in front of the door to his second-floor walkup and looked down at the key in my hand. He'd been trying for months to talk me into moving in with him, but I was too in love with Brooklyn to relocate to Harlem. I don't care how much more convenient it was to work and my hangouts.

I slowly opened the door. "Hello?" The apartment was quiet and dark. I felt along the wall for the light switch and walked further in after locking the door behind me. I looked around the kitchen, then made a beeline to the bathroom as I felt a sharp tingle that prompted me to take the first step of the pee-pee dance. I bounced around on the tips of my toes until I could pull my pants down without wetting myself. I hate to get into a "tight squeeze" but I knew it wouldn't take me long to get here and decided to wait. After I finished relieving myself, I was standing at the sink washing my hands when I noticed something floating around in the tub. At first sight, I was ready to break out, but upon better inspection I noticed the floating objects were beautiful pink, red and yellow rose petals in what had to be cold water now.

I walked out and headed down the hall to Johnny's bedroom.

"Baby? Where are you?" I peeped into his room where I found him stretched out across his king-sized bed with the remote clutched tightly in his right hand. I knew he was up from the moment my key was inserted into the lock. A detective? He sees and hears everything. Since he wanted to play, I decided to go along with the charade.

"Aww, look at my big baby." Just the sight of him made me go soft.

I bent over and kissed him on his slightly parted lips. He stirred and his eyes fluttered open. He was laying it on thick.

"You couldn't wait?" I said in a sultry voice that let him know what I had on my mind.

"Hey," he said as he stretched. He reached out for me and pulled me onto his bare chest. "I thought you were going to be here an hour ago."

"I didn't tell you that. Besides, we got into a deep conversation and I lost track of time. What happened with the movie?" I sat up and moved to the edge of the bed.

"I fell asleep. I knew you'd wake me up when you came in." He leaned up on his elbow and hit the power button on the remote. The blue light from the television lit up the room.

"Did you eat anything?" I stood up and walked toward the door.

"I picked up some chicken on the way home."

"You want something sweet?" I was walking out the door to the kitchen. I placed the white box on the counter and cut the strings away.

"What's that?" Johnny asked as he came up behind me.

"A special treat for my special guy."

He looked at the box carefully. He smiled at recognition of the name on it.

"You went all the way down to Veniero's?"

"Don't trip. I know how much you love these and I had a taste for one. No big deal." I shrugged my shoulders and continued to open the box and removed the strawberry shortcake.

Johnny grabbed a couple of plates and forks and handed me the cake cutter I'd given him as a gift. I was big on having the right gadgets in the kitchen.

"Oh, now I see," he said.

"See what?" I cut a nice-sized piece for him and a much smaller one for me.

"You're trying to butter me up so I'll give you some of my stuff."

"Your stuff?" I turned and looked at him.

"You know, my stuff." He gestured toward his midsection. Grabbing a handful of his crotch, I could see he was definitely willing to give me some.

"Oh, so now I have to butter you up to get some?" I seductively licked off the icing I'd managed to get on my finger.

"Naw, baby. All you have to do is ask."

"Ask?"

"I meant…"

"Have your cake now. Then we'll see about what else I'm willing to let you *eat* later." I smiled and placed a forkful of cake in his mouth. It had been hanging open since the licking of the icing.

"Let me hurry up and finish this slice so I can…"

"Take your time. There's no rush. I'll be here all night." I slowly brought another fork of cake to his mouth.

He leaned down and kissed me.

"Oh, and I have some things in mind I'd like to do to you." He gave me a seductive stare and then winked.

Oh, tonight was going to be a real marathon event and I was looking forward to every minute of it.

CHAPTER 3

YANI

"Do you think that's fair, Yani?"

"What do you mean, *fair*? Was it *fair* that she was fucking him and he was my *husband*? Was it *fair* for her to disregard me and *my* children when she decided to run off with him? Now all of a sudden I should be worried about being *fair* and embrace her and her kids with open arms? I don't think so, honey."

"Look, all I'm saying is maybe you should give the kids that choice. I think they should be the ones to make that decision. They are their siblings."

"As far as I'm concerned, they're nothing more than Jarrin's lil' bastard children. I can't believe we're even having this conversation. After all the shit he put us through—and that does include you in that us—you're here telling me to put it behind me and deal with the woman and children he chose over me and my children."

"That's not what I'm saying, baby."

"Then what exactly are you saying? 'Cause that's exactly what I'm hearing." I placed my hand on my hip for more emphasis. I didn't want him to misinterpret my feelings one iota on this subject. He had pushed into uncharted water on this one.

Alex looked at me sincerely as he searched for the right words to say next. I went back to making the bed. He went on his side and joined me. After watching me beat the shit out of the pillows to fluff them back up—more so to take out the anger I was going through—Alex finally said something.

"Look, I have cousins who were never given the chance to know their brothers because their mother didn't want them to have nothing to do with their father's outside children. I remember how they felt once they found out. How betrayed they felt about the *decision* their mother had made without giving them the chance to state how they felt. I guess you can look at it as a woman who badmouths her baby's daddy because she's angry with him about the way they broke up. Or the situation he's placed her in by not being there for their child like she feels he should be. Then when the kid grows up and gets a chance to know him, they see he wasn't as bad as she claimed. They become resentful and take it out on her. Now you don't want that, do you, honey?" He finished placing his pillows on the bed and came up behind me and grabbed me in a tight embrace. He kissed the side of my neck. I remained quiet for a moment. After everything Nat and Jay had been through, I definitely didn't want to be the source of adding anything else.

At sixteen, Nat was extremely mature and probably knew more about the trifling acts of her father than I cared to think. But Jay was my baby and I wasn't sure if his twelve-year-old mind could handle any more when it came to Jarrin.

"It seems like Jarrin is haunting me; even from the grave."

"He's not haunting you, baby."

"You're not the one faced with a decision like this…"

"I'm here with you. I'm faced with it, too. It's not like I'm going to disappear when they come over." He turned me around to face him. "I told you I would love you forever—no matter what—and I meant that." He ran his finger along the side of my face as he searched my eyes.

I looked away from him. "I have to give it some more thought, sweetie, before I can make a decision. You have to understand the hurt I felt when I first saw those kids. He duplicated our family." My tone pleaded with him to understand how I was feeling.

"Okay, okay. I'm not going to push you on it. You go ahead and give it all the thought you need. But remember there are four young lives hanging in the balance here. These kids never asked to come here. Not one of them asked to be in the situation they've been put in." He kissed me lightly on the lips. I placed my head on his chest.

"I love you, Mrs. Chance."

"I love you, too, Mr. Chance."

❖❖❖

"Can you believe that bitch Dede had the nerve to call me? I'm not even sure how she got the number." I leaned back in my chair.

"What does she want?" Asia turned her attention away from the papers she had been looking over.

"Check this; she wants the kids to have a chance to get to know one another. Is that a crock of bull or what? I bet that bitch is thinking she can get in good with me and maybe I'll give her some of that money. She can forget that shit. That money is going to *my* children. Her two will never see a dime of it." I took a sip of my tea.

"Maybe you're making more out of it than it really is, Yani. She may genuinely want them to know their big brother and sister. You said the kids were really cute once you thought about it."

I rubbed my temples and began to rotate my head to loosen up the stress that had settled in my neck area ever since I got the call.

"Being cute has nothing to do with what I'm talking about. There are plenty of cute kids out there."

"Yeah, but none of them are your ex's kids. Making them your children's little brother and sister. Maybe you should give her the benefit of the doubt."

"Benefit of the doubt? This coming from a woman who dismissed a man because a woman trapped him? Ah, hello, is my sister in there?" I reached over and pretended to knock on her head.

She placed the paper on the counter. "Look, what went down between me and Hayden is in no way, shape, or form, the same as this. So stop making comparisons. There's a lot of shit that was left wrong in the house Jarrin built, but you can work on making the home improvements needed to make things right."

"You know I found out that bastard married her?"

"And you married Alex…"

"Before he left us." I cut her off. A look of surprise registered on her face. "He was married to me *and* her for about six months before he made his great escape. For six months he fooled me enough to think I was the only one he loved and wanted to be with. Enough to make me waste five years of my life." I could feel the tears pooling. I thought of all the lies he'd told during that time.

Baby, I'm working on this case that's going to keep me out of town for a couple of weeks. I've got to go into the office earlier; now that I'm on my own.

The extended business trips, late nights, but he always managed to do something wonderful to make up for any of his shortcomings. I had been the biggest fool of all. The only one in the scenario who was clueless.

Asia walked over and wrapped her arms around me. "It wasn't him who made you wait so long. God knew you needed that much time in order to meet Alex. He made you wait so He could put the man you were meant to be with in your path." She hugged me tighter and helped me wipe away my tears.

"I can't believe this shit still fucks with me like this. I told Alex the bastard is still fucking with me from the grave! From the grave, Asia! How long must I deal with Jarrin's bullshit?"

She reached for the box of tissues on my desk, pulled out a couple, and handed them to me.

"As much as we both hate to admit it, Jarrin's a part of your past. A past filled with pain and regrets. You're going to have to deal with it, but it's on you *how* you deal with it. Remember how Daddy used to say, kill 'em with kindness? Kill her with a little kindness, Yani. Maybe God's testing you. Trying to see if you're worthy of the goodness He's bestowed upon you. You have to admit, you've got a great life right about now. What would it hurt for you to let these kids get a chance at knowing each other? Are you afraid you'll actually like them?" She helped me wipe away my tears with one hand as she rubbed my back with the other.

"I'm not sure I'm afraid of anything. I think it's more of an anger thing than anything else. I'm angry I was so blind I couldn't see what was real. That the man I'd trusted to take care of me and never forsake me could do something so unthinkable…"

"Then don't think with your anger."

I pulled away from Asia and looked at her.

"Is this my sister saying this? Ms., tell-it-like-it-T-I-is, Asia?"

"It's not like I'm getting soft or anything, but lately I've been starting to view things differently." She gave me a sympathetic smile.

"I guess Johnny is doing more than working your body right. He's even got your mind working differently."

"Forget you." She shoved my shoulder and we both laughed. I was happy to lighten the mood. I'd shed enough tears over Jarrin and just like Anita Baker said years ago, there would be *no more tears* for him.

I reached for the phone. "I'm going to give Carmen a call. You know I have to have an opinion from everyone."

"As much as I love the fact you treasure what we all think, the protocol changed when you got married last year. This is one of those times when whatever your husband has to say about the situation is the one opinion that should count more than any other."

"Spoken like a woman in love." I laughed as I dialed Carmen.

"Hello?"

"Don't try and act like you don't have Caller ID," I teased.

"If it isn't my oldest and bestest friend in the whole world. How are you doing in the big city?"

"The big city and I are doing just fine."

"And to what do I owe this unexpected call? It's been what? Almost two, three weeks since we last talked? I was starting to think you were a figment of my imagination for all these years."

"Stop with the melodramatics. It's time for some girl talk. I'm going to put you on speakerphone. Asia's in here with me."

"What's going on?" Her tone was now serious.

"I need your opinion on something."

"I'm listening."

I went on to tell her about the situation at hand. She sat silently on the other end of the phone and listened until I was finished.

"Well, I agree with everyone else on this, Yani. I mean, what harm could it do?"

"That's what I said, Carmen."

"I told you I don't trust her. Hell, she was the reason Jarrin left us. What makes you guys think she's not trying to pull something else?"

"Come on, Yani. I don't think she *made* Jarrin do anything. Think about how you were about Jarrin. No one could tell you anything about him. Maybe he had the same effect on her. Remember you're the one who said Jarrin had a certain way of pushing the right buttons. So, you weren't the only one it worked on."

I couldn't believe where she was going with this. "Well, thanks a lot, *friend*."

"Don't get an attitude with me because you don't want to see the truth. What were you expecting me to do? Agree with you just to be agreeable?"

"No, I guess I expected you to have my back a little more on this."

"And I do have your back." She took a deep breath. "Look at it this way, Yani..."

"And what way is that, Carmen?" My voice was laced with a hint of attitude; even though I didn't mean for it to come out that way.

"Maybe God is finding a way to make up for Jarrin taking the life of Angel."

I sat there quietly as I thought about the baby I would never have for Alex due to Jarrin. A beautiful baby girl who had been taken away with a bullet dislodged from the gun Jarrin pointed at me.

I took a deep breath.

"See, girl, even Carmen knows there's a higher order working on this," Asia said as she shook her head.

"I'm going to do this, since *all* of you think I should, but the minute it goes wrong..."

"We'll all still be in your corner, ready to do whatever is needed," Carmen replied.

"I'm going to do what Alex suggested and leave it up to the kids. Whatever they decide I'll honor. After all, they deserve that much."

"I couldn't agree with you more."

"Thanks, Carmen."

"You know how much I love Nat and Jay. I may not have given birth to them, but I was there when they were born and will always be there. I wouldn't tell you to do something that could harm them."

"I know. It's just… I don't know what her intentions are."

"Keep in mind this has nothing to do with her. It's about the kids. The four of them."

"I got you."

"We're going to let you go. We're here working on some pre-planning ideas. I'm sorry for not calling you since Monday. I know the code of honor says we must talk at least three times a week." We all laughed.

"Since today is Friday I'll let you slide. But don't do it again."

"Thanks for backing me up, Carmen," Asia said.

"We all love Yani, Asia, and she should know we'd never suggest anything that could harm her. Believe me; you'll only grow from this experience."

"Well, there's my cue. The baby just woke up from her nap, so I've got to run. I love you guys." We could hear Mya whimpering in the background.

"We love you, too, Carmen. Give Bryce and the kids my love."

"And mine, too," Asia called out.

"Will do, sister girl."

"Bye." I hung up the phone and looked at Asia, who had an "I told you so" look on her face.

"Whatever. It's still up to the kids. If they say no, then it's out of the question."

"I'm okay with that. At least you're giving them the option of having a say in it."

I would take their advice this time. And they—Alex, Asia, and Carmen— better have been hoping and praying things went the right way. 'Cause homegirl had one chance to come at me wrong. Then I was going to forget I was a lady and show her a thing or two. No one took me for a fool. At least not anymore. That stupidity had died with Jarrin almost a year ago.

CHAPTER 4

ASIA

"**A**re we still on for tonight?" I turned my attention back to Yani who was browsing over the contracts to make sure all the I's and T's had been taken care of.

"Um hmm. We're going to meet you guys there. Alex has a late meeting so we're going to leave from his office." She handed the file back over to me.

"Do you think we should call first? I'd hate to get there and they don't have any seats left."

"It's Tuesday. I don't think we'll have a problem."

"Did you let Mr. Carrolton know he needs to read the contract over? I'm not up for his crap this time. If he tries to pull that diva shit this time, I'll give his ass a cussin' he won't soon forget."

"Not you, Ms. Prim and Proper? He'd probably look at you and laugh or he might be shocked into silence." I chuckled at the thought of Mr. Flamboyant dealing with the wrath of Yani.

"I don't give a damn. I'm dead-ass serious. He has to realize we have a company to run. While we're here to serve him, we are not his servants. There's a limit as to what will be done when it comes to our clients. Being his personal shopper isn't in our contract. That's not the type of business we do."

"But you have to admit, his parties are off the chain and full of who's who in the theater."

"They're off the chain because *we* make sure they are. So don't try and make it seem like he has that much to do with it." She closed the folder and handed it back to me.

"I hear you."

"Make sure you let him know what duties we perform per our contract. I don't care if you have to outline them on a separate sheet of paper. Make sure he knows we mean business." She sat back in the chair. Her usual tawny-colored skin was two shades darker. A clear sign she'd spent quite a bit of time on the beach during her trip to Jamaica— a gift from Alex to celebrate their first-year anniversary.

"What's Alex working on these days?"

"He has quite a few offers after the success of the project from last year." She reached for the glass-covered candy dish on the corner of my desk.

"That's good."

"So, what happened when you got in the other night? Was Johnny up waiting for you?" She fished around in the bowl and pulled out a few foil-covered kisses.

"Actually, he was sleeping when I got in. What about you? Was Alex sitting at the door?"

"Cute. I have papers. You don't."

"What's that supposed to mean?"

She smiled and popped the candy into her mouth.

"If you're talking about being married, I don't have papers because I don't want them."

"Girl, tell it to someone who doesn't know you. You're starting to hear that biological clock tick. Loud and clear. I don't remember Old Maid listed as one of your life's ambitions."

"Maybe you should go up on stage tonight. Seeing that you've got the idea you're a comedian lately. Maybe you need to reevaluate your 'Life's Ambitions' list." I grabbed the candy dish out of her hand.

"You can be such a sour puss sometimes. Get real, Asia. You know you'd like to be married."

"Yes, Yani. I'd like to be married, but I'm not ready for that step just yet with Johnny."

"It's been ten months. How long do you expect to wait?"

"Some of us need time to get comfortable with people. Unlike you, we all don't have the ability to know what we want within a few months."

"Please. You're the only person I know who can go into the mall and come out in thirty minutes or less with a complete outfit."

"I'm not indecisive about shopping."

"Oh, only about men?"

I stopped twirling the pen between my fingers and looked at her. If she wasn't my sister I would've slapped that silly smirk off her face.

"Can we talk about something else?"

She scooted the chair back and stood up. "I'm going back to my office. I have a few calls I need to make. Aren't you going out on a site today?"

"Yeah. I have to meet with the manager for the release party next week."

"When's the last time you talked to Mama?"

"She called me last week. She's all in love now. Doesn't call every other day like she used to."

"Stop hating."

"Can you imagine Mama doing it with somebody?" She scrunched up her face. The upper left side of her lip was arched up.

"I said, stop hating. The old girl deserves to get her groove on. Mr. Towns is good to her and that's all that matters to me." I glanced at the clock on the wall. It was close to lunchtime.

"I'm meeting Linda for sushi. Want to come?" I unplugged my Palm Pilot.

"I have to take a rain check this time. I have some plans of my own." She winked at me and headed out the door.

"I don't know why you guys don't get a place in the city. You spend enough on hotel rooms."

"Mind your business," she called over her shoulder and kept going.

I grabbed my things and went to the front to the receptionist's desk.

"Betty, I'll be out of the office for the rest of the day. If someone calls and insist they need to talk to me, let Angie handle it."

"Okay, Ms. Fenton." Betty flashed me the movie star smile she wore and pushed the button to take the incoming call.

I walked to Yani's office before leaving. She was on her cell as she slipped into her jacket.

"Okay. I'll be there in no more than twenty minutes. I love you, too. Bye, Baby." She smiled as she placed her cell in her bag.

"You're glowing and the man hasn't even touched you yet."

"Hey, when it's good, it's good."

"Come on. We can ride down together."

"You don't have any plans to meet Johnny over at your favorite place?"

She was referring to the adult store Johnny and I frequented in the Village. I was a little apprehensive about going the first time, but that's all it took. I enjoyed myself so much that I took all the girls when it was my turn to choose the Friday night spot.

"No. Today I'm about business. Plus I need to get home and get ready for tonight." We walked through the glass doors that led to the elevators. A customer from the real estate office across the hall was standing, monitoring which floor the elevators were on as he anticipated leaving, as if his watching would make it get there faster. Everyone was always in a rush. Even with the things we had no control over.

"That's a first."

"I don't slip away every day to see my man. I'm not the boss."

"Don't start tripping. You know you have just as many rights to the company as me."

"In that case, I'm taking two weeks off then."

"Go ahead. As long as you make sure whatever you have on your agenda is taken care of." The bell dinged for the elevator.

"Yeah, you say that now because you're happy about going to see your man. Let me ask the same question in a few days when you first walk in the door."

"The answer will be the same."

"We'll see then."

CHAPTER 5

ASIA

I stepped out of my car and headed up the steps to my front door. My landlord opened his door and stuck his head out as I passed by.

"Hello there, young lady."

"Hey there, Mr. Brand. How are you today?"

"Oh, pretty much the same. Mrs. Brand says hello." He walked out on his porch. Age had caused his head to shine and his back to bend.

"Tell her I said hi and I'm still waiting to taste that punchbowl cake she told me about."

"I'll be sure to tell her. I stopped you for a reason though. I wanted to let you know next week a new tenant will be moving into the apartment downstairs."

"So you finally decided to rent it out. That must mean Charlie's gone for good." Charlie, their thirty-something-damn-near-forty-year-old son, was having a hard time staying out the nest.

"I finally convinced the missus we need to stop making things convenient for his return. So, if he decides to come back there won't be anywhere for him to come to this time." He hacked out a laugh laced with years of smoking.

The Brands were a nice couple who were first-generation native New Yorkers. They'd been married for more than forty years. Their parents had been a part of the "Great Migration" during the Harlem Renaissance Era. Mr. Brand loved to tell the stories of how his parents had been a part of many of the elite circles of that time. How as a boy he'd been privy to the conversations of Langston Hughes, Zora Neale Hurston, and Nella Larson to name a few. His father was really good friends with Walter White, the first secretary of the NAACP who also became the president after James Weldon Johnson stepped down. Mr. Brand once told us how Mr. White—who actually looked white, but was indeed a black man—would go to different places in the South to investigate crimes committed against blacks. Since he could easily pass, he would be able to talk to the white people and get the story right from the horses'—or the asses', as Mr. Brand was fond of saying—mouths.

Mr. Brand's father—while not as fair as Mr. White—could also pass and the same genes were passed on to Mr. Brand himself. His pale yellow skin, bluish-gray eyes, and the few fine strands of wavy hair left on his head were proof he came from a watered-down bloodline. He would often talk about how color-struck his family was.

"Yeah, Poppa's and Mama's jaws nearly hit the floor when I brought Pearl home," he fondly recalled and laughed about the first time his parents met his wife. Her rich, deep chocolate skin caused more than a ripple in the cream that separated them from other "Coloreds." Mr. Brand let them know he loved her and there was nothing they could do about it.

"I'll make sure to keep an eye out for the new tenant." I shifted the weight of my briefcase to the other hand so I could roll the key for my front door around the ring into my hand. The summer heat was making me wish the conversation would end soon, but I had to be polite. I started up the stairs in hopes he would get the hint.

"It's a man," he said to my back.

I turned back toward him slightly. "Excuse me?"

"The new tenant. He's around your age, I think." His eyes seemed to twinkle at the possibility of a "love connection" situation.

"He's also very good-looking, Asia!" Mrs. Brand yelled from inside the apartment. She was in her favorite spot—a LazyBoy recliner next to the door, facing the television. She was nosey like that. She was better than any neighborhood watch they could put together. She knew who belonged and who didn't on the block. And made no bones about letting the trespassing offender know she was aware they were out of place.

"That's nice, Mrs. Brand, but you know I have Johnny now!" I called out loud enough for her to hear.

"Oh, yeah. The nice officer," she said in a heavy Brooklyn accent.

"That would be the one."

"Well, I just wanted to let you know so you wouldn't be alarmed when you saw him," Mr. Brand said, cutting her off.

"That was really nice of you, Mr. Brand. Have a good night."

"You too, Asia."

I continued up the stairs after grabbing my mail from the box. I had two hours to get ready for my night out with Johnny and I had wasted more time than I planned talking.

You would think double dating would be a regular routine for the four of us. Since Johnny and Alex were friends, we didn't have to worry about any awkward moments. But with the busy lives they both led, Johnny and Alex were now more of acquaintances than boys. They would hold a conversation if they were in each other's presence, but there wasn't any shooting pool on certain nights, or meeting up for drinks. It felt as if Yani and I were their only link to one another.

It feels so good to be home, I thought as I walked into my room and kicked off my shoes. I peeled off the navy blue jacket of my suit and grabbed the hanger from the corner chair. I slipped out of my pants to add them to the hanger as well. Standing in the closet looking for something to wear, I grabbed a pair of black hiphugger jeans and a cutesy peasant shirt Yani had gotten for me. I hurried off to the shower so I could be ready by the time Johnny got there.

I told Johnny I would leave the door open so he could get in, so I didn't jump when I heard the bar door open and then close. I listened as he walked down the hall.

"Umm, something smells good in here," Johnny said as he walked into my room where I was lotioning up after getting out of the shower.

"Why don't you come closer and get a real good whiff." As I stood, my silk wrap floated to the floor.

"Woman, don't tempt me."

"See, that's the problem with you men. You can't handle when a woman is aggressive and voices what she wants. Here I am offering my goods to you on a platter and you're talking about being tempted. Do I have to come and take what I want for you to get the message?"

He was on me in two strides. Hoisted me up so I could wrap my legs around his waist as we wrestled to get his shirt undone. He never stopped kissing me as he kicked off his shoes and fumbled with his belt buckle.

"Remember we're meeting..." Before I could finish my statement he pressed my back against the wall and entered me. Legs hooked over his arms, he bounced me up and down in a slow rhythm, picking up the tempo in slow increments.

"See, Baby, I got your message. Loud and clear," he breathed into my neck.

Yes, he'd gotten the message all right. And he was responding good and hard. I prayed we weren't late.

❖❖❖

We arrived at Caroline's just as Alex and Yani were about to walk into the club. I pinched Johnny on the arm after he slapped me playfully on my rear.

"You know I love you in these jeans. They make your booty look nice and round. Just right for a good plucking." He slapped me on it once more.

"Behave yourself. You already got me walking wobbly kneed around here. Thinking about what you did to me makes my coochie jump."

"I promise to take care of that when we get back to your place."

"Oh, you better." I grabbed his arm tighter and smiled; shushing Johnny as we got closer to Yani and Alex.

"Well, don't we look all aglow?" Yani always knew when I got some, so she claimed. But she knew as long as Johnny wasn't working on a big case, I was getting it on a regular. And regular meant anytime we were together.

"I could say the same thing about you." I gave Alex a knowing glance.

"Hello, sister-in-law. How are you on this beautiful summer evening?" He kissed me on the cheek and hugged me. His way of shutting me up.

"I'm good, brother-in-law."

Johnny gave Yani a hug and kiss and then turned around and shared a brotherly love fist pound and back tap with Alex.

"Are we ready to go in?" Yani asked.

"You know I am. I can't wait to see Teddy. I'm telling you guys, he's off the chain."

"We know you are, Baby." Johnny placed his hand on my back and guided me into the club.

Just as promised, Teddy turned the place out. There was another comedian there, but he should've gone on before Teddy. I think half of the club left—us included—once he started this tired ass routine about ten minutes into his set.

"Where to now?" Yani asked.

"We can head over to the bar around the corner and grab a few drinks," Alex suggested.

"That sounds good. Is that good for you, Johnny?"

"I would love to, Baby, but you know I've gotta get up early. I've got some paperwork I need to get in so we can wrap up this case for the DA's office. You guys know I'd love to hang, but I really can't." He held his hands out as a gesture that it was out of his hands.

"Well, that means I'll see you at the office tomorrow, sis." I walked over and gave Yani a quick hug.

"We understand. Maybe we should head on home as well." Yani looked up at Alex.

"Just 'cause we can't go doesn't mean you guys shouldn't. Go and have an apple martini for me."

"Hopefully, by next week, we'll have this mess tied up and then we can go out and hang until they kick us out," Johnny said.

"You got it, man." Alex and Yani waved goodbye to us and went in the opposite direction.

"Now, was I right about Teddy or was I right?" I asked as we crossed over Broadway and 49th.

"You were definitely right about Teddy. The brother is mad funny. I don't know the last time I laughed that hard. Especially the part he did about the retarded cousin. Boy, I thought my side was going to burst open, I was laughing so hard." He started to laugh again from thinking about it.

"I wonder if he really likes big women. He's done that as a part of his act for as long as I've been watching him. I wonder if he's married and if so, is his wife a big woman?"

"Why you wondering about that man's love life? Don't tell me you're looking to…"

"With all this man I have here, why would I even consider that?" I stopped him and gave him a big kiss.

"Now that's what I'm talking about," he said as he unlocked the car and opened the door for me. "No need to look anywhere else. 'Cause Johnny takes care of it all." He winked at me.

"Get in the car," I said as I closed the door.

I smiled as I watched him walk around to his side of the car. In my heart I knew I loved him. Knew he felt the same for me. But things felt as if they were moving too fast and there was something waiting around the corner to throw us off course.

CHAPTER 6

YANI

It had been a step above being a madhouse at the office. All I wanted to do was go home, jump in the shower, and climb into bed. Since I'd promised Alex we would sit down and talk to the kids that night, my plan to relax wasn't going to happen. I'd kept putting it off in hopes Dede would just go away, but no such luck. The bitch was persistent. I guess that's how she was able to get Jarrin. Not that it mattered anymore.

I pulled up in front and climbed out of my car. I was absolutely spoiled when it came to my car. Alex had surprised me when the guy drove up with my special-ordered 740 IL. I couldn't believe he remembered that conversation we'd had at Carmen's about my obsession with BMW.

I climbed the steps and let myself in. "Hello?" I called out and waited for a response. I heard noise coming from the second floor where the kids were sure to be. I headed into the kitchen where I found Alex stirring the contents of a boiling pot.

"Umm, something smells good. What are we in store for tonight?"

"Nothing special. Just some black beans and rice, plantains, and stewed fish," he said in a Latin accent.

"Nothing special? Baby, my mouth is watering from the visual of that being on a plate." I walked over and gave him a smack on the lips.

"What'd you do, leave the office early today? For you to cook all of this, you had to." I walked over and took a whiff.

"While I did leave early, I only started dinner about thirty minutes ago. It doesn't take long to cook this."

"I wasn't hungry at first, but after smelling this, I feel like I'm starving. Where are the kids?" Just as I asked they filed into the kitchen. Jay following behind Nat.

"Hey, Mommy." Jay walked over and kissed me.

"Hey, Baby. How was camp today?"

"Good." He walked over to Alex and looked into the pot. I smiled as Alex let him stir while he pulled out the plates.

"I'll set the table," Nat volunteered.

We all worked together so we could sit down and eat. These were the things they'd missed because of decisions Jarrin made. Decisions that seemed like they were going to test me 'til the end.

"When we finish eating, Daddy and I need to talk to you guys."

"Okay," Jay said while Nat gave me a curious look.

"You're not in trouble, young lady. Unless there's something you want to tell me."

"I haven't done anything to tell," she said a bit too snappy for me.

"I keep telling you to watch your tone with me. Don't make me have a Janice flashback." My look told her I meant business.

"Grandma was not as bad as you claim. Gosh, Mommy." She smiled and looked down at her plate to say grace.

We met up in the family/entertainment room after dinner had been devoured and the kitchen was cleaned. I grabbed the remote for the television and turned it off. Natalia and Jay looked at me as they anticipated what was going on. I cleared my throat.

"I have something really important I want to talk to you guys about." I paused before continuing. Took a death breath, and then continued. "A few weeks ago, I got an unexpected phone call. Both of you know about what happened last year with your father and all. And you both were told about his new family. Like it or not, you have a little brother and sister."

Nat rolled her eyes and crossed her arms over her chest. Jarrin was a subject she wasn't crazy about discussing and thought it was downright disrespectful for me to even mention his name when Alex was anywhere in the vicinity.

"Well, the mother of those children has requested that her children be allowed to meet you guys. Have a chance to get to know you. Now, as upset as I am at the fact she had the audacity to even call, your daddy and everyone else has said this is a decision I should leave up to you guys. So, I want your honest opinion about how you feel." I looked at them to gauge their reactions. At first neither one said anything. They took a moment to process the information.

"I'm cool with that. I've been wondering what they look like and all," Jay said. I couldn't believe my son, who had taken a sudden turn onto goofy boy street, seemed so mature about the situation.

Natalia, on the other hand, only sat there and looked at us.

"What about you, Nat?" We all looked at her. She was silent for a minute longer before her unexpected outburst.

"How could you ask us this?! How could you even consider something like this?! Why on earth would I even want to see the little…"

"Watch your mouth. Don't forget your place," Alex reminded her.

"But, Daddy…"

"Listen, give it a try. Just see them. It's not going to hurt anyone to see them. Like I told your mom, these kids didn't ask to be brought into this situation."

Nat sulked for a minute, then sat up and nodded her head yes.

"That's my girl," Alex said and hugged her.

❖❖❖

"Yes, may I speak to Dede?"

"Yes?"

"Hi, Dede, this is Yani."

"I take it you've talked to the kids." Her tone was uneasy.

"Yeah. After some talking to, they've decided they're willing to meet your children."

"You mean their little sister and brother?"

"Look, don't make this something you'll regret in the long run. Believe me, you of all people don't want to piss me off."

"That's not my intention. All I'm trying to do is right some of the wrongs that were done to all parties involved. I know you may not believe it, but I'm not a bad person. All I'm asking you to do is give me a chance and allow my children to have what is rightfully owed to them."

"What is rightfully *owed* to them? And that would be?" She had one time to mention anything about the money and the entire conversation would be over.

"A relationship with their brother and sister. What else would I be talking about?" She knew exactly what the "what else" was, but she wasn't a fool. And neither was I.

"Only because the kids agreed to do this is it even happening. So, don't get it twisted, thinking you're in control of anything. Since you're up in Harlem, we'll be nice and come into the city to meet you. Say we meet up in Central Park at the fountain around two o'clock this coming Saturday? I'm only giving you fifteen minutes to get there. Not a second more."

"I'll be there. Or rather we'll be there."

"Goodbye then."

"Why are you so cruel to me?" she almost whined.

"Excuse me?" I brought the phone back to my ear.

"Yani, whether you believe me or not, I never set out to hurt you or your children. Jarrin was always in control of things. He made it seem like you knew what was going on. I was totally in the dark about a lot of things."

"If you say so. Besides, this has nothing to do with us. This is all about the *children.*"

"I do appreciate you making this happen. My son has talked nonstop about you since that night at the hotel. There was something about you he really liked." I could hear the traces of a smile in her voice.

The tightness in my face lessened at hearing that. As much as I hated to admit it, the lil' crumb snatchers were cute.

"We'll have a chance to talk Saturday. Then you can fill me in on the missing pieces of my life." I slowly hung the phone up. Providing me with answers to what had gone on during the years he was gone was the least she could do.

CHAPTER 7

YANI

The day started out as another scorcher, so I told Dede we'd meet her at the little water spot for the kids inside the park. That way they could play and keep cool. We found a nice spot on a bench that gave us a full view of their activities as we enjoyed our ice cream bars.

"I know I've said this already, but I really want to thank you for making this happen. Naya and Lil' Jay have been excited since I mentioned to them they were going to meet their big brother and sister."

I looked over and saw Nat helping Lil' Jay out of the watering hole. He'd stuck to her from the moment they'd gotten there. My Jay and Naya were over at the swings. I'd kept a calm composure about me the entire time. I wasn't sure what I was feeling as I sat next to this woman. "Kill 'em with kindness" kept resonating in my head. The only thing that kept me from giving her the cursing she deserved. At least the one I felt she deserved. One-word responses or body gestures were the most she'd gotten out of me.

Alex had offered to join us, but I thought it best he kept his distance from this tramp. No telling what she'd think once she saw him. She'd already gotten one husband of mine. Getting this one was not an option.

"So how long are you going to be in New York?" I finally asked. I know it shocked her to hear a full sentence.

"Not long. Maybe another week." She shrugged her shoulders.

"Umm," was my response.

"Yani, I'd really like for us to talk…"

"Remember what our purpose is. The children and that's it."

"But there are things I feel you should know. You're making me out to be the bad guy in this and…"

"Making you out? When you deliberately screw another woman's husband and turn up pregnant, then run off and live on the lam with him. Knowing he has another family he has made no contact with in years and you don't say or do anything. Oh, I'm sorry, I forgot the part where you married *my* husband."

"Jarrin never told me he was married until after Naya was on the way. Even at that point what he actually told me was he was getting a divorce. He even brought papers to show proof the divorce was final."

"Did it ever occur to you that he was a lawyer? He could get any type of papers and show them to you. Even if they weren't authentic you still wouldn't know because all of it was foreign to you."

"Put yourself in my place. Here was a man who was showering me with attention, expensive gifts, and paying all of my bills. I was pregnant with his child. While you may not think much of me, I'm not one of those women 'round here looking to be stuck with a baby and no daddy. The way he was feeding it to me, it seemed like you'd left him."

"I left him?" I grunted out a slight laugh. "Then tell me something, why didn't you try and do some type of research into what was going on? If a man told me he was married and then divorced in such a short span of a time, I'd try and see why he and the wife didn't make it."

"You can't be serious?"

I crossed my arms and stared her dead in the face.

"In the society we live in, women aren't making appointments to meet the ex. She's the last person you wanna have to deal with."

She had a point. I mean, it wasn't like I'd called Taylor to find out what the status of her relationship was with Alex when I was about to marry him, but he wasn't married to her either.

I relaxed against the bench and looked up into the clear sky. Other than the heat, it was a beautiful day in the city. Being in the park was like being in a sanctuary. If it wasn't for the honking of car horns in the background, you would never really know you were in the midst of the largest concrete jungle.

"I do have something I'd like to ask you about," I said as I brought my head out of the clouds.

"I told you I'd like to clear the air with you, so ask away."

"I'm curious as to why the authorities never came to my house looking for him. If he actually had people looking for him like he said, why didn't the DEA, the police, or anybody else come knocking on *my* door? I'd filed a missing persons case for him and all, but never once did I get a call, a letter, or anything."

She shrugged her shoulders and shook her head. "Did he ever bring you in on anything that was going on with his office?"

"No. He never told and I never asked."

"Did you know he had a condo on William's Island?"

The widening of my eyes answered her question.

"This is why I never questioned his marital status. Not only was it nicely furnished, he had a housekeeper and all. Pictures of the kids all around the place."

"When did you find out the truth about me?"

"A few months before we skipped town."

"Did he know he was going to leave? Was it planned or was it a spur of the moment thing?" She had my full attention now. I took a bite of my melting ice cream bar before it started to run down my arm.

"It was planned. He knew the heat was coming down and had gone back and forth about leaving before it came down on him."

"He never once let on…"

Nat walked over with Lil' Jay in tow.

"Mommy, I'm hungry." He climbed up on the bench and sat between us.

"You guys hungry too, Nat?"

"I guess. I'll go get the other two." She turned to walk away, but stopped and turned back.

"Mom, remember I'm supposed to meet up with Kayla at the movies around six."

I glanced down at my watch and saw it was almost four. "Get your brother then. We can start heading back now."

"You leavin'?" Jay looked up at me with a softer, smaller set of the eyes that had haunted my dreams for months.

"Yes, sweetie. But, we'll do this again soon. Okay?" I smiled at him. It was hard to take out your anger on a child so young and innocent. Both of them had this endearing quality about them which prevented me from really being the witch I thought I would be. Now girlfriend was another story.

"Can I go to your house with you?"

I laughed. He was the cutest lil' thing. "We have to see what Mommy says about that."

"Mommy, can I go to her house? I promise to be a good boy and go to the potty and all." He shook his head while he spoke.

"Ms. Yani doesn't want to be bothered with you all day."

I hated it when people talked to children like they had no understanding of what was being said and how it made them feel.

"Ms. Yani would love to have you at her house. Only I think we should plan it better, sweetie. That way Mommy will bring you enough clothes and anything else you may need. Okay?"

He nodded his head and smiled, then looked back at his mama.

Jay and Naya came over with Nat.

"If you ever want to finish having this conversation, give me a call. I'm going to be here until sometime next week and then I'm going out to California."

"California? What's out there?"

"I have a few things lined up."

"Have you lined up a job yet?" I was wondering what type of work she was doing these days.

"I have an interview with an employment agency when I get out there."

"That's good." I nodded my head and continued to look at the children. When I looked at her I felt a little hint of jealousy as I tried to figure out what was it she had that I didn't. What was it about her that made my husband, the man who promised my father on his dying bed he would take care of me until the day he himself died, leave and not look back. If anything, she was the total opposite of me.

She wore a full weave—the wavy look. Was maybe a shade or two darker than me. A few inches or more taller than me—around 5'6". Those things were nothing extraordinary. The only thing I could think of was sex. Jarrin always made me feel anything other than missionary was dirty. Being he was the only source I had to pull from when it came to sexual relations, I went along with it. That was always my problem when it came to him. I always went along with what *he* said. Never once questioned any of his reasoning. I guess girlfriend blew his mind with the tricks she'd picked up while dancing.

"Thanks again. I think today was a success. Is it okay for the kids to call?" She stood and started gathering up the kids' things. She pulled Lil' Jay's shirt over his head and put on his sandals.

"I guess it would be okay." I looked at Nat who was helping Naya put on her shoes.

"Tell your brother and sister bye, kids," she instructed her two.

Lil' Jay walked over and gave Nat and Jay a hug. He surprised me when he tapped me on the leg and reached up for me. This baby had melted my heart without me knowing it. I reached down and lifted him up for a big hug.

"You be a good boy for Mommy and maybe we'll see you next weekend. Okay?" I looked at him. His eyes widened and a big smile crossed his face as he nodded his head. Naya then followed his lead and offered me a hug. Not as endearing as his, but she was older and a little more reserved. She'd probably been schooled on the situation to a certain point, so she couldn't help it.

❖❖❖

"So, what did you guys think?" I asked as I pulled out into traffic.

"They're cute. Especially Lil' Jay," Nat said as she bopped her head to the music.

"Would that be because he sorta, kinda, looks like you?"

She smiled. "No, Mother. I'm not just saying it because he and I happen to get more genes from that man than the other two. I really think he's cute."

"What about the little girl?"

"Naya? She's cute, too, but not as cute as Lil' Jay."

I looked in the rearview mirror at Jay. "You're awfully quiet back there, son. What's your opinion?"

He hunched his shoulders upward as he continued to look down at his handheld game. "They're okay. But what does it matter anyway? They're leaving to go back to wherever it was they came from. We probably won't ever see them again anyway, so what's the big deal?"

I hadn't thought that far along. Well, maybe I had. You know that wishful kind of thinking. Wishing she'd go back to wherever it was she'd come from and leave me and mine alone.

I was also smitten with the little boy who had the same eyes and smile as Jarrin. The smile that had swept me off my feet the first time he flashed it at me as I passed him in the hall. Maybe that's why the baby was able to tug at my heart strings. He reminded me of a time when Jarrin made me happy instead of sad.

❖❖❖

The entire transition to high school had been a big ordeal for us. Most of my friends had ended up at Carol City High while I was bussed off to American. American was a new school. Built in '76, it had only been open four years when I got there.

I'll never forget the first time I heard his name. School had been in for three weeks.

"Have you seen that cute tenth-grader?" Friends since elementary school, Mimi sat down next to me on the bench during lunch.

"What tenth-grader?"

"I think his name is Darren or something like that. At least that's what it sounded like the girl called him."

"I don't know." I took a bite of the sausage sandwich I'd gotten off one of the many ice cream trucks lined up in the rear of the school to serve those of us who were against partaking of the cafeteria food.

"Wait. Here he comes."

I looked up in time to see a group of guys walking by. I looked at Mimi and asked her which one without saying a word. She pulled on her top to signal the color shirt he had on. There he was, laughing and talking loud with his friends as they passed by. Yes, I knew who he was. I mean, what girl didn't? He was the best-looking boy in the whole school. From the stories I'd heard, he even had seniors trying to get with him. What I was trying to figure out was why?

He was cute, yes. But he was always talking loud and goofing off with his friends. Myself, I preferred a boy who was mature. One who knew how to go out in public without drawing attention to himself.

"His name is Jarrin. Jarrin Miller," I dryly replied.

"Well, Jarrin Miller is cute as hell."

"Then I say you go for it," I encouraged Mimi.

How was I to know that I would be the one to fall under the spell of Mr. Cutie? And when I say under the spell, I mean it. Jarrin had girls who were at his beck and call. When I became the target of his interest I decided to play the indifferent role. I couldn't care less one way or another about him or the fact he was the most popular boy in school. I later found out my decision to ignore him was what made him want me more. He worked overtime to woo me until he wore me down. The key to us lasting was my holding out on giving up the goods too quickly.

We'd been dating for three years before I blessed him with the gift of my virginity. And the only reason he was able to get it then was because I'd been listening to Mimi and the rest of my friends about how he was off in college and could get any girl to give him what I wasn't. Peer pressure is a bitch. But they were right. He had girls practically throwing themselves at him; even while I was holding hands with him. I could only imagine what happened when I wasn't around.

I trusted him, but I wasn't so trusting of the girls he would encounter while in Atlanta attending Morehouse. It would be an entire year before I got to Spelman, so I decided Mimi and them were right. I gave him something to look forward to coming home to before he left. And I started giving it to him on the regular before he left at the end of the summer.

Since he was an only child and his mother was a widow, we had plenty of opportunities at his house when she was at work. Which was the only time I went over there considering the witch—and I'm being nice about her— didn't like me.

I shook the thoughts of long ago out of my head and pulled my cell from my purse. Since we were in the city and Alex was working, I thought it would be nice to meet him at his office. Since he wasn't invited on the outing, he decided he would go into the office and get ahead on some of his work. I thought now was a good time for him to take a break to eat.

"Hey, Baby. We're all done here and thought we'd come and treat you to lunch. We'll be there in a few." Before he could respond either way I hung up and drove the few blocks to Midtown and found a parking space without the possibility of being towed as soon as I stepped out of my car.

I couldn't wait to tell him how things went and the juicy information I found out from Dede. Here I was beating myself up for moving on and come to find out that bastard had moved on while he was still with me. I would leave out the part about how my heart sank as she told me these things.

CHAPTER 8

ALEX

"So how are things on the home front? Still enjoying the married life?"

"What kind of question is that? Is there a pool or something going around here for how long I'll stay married?"

"It's not like that. Everyone around here *wants* you to stay married. Hell, I'm glad to have you in the ranks with me." Ed sat back in the chair. We were in the conference room after wrapping up a mandatory Saturday meeting.

"You make it sound as if it's some kind of elite club I've become a member of. I love my wife. Man, sometimes I wish I had met her sooner. Would've saved myself a lot of wasted time."

He mimicked the playing of a violin. "And money." He laughed. "Yani has you wide open, man."

"Like Jen's not running things in your house."

"That's in the house. When we're out in public, I get to play the role of the man."

We both laughed. Just like Ed to add humor to things.

"Have you heard anything else about… you know…"

I gave him a quizzical look.

"The situation you guys are dealing with?"

"Oh, you mean the baby?"

"You said that like there's another situation you haven't told me about."

"Well, in so many words, there is."

"What is it now?"

"Nothing too bad we can't deal with it. I don't see anything wrong with it. Yani, on the other hand, is the one having a problem with it."

"Don't tell me your shit ain't working." He sat back and looked at me for confirmation.

"Now why you wanna try me like that? My dick is working just fine." I threw a pen across the table at him.

"You said Yani is having a problem with it. I thought…"

"Stop thinking and listen for a minute." I leaned forward on the table.

"I'm listening." He leaned toward me.

"Tell me if you think I'm wrong or not. The other wife called Yani about the kids being able to see each other. She nearly hit the ceiling when I told her she should allow them to have a relationship. So, am I wrong?" I looked at him, waiting for his take.

"You're asking a man who knows the meaning of papa was a rolling stone. I have a couple of half-brothers myself. When their mother decided being the other woman wasn't quite what she was going for, she gave Pops up and her boys. Pops brought them home and told my moms they were going to live with us. No questions asked. But we came from a different time." He shrugged his shoulders.

"So you feel me on this?"

"I can see where you're coming from, but…" He looked over at me seriously. "I can also see where Yani's coming from. My mom showered them with the same amount of love as she did us, but their presence did do a number on her in the beginning. Moms came from the old school. A time when women stood by their men no matter what. Took the good with the bad. Nowadays, women don't have the tolerance level of our mothers."

"I told Yani she should give Nat and Jay the choice."

"And what did they choose?"

"They're out right now. I'm waiting to hear how it went."

Just then the cell phone on my hip began to vibrate. I checked the Caller ID. *Wife.*

"This is her now." I answered. "Hey, Baby."

She quickly informed me she was on her way to get me for a bite to eat and, more than likely, to give me an earful for making her go.

"Bye." I closed the phone and placed it back on the clip on my hip.

"What's up?"

"They're on their way up."

"Who are they? Yani bring the chick with her?"

"I doubt very seriously if Yani is rolling like that with her this soon." We both laughed.

"I'm about to get out of here myself. Enjoy what's left of my weekend."

"All right, man. Catch you later."

We gave each other dap and stood up. I started toward my office to grab up my things. By the time I made my way out to the elevators the doors were opening. Yani and the kids stepped off.

Her skin seemed to glow from the short outing. I wanted to walk over and kiss her exposed shoulders.

"Hey, Baby." She wrapped her arms around my waist and kissed me.

"Do you guys have someplace in mind you'd like to go?" I placed another soft kiss on Yani's lips.

"Aw, we can't hang out for a minute?" Jay asked.

"Hang out here? Everyone's gone but me and Ed."

"Boy, quit whining. Daddy's been here long enough and I'm starving," Nat nearly barked at him.

"Did you drive in today?"

"Nope. I was thinking ahead and since you drove and I knew you'd want to talk, I caught the train."

"Can we go over to Times Square?"

"For what?" Yani asked Jay.

"I was hoping Daddy could get us into the MTV building. I'd like to be on *TRL*."

"*TRL*? We need to head uptown so we can get on 106 & Park."

I laughed at the back and forth banter. I knew it was only going to last for a short minute before Yani intervened.

"That's enough, you two," she said as we got on the elevator.

"Ready?"

❖❖❖

"You haven't mentioned how today went." I'd waited until we were alone before asking.

"It was nice. The kids seemed to pair off."

"Pair off?"

"Yeah. Lil' Jay had Nat at his beck and call and Jay and Naya went off and played."

"Oh, I was thinking they paired off like our two and then the little ones. Sounds like things were cool then."

"Pretty much." She flipped through the pages of her monthly magazine. "Lil' Jay asked if he could come home with us."

"Really?"

She nodded her head without looking up.

"What did Dede say to that?" I climbed into the bed with her and picked up the book I'd been reading for the past week.

"Told him I wouldn't want to be bothered. She kind of pissed me off with that. She didn't even ask me. But I told him he could come over another time."

"You know he's a baby so he's going to hold you to that promise."

"I meant it. I only wanted to talk with you first."

"Talk with me? You know I'm behind you in any way you choose to handle this."

"Thanks for staying on me about this. You have to see him, Alex. He's such a cutie." She began to smile and look off and then picked her magazine back up.

"A cutie?"

"Lil' Jay. He's such a cutie. Don't get me wrong, Naya's pretty also, but there's something about the little boy. He has such a personality; it's almost as if he's a little man." She continued to smile as she talked about him.

"I take it you had a better time than you let on." I placed my book on the nightstand and reached for her.

"Honey, I'm reading," she tried to protest.

"Nothing in that magazine can rival with what I've got," I teased.

"This magazine is feeding my soul."

"I'll feed more than your soul." I kissed her on the neck.

"Just let me finish this article, then I'm all yours," she breathed heavily.

"You sure about that?" I continued to kiss her on various spots I knew would get the response I wanted. Releasing her ponytail, I began to massage her scalp with gentle strokes. She was putty in my hands after that. The magazine fell to the floor as she climbed on top of me.

"Ready to feed my soul?" She slid her hands down my chest and grabbed my crotch. My dick was at full salute.

Feed her soul? She would be treated to a meal that consisted of an appetizer of foreplay and a generous helping of lovemaking.

"Do you know how much I love you?" I asked her as I kissed my way down to her breasts.

"How much, Baby?"

"More than anything." I slipped the first nipple inside my mouth and then the other. Going back and forth between them until I was satisfied. Then I traveled further south until I reached her valley. The sweetest of sweet honey flowed all for my enjoyment.

She pulled me up and rolled me over on my back so she could give me the same pleasure I'd given to her. My head rolled back as I enjoyed the pressure she applied with her cheek muscles. She pulled away and smiled up at me.

Our lovemaking was beyond intense. We both gave our all to please one another. I pulled her up and rolled her over and filled her with my hardened flesh. I pushed up inside her, wanting to fill her with all my love until she burst.

I awoke an hour later. The television on full blast to drown out the loud moans and other sounds that gave away what we were up to. I pried my arm from underneath Yani so I could turn the television off. As I pulled the covers up to search for it she woke up and looked at me.

"What's wrong?" she sleepily asked. I could see the satisfaction on her face.

"I'm looking for the remote. Go back to sleep."

"I love you, Alex," she said as I kissed her on the forehead and covered her up.

"I love you too, Baby."

I found the remote lodged between the mattress and the footboard. I was about to click it off when I noticed the next movie coming on—*Love Jones*. I smiled as I thought about the first time we'd made love. The movie was a backdrop. We'd come a long way since then.

I climbed back in the bed and turned the volume down a bit and lay back to enjoy as much of the movie as I could before sleep took over.

CHAPTER 9

ASIA

"Hey, Baby, what've you got planned for tonight?"

I'd just walked in the door from getting my hair done. I had a standing Saturday appointment for the past six months. When I found someone who could really do my hair, I was loyal.

"I was going over to Yani's so I can be nosey." I kicked my shoes off at the door and walked into the kitchen to put the bags of food on the counter.

"Be nosey? What's going on over there to be nosey about?" Johnny was lounging on the sofa while reading the paper.

"She's getting Jarrin's other kids today."

"Getting them?"

"They're coming over to spend the day." I closed the fridge and broke the seal on the water bottle I'd taken out. "Don't you want to ride with me over there?"

"Don't try and pull me into this."

"I'm going over to visit my niece and nephew. Is there something wrong with that?"

"And why do you need me to drag along?"

"Because, you're part of the reason I'm stopping by. We were on our way into the city to spend the day."

"Is that the best excuse you can come up with? Yani's going to see right through it." He placed the paper on the coffee table. "I won't lie. I'm curious, too. Come on, let's go." He laughed.

I walked over and popped him playfully on his shoulder.

"Why'd you make me go through all of that if you wanted to go? That was really mean."

He pulled me down into his lap. "I wanted to see you squirm. Test your ability to come up with a lie on the spot." He kissed me on the neck.

"And how did I do?"

"You wouldn't make it through the first hour of an interrogation."

"See, that's where you're wrong. If I'm trying to cover up something serious, I'm going to have my story together before I walk out the door."

"Oh, so what are you sayin'? If you have to, you can lie with the best of them?" He started to tickle me.

"It's in our nature. We will protect ourselves at all costs when we have to." I giggled and squirmed around.

"You women are some sneaky creatures."

"No, we're smart. Plain and simple. Now let's go. I want to be there when they arrive. Might as well see what she looks like also." I loosened myself from Johnny and went to the bathroom.

"You're a nosey ass," he called to my back and started laughing.

Yani and I sat in the kitchen while Johnny and Alex had retreated downstairs to watch a Jets game on TV. Yani held Lil' Jay in her arms. He had been all over her and Nat the entire day. Alex and Jay had worn him out at Sesame Place. Yani said he almost lost his mind when Big Bird came around the corner.

"Wasn't that cute how his eyes got really big and he couldn't get the words to come out of his mouth? He stood there smiling and shaking. I thought the boy was going to pass out for a minute there."

"He's going to be a lil' handsome thing when he gets older."

"Yeah, just like his daddy was." She slowly stroked the curly head lying on her lap.

"So the little girl didn't want to go with you?" I quickly changed the subject. No need in me trying to fake the funk. Jarrin was not a subject I liked to discuss. At least not in any good type of way. I wasn't able to get over his wrongs to make an attempt to remember the good about him.

"She was fine, if her mommy was coming. But him…" She pointed at the top of his head. "He told her bye just as big and walked right out the door."

"You're not hooked on him because he looks like…" I looked at her and nodded my head forward a bit. No need in saying his name.

"Of course not. You saw him in action. It's hard not to be affected by his sweet innocence. I can't believe you even asked me that. You of all people should know Jarrin is water under the bridge as far as I'm concerned." She readjusted the sleeping child in her arms.

"Just checking."

"No need to worry. Like Jay said yesterday, what's the use in getting all used to them when they'll be gone soon."

"Gone?"

"Yeah, they're going to California."

"I commend you for doing what you're doing."

"If you had stayed with Hayden, this is what you would've had to look forward to."

Alex walked in and headed for the fridge.

"He's knocked out." He reached in and grabbed a couple of beers.

"Yeah. You mind taking him upstairs to Jay's room? My arm is starting to get a bit numb." She repositioned his head again.

"No problem." Alex came over and placed the beers on the table and scooped him up.

"You guys look so natural." They both were smiling.

The phone began to ring. Yani reached for the wall phone near the fridge.

"Hello? Yes, this is Yani Chance."

I watched as the bright smile she'd had slowly faded from her face and was replaced with a look of worry.

"What hospital? We'll be right there. No… No… Thank you."

"What's wrong?" I was now standing beside her.

"Dede was in an accident. She's over at Harlem Hospital."

❖❖❖

Yani stood down the hall talking with the doctor as I sat between Johnny and Alex. We'd left the kids at home because we didn't know what we were dealing with.

We all stood as Yani slowly walked back toward us. The grave look on her face told us the situation was bad, but her words revealed how bad.

"The baby… Naya…" She shook her head. "She didn't make it."

"What?!" Alex and I asked.

He ran over and guided her to one of the uncomfortable plastic chairs that were a uniformed part of the hospital's décor.

"Dede's in critical condition. They're not sure if she'll make it through the night. She came out of surgery an hour ago."

"Where's her girlfriend she's staying with?" was my question.

"The only contact information they found on her was mine. That's why they called me. The only phone number I have is her cell number and I never asked her where she was staying. I really didn't want to know." The shame on her face spoke volumes.

Alex gathered her up in his arms. My sister seemed really distraught over the whole thing.

"Did she have any family here? If we can get her ID and what not I can run a check and see what I come up with." Johnny's detective mode was always on.

"They actually think I'm her sister. I didn't tell them any different so they'd let me know about her condition."

We sat there for a few minutes as we tried to figure out what would happen next.

"Mrs. Chance," the doctor called out.

Yani got up and met him.

"You can go see your sister. But only for a minute. She's still weak, but when we told her you were here she asked to speak to you."

Yani grabbed my hand tightly.

"Can my sister come with me?"

"Usually we only let one person at a time go, but seeing her condition could go either way, I'll allow it. Just promise me you won't stay too long."

I followed hand in hand with Yani behind the doctor as he led us to the ICU ward. The corridor was dark. I guess they kept it that way because it was soothing. The sound of beeping machines could be heard in the hallway as we passed each room. As we approached the middle of the hallway the doctor pushed open a door that had Miller in the name slot. Yani and I crept in slowly behind him until the bed came into view. Neither of us was prepared for what we saw. We gasped and couldn't believe the severely swollen and bruised face that stared back at us.

"They were ejected from the car as it flipped over. That's why she's cut up so badly. We have her heavily sedated, because she's in a lot of pain."

We walked closer to the bed. Yani stood over her and said her name. We could see her eyes as they rolled back and forth behind her lids. Yani gently grabbed her hand.

There's something about the nature of a human being when they're put in a situation like this. After all of the heartache Yani'd experienced behind this woman, she still found it in her heart to have compassion for her.

I rubbed Yani's back as she stood there. Both of our eyes were filled with tears as we realized how much Dede was suffering.

Her eyes slowly opened. She looked at both of us through heavy lids.

"Yani…" She blinked her eyes closed. It was almost as if she was relieved to see her.

"We're here. My sister and I came…" Yani's tear fell on their hands. She took the free one and wiped away the moisture.

"I'm not… I'm not going to ma…"

"Shh, don't talk like that. You'll be fine. Soon as you get better I'll bring your baby to see you. You'll see. Everything is going to be fine." Yani was trying her best to be strong. She and I both knew from looking at Dede it would be a long road to recovery, if she lived at all.

"Lis… Listen to me…" She was struggling with her words. "I want you to… take care of him."

"I will. Until you get out of here, he'll be fine with us."

"No." She shook her head slightly; as much as she could without causing too much further pain.

"Who do you want me to call and let them know…"

"I don't… my family." She took a deep breath.

"Don't worry; we'll take care of everything. You just lay here and take it easy so you can get better."

"Naya..." she looked at us with asking eyes. It was then we realized she had no idea of the fate of her little girl.

Yani looked at her for a long time before she shook her head. A tear slipped from Dede's swollen eye.

"I'm... sor... sorry, Yani."

"For what? Don't worry about it. That's the past. And that's where it's going to stay."

"I never... meant... hurt you. Thank you."

"When you get out of here, we'll go hang out at the spa. Get your strength back. One day we'll look back on all we've been through and laugh about it." Yani forced a smile on her face.

"I... wish... we could." Dede attempted to smile. The pain made it almost impossible. "Promise me... be... good... life." She began to fade out.

Yani squeezed her hand reassuringly. "You need to get some rest, Dede." The monitor told us her heart rate was beginning to slow down.

"Lil' Jay needs you, too. You can't go! Come on, Dede, hold on!" Yani's voice rose with each command. She knew she was slipping away and thought she'd remind her of her reason to live.

The door burst open with the doctor leading the pack. They quickly began to attempt to save her. I pulled Yani back toward a corner in the room. The nurses and doctors went back and forth with medical mumbo-jumbo as they prepared to hit her with the paddles. They inserted needles into her IV to inject her with the needed medicine to keep her heart from stopping. No matter what they did it wasn't enough. Dede had made her peace with Yani and was sure Yani would do whatever was needed to assure the welfare of her child.

Yani began to sob uncontrollably. I held in my emotions to be strong for her.

"I'm sorry," was the doctor's response to us as they called out her time of death.

I wrapped my arm around Yani's shoulder and guided her out of the room. As soon as we parted the doors to the waiting room Alex ran to her side and she collapsed in his arms.

"It's okay, Baby. It'll be okay," he reassured her.

I looked at Johnny standing in front of me. He reached out and pulled me into his broad chest. Once I hit my place of comfort the tears flowed from me. Even though I didn't know Dede, I was still affected by the experience. It had been a long time since I'd experienced death, but never this up close and personal.

Dede's personal effects were given to Yani. Before we left, the hospital asked Yani to identify the body of Naya. It was more heart-wrenching than the episode with Dede. Her tiny mangled body lay on a cold steel table covered by a white sheet. The impact of hitting the windshield and then the street caused the right side of her tiny head to burst open. If I lived a hundred years, I never wanted to experience that again. She was so helpless.

Johnny went through Dede's belongings and found her purse. He told us he would go over to the station and see what he could come up with. See if he could find any of her living relatives or someone we could contact. He promised to meet us back at the house once he found something.

The ride home was extremely silent. Alex drove, his hand covering Yani's. The most we could do was stare out the window and watch the landscaping pass by in a blur.

"What am I supposed to tell this baby when he asks about his mommy and sister?"

"We tell him the truth, honey. Just because he's four doesn't mean he can't understand."

"It'll be okay, Yani. Jay was younger than him when Daddy died and he dealt with it well."

"Daddy didn't live in the house with Jay every day. This baby has lost his entire family in less than a year."

I hadn't thought about that up until that moment. It was not quite a year since Jarrin was killed and now this.

"Not his entire family," Alex said as he looked over at Yani.

"He still has Nat and Jay," I added, following Alex's cue.

"He's got us also," Yani said and for the first time since it all began she smiled a little.

I thought about the conversation we'd had earlier about how much she adored this baby. I hoped Alex knew what he was about to get into as he smiled back at Yani and squeezed her hand. I prayed she knew what she was doing as well.

CHAPTER 10

YANI

Breaking the news to the baby was one of the hardest things I think I ever had to do. Telling Nat and Jay about Jarrin had been much easier. He cried about it, but I don't think he really understood the seriousness of what had happened. He'd ask for them from time to time throughout the passing weeks. We'd tell him they were both gone to sleep and he would see them later when he got older. I know it may sound corny, but how do you help a child that young deal with death? Alex found a therapist who specialized in it. Dr. DeVaughn had been a blessing in more ways than one. He would see Lil' Jay, whom we'd decided to call Corey—his middle name—to keep the confusion in the house to a minimum, three times a week in the first month. Then he incorporated the whole family into it. This process helped us deal with unforeseen problems we would've never thought about. Even preexisting problems we weren't paying attention to.

"So how's my favorite family?" Dr. DeVaughn gestured for us to have a seat.

"Pretty good. Still pretty much in the transitional stage, but I think things are going very well," I said as I sat down next to Alex and held his hand. Dr. DeVaughn had asked for us to come in without the kids, so I was pretty nervous.

"I know you're wondering why you're here." He continued to look over the papers he held in his hands.

We sat quietly waiting for him to continue.

"I've been going over my notes and I wanted to talk to you about something that has come to my attention." He placed the papers on his desk and looked at me and Alex.

"Is it something serious?" I finally asked.

"Not too serious, but if ignored it could become a problem in the future."

"Well, lay it on us, Doc. That's why we come here, so you can help us." Alex tightened his grip on my hand slightly.

"Mr. and Mrs. Chance, I'm noticing a bit of friction that may become a problem with one of the boys." The serious expression on his face made my heart race a bit.

"You're talking about Jay?" Alex asked.

"Well, during my sessions with him I've asked about his feelings of Corey becoming an addition to the family. While he's saying he's fine with it, I sense there's something else underlying. From the history of this family…" He shuffled the papers again. "I think he's dealing with the issue of abandonment by his own father. When he looks at Corey, he feels he's the reason for the abandonment."

"But it's not like we haven't talked about what happened with Jarrin."

"I know, Mrs. Chance, but I think he somehow blames himself for his father leaving. After meeting Corey and his sister…" He looked at the papers again.

"Naya," I offered.

"Yes. And their mother, his perception changed. He began to see them as the source. So unconsciously he's still harboring those feelings toward Corey."

"Is this something he told you? Or… I mean, what led you to this…" Alex looked at the doctor for some answers.

"There's a series of questions I asked all three of the children. Jay's answers gave me cause to look at him a little closer. Also, Mrs. Chance, I'm also sensing a hint of jealousy about the time and energy you're spending with Corey."

I was shocked. I spent more time with the kids than the one hour a week he did, but he was telling me there was a problem in *my* house.

"I don't understand what you're talking about. I spend an equal amount of time with all of my children." I was a bit on the defensive now.

"Be that as it may, your son feels once again, this baby is coming in to take another one of his parents away from him. In his mind, Corey is not your child and never will be."

"But he hasn't voiced this to me. Matter of fact, he was given the choice of whether or not he wanted to meet them. He was all for the meeting and them coming to spend time with us."

"Spending time is one thing. Now Corey has become a permanent fixture and he's not sure how he feels about that." He repositioned himself and leaned forward a bit.

"Let me ask you something. Who plays the more dominant role in what's going on with Corey? Do you seem to handle everything? Do you and your husband do them together or equally?"

"No, I handle the bulk of everything. But, Dr. DeVaughn, my husband is a very busy man and he doesn't have..."

"I understand..." He cut me off. "But you also run your own business, do you not?"

"Yes, but..."

"Mrs. Chance, I'm not attacking you. I'm only trying to get you to see what your son is seeing and how he feels. His mother has taken an extra amount of interest in this kid that's not really hers. While he is his half-brother, in his mind all he can think about is he's not anything to his mother. So why is she spending so much time with him? Why hasn't she found his own family so he can live with them?"

"We did search for his mother's family."

"Mrs. Chance, once again, I'm not attacking or accusing you of anything. I understand you've done what you have out of love and sympathy for a child who has, in your eyes, lost everything in his short life span."

Tears began to well in my eyes. Was I wrong for wanting to nurture him? I'm a mother. That's what mothers do. They nurture their young. No exceptions.

Alex wrapped his arm around me. Wiped away the tears.

"So what are you suggesting we do to keep this from becoming a problem in the future?" Alex asked.

Dr. DeVaughn went on to explain how we should create "me days" with Jay; especially me. A day where he and I would do anything he wanted to. We had to reassure him nothing was going to change.

❖❖❖

"Okay, Baby?" Alex reached over and grabbed my hand.

I stared out the window as we crossed over the Brooklyn Bridge.

"Hmm?"

"It's all good, Baby. Don't even let this worry you. We got this. Me and you, Baby." He was doing his best to get a smile out of me. I gave in. The corners of my mouth turned up.

"That's my baby." He reached over and rubbed my cheek.

"Do you think I should sit down and talk with Jay? I think I should explain to him why I…"

"We'll talk to him; both of us. We're a team, right?"

"Yes, Baby. We are a team."

"Then we'll handle this like parents. We'll talk to *our* son and get him to understand what's going on."

We rode the rest of the way in silence. I couldn't understand why the doctor had said what he'd said. I was a good mother. Jay understood what was going on. At least he told me he did. We'd soon find out though.

CHAPTER 11

ASIA

"So what are the dates for this cruise?"

"Next month. I have all the paperwork." Linda slid the brochures across the table for everyone.

"Girl, it's really nice to have a friend who can hook us up like this." Brina threw back the remainder of her drink and got up to get another.

We decided to meet at my place instead of some noise-filled restaurant or club after Linda said she needed to talk with us about the cruise. As hard as we'd all been working the past few months, we wanted to be able to hear every word she had to say.

"Is this a new ship?" I asked as I scanned the brochure she had given to each of us.

"No, this is a convention I attend every year. I thought it would be fun if we could all go. It's affordable and it happens to be one of their nicest ships. What more could you ask for?"

"I'm in," Yani said.

"Me, too," Brina added.

"How many people can you take?"

"I think six. Why?"

"I wanted to invite Carmen to join us; especially since we're leaving out of Miami."

"That's fine with me. I need her answer by Monday, is all."

"I'll call her right now." Yani pulled out her cell phone.

"Why are you wasting up your minutes? You can use my phone." I handed her the cordless from the kitchen.

"Thanks."

"What about you, Ms. Asia? You in or what?" Linda looked at me over the rim of the glass in her hand.

"I have to check my schedule."

"What could you be doing that will keep you from being with your girls?"

"I think it's more of a *who* than a what, Brina. Girl, we're only going to be gone for four days. We leave out on Friday and get back on Monday. So technically he'll only be without you for three days."

"You bitches are trippin'. I haven't said no. I just said I needed to check my schedule. I might have an appointment or an event…"

"Your sister doesn't have a problem with going." Brina pointed over to Yani, who was on the phone and oblivious to our conversation.

"My sister is the owner. So that means us peons are left to do the work."

"Girl, it's us you're talking to. We know you carry more weight than what you're saying." Brina got up and walked into the kitchen to refill her glass.

"I heard that shit, Asia," Yani said and went back to talking to Carmen.

"Well, like I told Yani, I have to know by Monday. If you don't let me know before then, the ship will sail without you."

"You'd do your girl like that, Linda?" I playfully asked.

"I should be asking you the same question." She gave me a look that screamed challenge.

As much as I wanted to spend that weekend with Johnny at his parents', I knew I couldn't go out like that. I had to commit right then. I'd never give them something they could bring back and throw up in my face.

"If you ladies would let me finish what I was trying to say…"

"What? That you have to check with your man first?"

"I know you're not talking, Ms. Brina? Don't let me remind you of Patrick, Michael, Devon…" I flipped out a finger for each name.

"Whatever, Ms. Bitch." She sat down and placed her wine glass on the table.

"As I was saying, before I was so rudely interrupted." I looked over at Brina and rolled my eyes. "I'm in."

"That's all you had to say from jump. A simple yes with no drama."

"It wouldn't be her without the drama. I thought you knew, Linda."

"Okay, Carmen's in also!" Yani said as she rejoined us.

"That leaves room for one more. Any ideas?" Linda looked at all of us.

"Did you guys call Cheryl?"

"Please. She's got it worse than you."

"Stop trying me, Brina."

"I'm serious. We've already had this discussion. We haven't seen Cheryl in more than a month of Sundays. It's not like she got a new job. But she has gotten a new man. Need I say more?"

"We could still call and ask."

"Well, if she can't go, we can invite my sister-in-law," Yani said.

"Oh yeah. Lucia is mad cool. Hell, I'll even bunk with her. Yani, give me her number." Brina grabbed the phone off the table.

"I'll call," Yani said as she grabbed the phone back from Brina.

After a few minutes on the phone, it was all set. The final six had been chosen. All Linda had to do now was put in the request.

We spent the rest of the night playing name that tune with the collection of records I'd accumulated over the years on top of what I had inherited when Daddy died. That alone brought my collection to over a thousand. And that's before counting the CDs.

Since Brina was in no condition to make the trek back to the Bronx, I pulled out my sofa bed for her. Yani and Linda were each one drink away from spending the night themselves, but chose to take that chance. I made them promise to call me when they got in so I'd know they'd arrived safely. After receiving those calls, I made the one I'd been thinking about making all night.

"Hey, Baby," I sang into the mouthpiece.

"Hey. How'd everything go?"

"We had a really good time. Brina's out on the sofa."

"One too many?"

"Try four too many." I curled up in my bed and grabbed the remote.

"So, I guess that means I'll be sleeping alone tonight?"

"You don't have to."

"You're going to come over here?"

"Don't ask crazy questions."

"Oh, so I guess I'm supposed to drive over there?"

"Well…"

"See, if you'd simply take me up on my offer, you'd already be here with me. Where you should be."

"You know how I feel about Brooklyn."

"I know, but you're in the city more than anyplace else. You hang out over here. You work over here. You even shop over here. So what's so wrong with sleeping over here?" I would've given him points for persistence, but he was fighting a losing battle.

"It's not Brooklyn."

"What would you do if we were married?"

"I guess we'd find us a nice place in Brooklyn."

He laughed. I stayed silent. He had asked me to marry him twice before. First time was three months into our relationship. The second at six months. When we made it through the ninth month without a proposal I thought he was tired of trying.

"We're going to have to come to some type of compromise then. 'Cause see, I'm straight up Harlem World, Baby. Born and bred. While you, on the other hand, are an import."

"I guess we'll cross that bridge when we get to it."

"Yeah, the Brooklyn Bridge."

I got quiet. He changed the subject.

"Are you all set for tomorrow?"

"I sure am. Got my clothes all laid out. My shoes by the door."

"Now see, if you came here tonight, we could walk over to the park."

"I'm not driving over there this late, Johnny."

"It was worth another try." He took a deep breath. "I'll see you in the morning. The picnic starts at noon."

"I'll see you by eleven then."

"Asia?"

"Yes, Johnny?" I said, trying to keep the annoyance I was starting to feel out of my voice.

"I love you, Baby."

I paused and smiled. He had a way of melting my heart whenever it seemed that wall of ice would try to creep in.

"I love you, too."

We hung up and I thought about how serious my relationship with Johnny was. I wasn't quite sure I was happy with how fast it was moving. I did love him, but I wasn't sure how much.

CHAPTER 12

ASIA

The day turned out to be a borderline scorcher. Typical of summer days in New York. People had the tendency to think because I was from Miami I was more adept at dealing with heat. Please. If you asked me, the summers in the northern part of the country were much hotter than any I could ever remember in Miami.

"You want something to drink?"

Johnny had been very attentive to me. It was nice to finally be able to put faces with some of the names I'd heard for almost a year.

"I'm good, Baby."

"You sure?"

"Johnny, I'm fine. Go over there with your buddies. I'm going to go sit in the shade with some of the other ladies."

He pecked me on the lips before walking away. I made my way around the small groups that had stopped everywhere to talk to each other. Giving the plastered-on smile I was known for to anyone who greeted me.

"You know she has no business wearing that," I could hear one of the ladies say about the busty blonde who seemed to hug every man she came in contact with.

"Girl, don't she look a mess? If you're going to get them, at least know how to control them. Ya know, learn what you can and can't wear."

"See, mine are natural. I've been dealing with them all my life," the heaviest one in the group said. She emphasized it by jiggling them for everyone.

"Girl, you didn't have to go there." They all laughed.

"Hi," I said as I joined their little group.

"Hi. You're JJ's friend, right?" the one who seemed to be the leader asked.

"Yes. I'm Asia." They all seemed cordial, but there's always one in every crowd.

"He seems to bring a new one every year."

"Don't pay her any mind. I'm Melissa. This here is Tracey, Shavonya, Mary, and that over there is Tonya." She pointed to the tallest of the group. The one who seemed to have her eyes on me from the moment she spied me and Johnny walking into the park.

"It's nice to meet *all* of you." I made sure to look at Tonya.

"So how long have you been seeing JJ?" Tonya asked with much bitch attitude.

"You don't have to answer," Melissa interjected; even though I could tell they were all eager to find out.

"No, I don't mind. It'll be a year next month." I eyed Tonya down.

"I think you've got the record then." Tonya took a sip from her cup.

Did that bitch roll her eyes at me?

"Do you ladies work for the department, wives, or girlfriends?" Hey, since she wanted to roll like that, I could roll, too.

"We're officers. We work at the station with JJ," Melissa said as she pointed to Mary and, of course, Tonya.

"I'm a wife," Tracey said.

"And I'm on your team—a girlfriend," said Shavonya.

"A longtime girlfriend," Tonya added.

What the fuck was her problem? I decided to ignore her slight. I wasn't in the mood to cause a scene in the middle of a police function. I could see it on the evening news now.

Woman goes berserk at police picnic and beats the shit out of one of New York's finest.

I know you didn't expect me to say she was going to win? Hey, I may not be the biggest thing, but I can definitely handle mines.

"So what do you do? Where do you work?" Melissa was trying to keep it civil.

"I'm VP of an event planning company owned by my sister."

"Event planning? What type of events do you plan? If you don't mind me asking."

All eyes were on me as they awaited the answer to Shavonya's question.

I decided to throw my weight around and let that bitch Tonya know who she was dealing with.

"Oh, I don't mind. We do all types of events. But we mainly deal with entertainers, writers, you know. People in the industry."

"Like who?" This time Tracey was in line to ask the question.

"Well, my sister is married to Alex Chance…"

"You mean *the* Alex Chance?"

They all seemed to perk up. All except Tonya who seemed to get more annoyed with each question they asked me.

"That was your sister on the cover of *Essence* with him?"

"Wasn't she a beautiful bride?"

I beamed as they went on and on. Now I was the center of attention. Which isn't what I was going for, but to see that big-boned heifer sit over there and squirm, I was willing to allow them to keep talking.

"So who have you met? Anybody we would know?"

"Oh, I've met plenty of people that you'd know. Even some you wouldn't who happen to have bigger bank accounts than those you do know." They all laughed. Well, almost all of them. But at this point, no one was really paying her any attention.

By the time Johnny came over to retrieve me, we were really deep into a sistah girl conversation.

"So you're telling me the rabbit is the best one?"

"Oh by far…"

"Am I interrupting something?"

"Hey, Baby." I kissed him. He then said his hellos to the ladies. Ms. Tonya, who had been quiet for quite some time, suddenly perked up.

"Hi, JJ."

He gave her a nod and then looked back at me.

"Ready to go?"

"Aww… we were just getting into a really good conversation," Melissa said.

"Sorry, ladies, I can't stand to be away from her any longer." He wrapped his arms around my waist and pulled me into him.

"It was nice meeting you guys. *All* of you," I said as I looked at Tonya.

"We have to do this again. Do you have any cards on you?" Shavonya asked.

"I didn't bring any today. Maybe we'll see each other at the next event you guys have."

"Okay." Melissa jumped up to hug me bye; totally catching me off guard. I hugged her back. This seemed to be a signal that it was okay for everyone else to follow suit.

"I'd take that as being you were a hit," Johnny said as we walked away.

"Well, not at first. You know, since you seem to show up every year with someone new." I poked him in the ribs playfully.

"I don't have to ask who said that bullshit."

"You mean your biggest fan?"

"Chick has got some serious problems."

"She's was about to catch the antidote for them if she kept fucking with me."

"What kept that from happening?" He smiled slightly.

"Now how would that look to your colleagues? They'd talk about you for years to come. Yo, remember when JJ's girlfriend beat the living shit out of Tonya at the annual picnic?" I said in the manliest voice I could conjure up. I gave him my B-Boy stance to go along with it.

"You do know she's a cop?"

"I don't give a damn. What *she* needs to know is that I have a black belt, which is a license to kick a bitch's ass."

"You never told me that."

"Never was important. I only use it when I have to and that's rarely."

"So, all in all, you had a pretty good day?"

"Pretty much. I mean, at first they were trying to give me the cold shoulder in a show of support for their girl. But once they found out what I do for a living and who I knew, they were hooked." I smiled in spite of myself.

"You played the name-dropping game?"

"Yes, I'm sad to say I had to stoop to that. But sometimes you have to pull out the big guns."

"The big guns? I take it that Mr. Chance's name was mentioned."

"It's the biggest gun I carry." I winked at him as I blew smoke from my imaginary smoking gun and pretended to place it back on my hip.

Johnny grabbed my hand and playfully spun me into him. "What am I going to do with you?"

"I don't know, but I hope it's something good."

We strolled hand in hand out of the park toward the train station that would take us back up the few blocks to Harlem. It was still hot out and I wasn't up to walking.

I tried to think of how I was going to approach him about the stank ass attitude I received from Tonya and what it had to do with him.

"What's on your mind, pretty lady?"

"Hunh?"

"You're too quiet. So that means you have something on your mind."

"Oh, so now you know me like that?" I teased.

"I think I know you well enough."

"I was just wondering about something."

"Would that *something* be named Tonya?"

"She's a part of it." I looked at him. "What's with her? She gave me bitch-tude from the moment I walked over to her and her little clique."

"Now I take it you want to know the history between us?"

"I think I deserve to know. You know all about my past relationships. You can at least give me one. I'm starting to think you're hiding something from me."

"I'm not hiding anything."

"So you shouldn't have a problem telling me about Tonya then."

"We went through the academy together. And yes, I dated her, but only for a minute. She became possessive and I couldn't deal with it."

"So you gave her some of Johnny's good dick and she hasn't been the same since?"

"Damn, why you gotta say it like that?"

"I calls it like I sees it. After the way that bitch acted today, I knew for a fact she'd had some."

I saw his mouth curve up at the corners into a devious smile.

"Umm hmm. I knew it! I knew it!"

"I was young. You know, thinking with the other head first. How was I supposed to know she'd have a problem moving on?"

"Are there any others I should know about? I mean, you have to give a sistah some type of warning. I need to have my stuff together beforehand. Ya know? Got me walking into hostile land without a clue."

"Baby, you're all that matters to me. So there's no need for you to worry about anyone else." He held me close to his side.

"That's what your mouth says, but I know better."

"You can't compare our thing with you and dude before me." He said it as if he didn't know Hayden's name. I had been upfront with Johnny from the beginning so, he knew damn well what *Dude's* name was. I gave him a look that told him he was treading on thin ice.

"We need to talk, Johnny. There are some things we need to get out in the open or we'll never be able to get to the next level."

"And what level would that be?"

"It's not something that has to be defined. So, don't go thinking I'm pushing up on the marriage thing."

"I never said that."

"I'm simply letting you know. I'm not saying this in an attempt to steer you toward it."

"You don't have to steer me. I've been there for quite sometime. You're the one who needs steering. So stop being defensive."

"I'm not being defensive." I stepped away from him.

"Yes, you are. Anytime someone says anything against you, you go on the defensive. And before you say one word, it's natural. It's in our nature to want to protect ourselves." He pulled me back into him. "Besides, what if I wanted to have the marriage talk?" He made quotation marks with his fingers.

I didn't respond.

"Hmm. What would you do if I were to drop down on one knee right now and ask you to be my wife?"

My heart began to beat at a faster rate. I looked around at the faces passing by us unknowing of the conversation going on.

"Are you going to answer me?"

I looked back at him to find that he'd started to make the descent toward the ground in that too familiar stance of one knee up and the other down. I could not believe this was happening. Right on the street in front of people we'd probably never see again.

He was putting me on the spot. This time he'd asked in front of people. Not like the other two times. Those were after we'd had a marathon session of sex or spent a nice quiet day enjoying each other's company.

"Johnny?"

"Asia, I'm asking you to marry me. I know we've been here before, but I'm serious. Are you willing to spend the rest of your life with me? Forsake all others for our love?"

"You're really serious?" I didn't know what else to say.

"You're asking a man who has knelt down on a busy street in front of strangers if he's serious?"

I loved him and Yani had told me to stop denying myself. What was I to do? We'd done enough time to know this is what we wanted. Eventually. But I was still unsure. I looked up at the crowd forming around us.

How could I embarrass him like this?

"Yes," was the response that came out of my mouth. The response that was in my head. My heart, on the other hand, was saying something else.

"Yes? You said yes?!" He got off his knee and looked into my eyes.

"Yes, I'll marry you. Yes, Johnny." I gave him the most convincing smile I could come up with.

He scooped me up in his arms. "She said yes!" we heard in the background as someone announced the outcome to the other onlookers. An approving chorus of clapping followed.

"I love you, Ms. Asia Fenton. I promise to always love you."

I continued to smile as my brain seemed to be deep in a wrestling match with my heart.

What have I done?

CHAPTER 13

YANI

I sat waiting for Asia to walk out of the dressing room wearing what would be the seventh gown she'd tried on that day. While we knew she wasn't going to buy the dress at the shop, I wanted her to be able to try on a few to get an idea of what she wanted Jeanette to make. I jotted down the things we liked about the gown so we could relay to Jeanette exactly what she was looking for. While I wasn't an artist, per se, I did well enough to get the point across. As long as it was in front of me I could work with it.

"What do you think about this one?" Asia spun around slowly; examining every side in the mirror.

"I'm still leaning more toward the second one. I really like the neckline on it and the back is beautiful." I stood up and felt the satiny material of the dress. The humungous bow in the back was too ugly for words. It screamed eighties loud and clear. "Look at these puffy ass sleeves. Girl, go take it off. Please!" She walked away laughing.

"I don't know why I let you talk me into this. Johnny and I wanted something simple. But you've gone crazy and we haven't even set a date yet."

"Girl, hopefully, you'll only have to do this once. Besides, this is your first time so it has to be special." I worked on a few of the sketches I had as I waited for her to come out of the dressing room.

"Still, Yani, I think you're going a bit overboard."

"The way you're talking you might as well go on down to the courthouse and get it over with."

"You have some nerve. Have you forgotten where you and Jarrin were married?"

"Exactly. And you know the ending to that story."

"Yani, Mama and Daddy were married at the courthouse and if Daddy hadn't died, you and I both know they'd still be together."

Talking about Daddy was always a soft spot in my heart. Even though he'd been dead for more than a decade I still got a certain feeling when I thought about him. I could still hear him telling me to do what was good for me as opposed to trying to please others. I'm glad he wasn't alive when my marriage to Jarrin went wrong. He really loved him. Jarrin was the son he'd never had. But I know he would've loved Alex even more.

"Asia, for years I felt I had been cheated out of something that meant the world to me. To get married in a place filled with your family and friends, there's nothing like it. I love Alex for giving me another opportunity to experience that. Even though I'd been married before, he wanted to make me happy."

She'd changed back into her street clothes. A pair of khaki-colored cargo pants and white tank top. Her cap covered her head while her ponytail hung from the opening in the back of it. She slid her feet into her sexy sandals. She handed the last dress to the attendant.

"Well, sister dear, we need to get a move-on. I told Jeanette we would be there at two." On cue, we both looked at our watches.

"You're the one who wanted to try on all these dresses. I told you the last ones were ugly before you even put them on." I pulled my purse up on my shoulder and stuck the pad under my arm.

"Regardless, we need to get a move-on."

We thanked the store attendant for her help and made our way out to the street. We turned right and headed back to the block where we'd parked.

I pulled out my Palm Pilot and flipped it open. As I began to check things off, Asia's cell rang. Before she said hello, I knew it was Johnny from the way her eyes lit up when she checked her caller ID. We reached her car. I stood waiting for her to unlock the doors as she snuggled the phone between the side of her face and her shoulder.

"Okay, baby. Love you, too."

She hit the alarm box on her key ring. I slid into the car as she ended her call.

"Your sweetie?"

"Umm hmm. We have dinner plans tonight."

"That's nice. You know I'm nosey so embellish." I pulled the seatbelt across me and placed my purse on the floor at my feet.

"Nothing special. We were thinking about driving to Atlantic City and hanging out there for the weekend." She strapped in also and adjusted her mirrors.

"If you're going to Atlantic City, why would you say nothing special? You act as if you go there every day or something."

"I stand corrected then. Actually, any time I spend with Johnny is special so you're right." She smiled and pulled into traffic.

"Why does it feel like you're not telling me everything?"

"Yani, don't start. I don't have to tell you everything that goes on between my man and me."

We both burst into a verse of Aretha's "Dr. Feelgood."

"Boy, does that make me think about Daddy."

I looked out the window. A simple smile adorned my face as I thought of the record collection he had. I was willing to bet there wasn't a DJ in town that could rival it.

"Has Johnny picked out the place where they're going to get the tuxes?"

"Yes, Ms. Wedding Planner. He got your email, phone messages, and the postcard you dropped in the mail."

"You know I'm big on follow-up. Have to make sure everyone is on the same page."

"We are, Yani.

"On a different note, where did you get those from?"

I looked down at my jeans.

"What's so special about these?"

"I've never seen you with hiphuggers on before. Got your ass looking like it's about to spill out the back. Alex is okay with you dressing this way?" She took her hand and pulled at one of the many straps crisscrossing across my back.

"Alex is fine with the way I dress. And you, for one, know it's never about what someone else thinks with me. I'm classy enough to pull off any look without it looking too hoochie."

"Now did I say you looked like a hoochie? No. Here I am trying to give you a compliment and you wanna go and switch up on me."

"I never said you weren't complimenting me, but I was setting the record straight before you tried to switch it up on me."

Unconsciously I pulled my jeans up a bit and made sure my shirt was adjusted. No need for showing more skin than was needed. I did feel sexy as hell though. And my husband definitely approved of it. So much so, he stopped me for a quickie before letting me leave out the house. I smiled as the stirring between my legs reminded me of just how much I enjoyed it.

"Looks like you're enjoying your own private joke over there."

"Just thinking about something Alex said."

She pulled up to the curve in front of Jeanette's and parked. Killing the ignition she turned to me.

"Can you believe I'm getting married?"

"I know. I'm so happy for you, baby sis." I reached over and hugged her.

"I have something to confess."

I pulled away slowly and looked at her as I waited for her to tell me what was on her mind.

"I'm scared, Yani. I don't know if I really want to do this. What if things don't work out? If he realizes I'm not the one. Or…"

I put my hand up to protest. "You stop this right now. There's no reason Johnny is going to turn chicken and run. Asia, he loves you. This isn't Hayden. You have to realize things didn't go the way you wanted them to with Hayden and you both moved on. But don't forget you guys were young then. And like you made me see, God does things His way, not yours. I couldn't be happier right now than I've been in my entire life. So, stop second-guessing yourself. It was meant to be this time, Asia. Trust what you're feeling." I hugged her and then reached over and opened my door.

"Now, we have an appointment we're about to be late for."

"But…"

I waited for her to finish.

"I'm... I don't know. For some reason I'm feeling this isn't right. With Hayden, I knew, Yani. Deep in my soul I knew he was right for me. Everything about him felt right. I know things didn't work out, but it's been eating at me. For some reason I'm having second thoughts."

I didn't know what to say to her. It wasn't like she was saying she didn't love Johnny.

"Does it have to do with his job?" It was the only thing I could think of that would give her any doubts.

"I don't know."

"Then why did you tell him yes, Asia?"

"Because he'd asked two times already. We were in a public place. This man humbled himself for me. What was I supposed to do?" Her eyes began to tear up as she chewed on the tip of her finger.

"Oh, baby sis. You have to do what's good for you." I reached over and hugged her.

"Johnny is good for me. I love being with him, but I'm not sure if I want to spend the rest of my life with him. Does that make me a bad person?"

"No. I wouldn't say that. Maybe you need more time."

She hung her head, then looked at her watch.

"We better get in here." She signaled to Jeanette's with her head.

"Are you sure you want to go through with this?"

"I told the man yes already."

"It's not like signing a contract. Doesn't mean you have to go through with it."

"I'll be fine. Besides, I need a new dress anyway."

"Now you're being silly."

She opened the door and got out.

I tried to think of something I could say or do to make her realize she needed to hold off on this until she got her feelings in check. I got out of the car.

"Asia, you should talk to Johnny before you make Jeanette waste her time."

"Yani, you worry too much. Everything will be fine."

Her demeanor had gone from night to day.

"No, everything will not be fine. You *need* to talk to Johnny."

She took a deep breath and looked around. She nervously bit down on her bottom lip. Looked over at me and shook her head.

"Let's go tell Jeanette we'll catch her later." I held out my hand for her and led her into the boutique.

I had to help her get over whatever was holding her back. For some reason I felt it was more of a "someone" than a "something."

CHAPTER 14

ALEX

"Man, better you than me," Mike said as I plopped down on the tan leather sofa in Ed's house.

Michael, or Mike as we called him, would roll with us every now and then when his playa playa lifestyle allowed him to. Since I'd gotten married he'd made himself a bit scarce. He was the dude who was physically fit or, as women would say, buffed. Being a personal trainer allowed him plenty of time for working out. The sleeve of his T-shirt, which advertised his services on the back, seemed to have a chokehold on his muscular bicep. He was the shade of dark brown that was, as he often reminded us, *in* right now. I'd been labeled the "beige" brother of the group while Ed was brown sugar.

"What am I supposed to do? Throw a fit?"

"I'm not saying you have to go out like that, but you do need to let her know how you feel. Keep bottling this shit up inside of you. Next thing you know you'll be in the hospital or something."

Ed handed me a cold beer and joined us.

"I'm cool with it, man. He's only four and he's been through a lot in those short four years. He needs her."

"And you don't? Man, please. Tell me something, how does it feel raising a houseful of another man's children? Man, he stepped out and you stepped right in."

"That's not how it is."

"Oh really? Let's see…" He held his fingers up and prepared to count off a list of things to me.

"When I married Yani, I knew the kids came with it," I said before he got a chance to start.

"Yeah, *her* kids I can understand. But this other kid, yo, I'm not feeling that one."

"The kids are the only family he has left."

"Are you sure?" He took a swig from his beer and stared at me over the bottle.

"Yani had it checked out."

"Yani had it checked out? What kind of checking did you do? Homegirl had to have some friends or something. I don't know any woman who doesn't have at least one girlfriend she talks to about everything." He gave me a questioning stare.

"Stop trying to start something, Mike," Ed said.

"I'm not trying to start anything. I'm only making my boy look at all aspects of this thing. Look at him. Homeboy came in here looking like a sick puppy 'cause his wife doesn't have no time for him. Boo hoo." He held his fists at his eyes. "Told you negros to stay clear of that marriage shit. It ain't for everyone." He reached into the bucket for another hot wing.

"Don't start stepping on toes in here. I've been married for a long time and I'm happy as a fucking lark." Ed kicked back in his recliner and reached for the remote to his 52-inch.

"You are now, but I remember when…"

"Keep your tongue in your head." He pointed his finger at Mike as a fair warning. "Alex, every marriage has those trying years, especially the first ones. Don't listen to numb nuts over here who hasn't had a relationship to last long enough for him to develop enough feelings to even think about marrying someone."

"And believe me, that shit is by design."

Ed shook his head and took a drink of his beer.

"Mike, don't you ever long for someone to go home to?"

"Hell naw. I love having my *own* space. Women are some fickle creatures. One day they love the shit out of you and the next one they talking about cutting your dick off or some other crazy shit. Naw, man, let me deal with them on a *need to* basis. When my dick *needs* wetting, then I *need to* deal with them."

"No wonder your ass is alone. Uncouth bastard." Ed tossed a pillow and whacked him on the head.

"Yo, I'm just keeping it real."

"Yeah, *real* stupid," I said.

❖❖❖

On the drive home I couldn't help but think about some of the things Mike had said. Did Yani really check out Dede's past? Could there actually be something else that motivated her to take in the child of her dead ex-husband? The same man who had taken away the life of my seed. Of our chance at bringing a life we created into the world.

Every now and then I thought about Angel. She'd be five, almost six, months old now had Jarrin not come into our lives with his madness. We were coming upon the one-year anniversary of the nightmare that also took his life and like Yani had said when Dede first showed up, he's still somehow got a hand in our lives. While I know Yani needed the closure, I wished his ass would've stayed under the rock he'd been hiding under those five years. If only I'd gone with her to Florida maybe none of this craziness would be going on.

After returning home from the hospital Yani never talked about it again. It was almost as if the whole thing was a bad dream. If it weren't for the tiny scar on her abdomen, it would've been just that.

I pulled up in front of the brownstone. The wedding gift I'd given to my beautiful wife. Suburban life was cool, but more often than not, I was beginning to miss the loudness of the city. Missed stepping out my door and being right in the mix of things. But married life changes things. With the kids being in school and all, I couldn't uproot them and expect them to adjust. Moving to New York was a big enough adjustment. Maybe once Jay graduates… Damn what am I thinking about? We now have Corey to think about.

I unlocked the door and let myself in. The parlor light was on. I placed my keys in the bowl on the table and went to investigate. No one was in the kitchen, but the door leading downstairs to the media room was open. I was surprised to find Natalia curled up on the sofa with a book.

"You're up pretty late."

"It's summer, Daddy. It's not like I have to get up early in the morning. What about you? Had a late night at the office again?" She placed the book on the table.

"Not tonight. I was over at Ed's house. What'd you do today?"

"Nothing much. A few of my friends and I went over to the mall. Then we caught a movie."

"What're you reading?"

"One of the four books I *have* to read for school. You know they're doing that summer reading program now."

"Is it a good book?"

She picked it up and showed it to me. *Sula* by Toni Morrison.

"So far so good."

"Well, I'm tired and unlike you, I've got to get up early in the morning. Since you know I'm home, you can go upstairs to your room." I smiled and stuck out my hand to help her up.

"There's no fooling you, hunh?"

"Nope. Goodnight, sweetie."

"Goodnight, Daddy." She kissed me on the cheek and hurried up the stairs.

I checked around and made sure everything was secured before heading upstairs. When I got to the floor where our bedroom was I could see the light from the television seeping through the crack at the bottom of the door.

Maybe she's still up.

I walked in and my hopes were dashed before they could ignite. Yani was protectively wrapped around Corey. The TV was on the Disney Channel. One of the few channels he watched.

As I stood there and looked at them, Mike's words were ringing loudly in my ears. I knew I needed to get to the bottom of it before it ended up driving me crazy.

I walked into the bathroom to get ready for bed. Brushed my teeth, washed my face, and then jumped in the shower. I wrapped the towel around me and went to get my bed clothes. That also was something I didn't need until Corey got here. At the suggestion of Dr. DeVaughn, Yani had allowed him to sleep with her as a source of comfort. I went along with it. I didn't expect it to last this long. I'd mentioned to Yani the week before it was time for him to get accustomed to sleeping in his own bed in the room with Jay, but she hadn't been able to wean him from our bed as of yet. It was at the point that it was starting to cause some serious interference in my love life. If he was in the bed, which seemed to be every night, I definitely wasn't getting any.

The good doctor. I thought about what he'd said at the last session I had with him.

❖❖❖

"Mr. Chance, how are you adjusting to the change in your house?" His trusted tape recorder sat on the table in front of us. His pad in his lap, he scribbled away while I talked. I realized he never really looked at you. Just sat there scribbling on that pad.

I'd seen in a movie once where the therapist was doodling or sketching during the sessions. I began to wonder if Dr. DeVaughn was doing the same.

"It's a big change, but I'm adjusting fine."

"Umm hmm. I'm sensing you're not being completely honest with me." His attention was still on the pad in his lap.

"Completely honest?" I sat up straighter and intertwined my fingers and rubbed my thumbs together.

"If I'm going to help you, Mr. Chance, you have talk to me about what's bothering you. And from the responses you've been giving me, I have the feeling something is really bothering you." He looked up at me. His eyes seemed to bore a hole through me.

I thought about the characters I used to read about in the comic books I collected as a boy. They all had some sort of special power. Sometimes they had special props that gave them those special powers. If Dr. DeVaughn were a superhero from one of my old comics, I thought his special powers would come from his glasses at that moment. They seemed to give him some sort of power to see through you. At that moment I felt naked. Stripped of all my protections. Making it possible for him to see right through me.

"I know we talked with your wife about how Jay was feeling about Corey being added to your household, but I thought I'd talk with you one on one. I don't think she's ready to hear you also have a problem with the attention she seems to be showering on the son of her dead ex-husband." He tore his haunting stare away from me and scribbled something else on his pad.

"The baby is adorable. It's hard not to love him…"

"But?"

I took a deep breath. How was I going to tell my feelings without sounding petty? Being jealous of a four-year-old is as petty as it gets.

"When I look at him all I see is his father. A man who happened to blow into my life and change the course of things. A man who wreaked havoc on her life. But here we are now faced with the responsibility of raising *his* child. A child that was conceived during a time when she was in mourning. Mourning over him. But, thanks to me trying to be a good guy, she has closed her eyes to everything bad he's done." I could feel my anger rising with every word I said. I didn't like this feeling. Especially when it came to Yani. But hell, I was mad! Damn mad!

"And when you told your wife about this, Mr. Chance…"

"Told her? I haven't told her."

"You mean you've been keeping all of this bottled up inside of you?"

"She's so into this baby… I wouldn't know how to tell her if I wanted to. She's been through enough heartache…"

"But what about you, Mr. Chance? You, too, have suffered. The loss of your baby. Almost losing your wife? Why do you discount your pain? Your loss?"

I placed my head in my hands for a minute. Slowly I dragged my palms over my face. Took another deep breath.

"Because I'm the man. As the man I have to take care of my family. I have to make sure my wife and kids are happy."

"But at what cost?"

"I don't know! All costs!" I stood quickly. Paced back and forth in front of the fireplace with the array of diplomas posted on the wall from the various colleges he'd attended.

"Mr. Chance, do you see another solution to the problem?"

"If I had the answer to that why would I be here talking to you?"

He looked at me over the rim of his glasses. I guess that was a low blow in his book.

"You have to have some sort of idea. Something you would have done."

I looked over at the clock. My time was running out. It was the first time since we'd started seeing him I didn't want the session to end. I needed him to help me figure this out. Figure out what I needed to do to make things better. To make everything right.

"I would've had Dede's background checked out better. I just… Just feel we somehow might have overlooked something. Or didn't look hard enough." I placed my hands in my pockets. Hung my head until my chin hit my collarbone.

"Then, Mr. Chance, I suggest you do that. Check this woman's background so you can put this thing to rest that is plaguing you. If you don't, there's going to be more havoc wreaked upon your house. And this time it won't be by the ex-husband."

The alarm clock went off signaling our time was over.

"Mr. Chance, I'd like to schedule another session with you later this week. Please stop in with my receptionist on your way out."

I nodded my head and headed toward the door.

"Mr. Chance." He held out his hand.

I looked down at it and then back up to him before shaking it.

"I promise to help you get to the bottom of this. Help keep your family together."

"That's all I want, Doc."

CHAPTER 15

ASIA

I pulled up to the curb in front of my place and noticed the furniture truck. I'd almost forgotten about the new tenant Mr. Brand had told me about. The man had been here for more than four weeks and I hadn't caught a peep of him. Other than a new car being parked around the back, it was almost as if it was still just me and the Brands living there.

I messed around in my car for a few minutes trying to waste time in order to finally get at least a glimpse of him. I grabbed the sketch pad Yani had been doodling on from the passenger seat and gathered up the rest of my things. I flung open my door only to have it abruptly stopped.

"What the…" I looked up to see what or who had caused the door to jerk back. "I'm sorry. I didn't see you standing there," I began to apologize.

"No, it's my fault. I shouldn't have assumed the car was empty and walked this close to it."

"I don't see how I didn't see you. I'm always careful to look and make sure no cars are coming or anything."

He gave me a toothy grin.

"I'm Raymond. But obviously my friends call me Ray."

I looked at the outstretched hand sitting patiently waiting for me to grab a hold and reciprocate the friendly gesture.

"I'm Asia."

"Ah, top floor?"

"That would be me. And I take it you're the mystery man from the bottom floor? Nice to finally meet you." I put the sketch pad under my arm and finally shook his hand.

"Where are my manners? Can I give you hand with something?"

"No, I'm fine. I'll…"

"It's not like I'm not going that way." He smiled again and held out his hand.

I smiled back and gave in. I handed him the sketch pad and another bag I was carrying.

"Are you an artist or something?" he asked as he glanced down at the sketch pad.

"I wish. No, I went looking for a wedding dress today."

"Wow! Who's the lucky man?"

"What makes you think he's lucky?"

Raymond gave me a questioning look.

"I'm just messing with you. He is lucky. Very lucky." I playfully winked at him, then continued to gather my things from the car.

"A beautiful sister like yourself, any man would be lucky to call you his. Let alone have you as his wife."

"Now you're laying it on thick. You don't even know me, but you're standing out here spewing compliments like we were once lovers or something."

"It's not like that. I'm a pretty good judge of people. My intuition tells me you're all the things I said and more."

I gave off a slight laugh, turned away from him and continued toward the building.

"Ooh-kay then." I headed up the stairs with Raymond in tow.

"You still haven't answered my question."

"I doubt if you would know him, but his name is Johnny Johnson."

"Oh, the detective?"

I stopped and turned around to face him. "You know Johnny?

"I ran into him the week after I moved in. He seems pretty cool."

I couldn't understand why Johnny never mentioned to me he'd met Raymond. We'd talked a few times about how I had yet to meet someone who basically shared the same roof with me. Never once did he come out and say he'd actually seen him himself.

I continued the trek up to my apartment. I fiddled around for my house key and unlocked the doors. I turned to retrieve my things from Raymond and damn near kissed him, as close as he was to me. I was unnerved a minute and stepped to the side to put some space between us.

"Uh, thanks for the help. I think I can handle it from here." The attraction between us was almost undeniable.

"Oh. Yeah, yeah. Here you go." He handed my things to me. "Don't be a stranger."

"I'll try not to."

He started walking back down the stairs.

"Welcome to the neighborhood," I called down to him.

"Thanks." He smiled again, then turned back and kept going down the stairs.

I did the normal female thing and gave him a quick once-over. The baggy pants he was wearing gave no real hint at what was hidden underneath, but the loose-fitting sleeveless T-shirt gave clear indication he worked out in some form. The muscles in his arms were nice and just the right size. I don't know how many of you watch the *Soul Food* series, but homeboy was giving Lem a run for his money. And those of you who do watch it know exactly what I'm talking about! Now that I thought about, he and Lem shared a few more physical features. The toothy grin and neatly trimmed goatee. Raymond's smooth skin was a shade darker than Lem. They'd easily pass for at least cousins.

Girl, get your ass in the house. I smiled and walked in and grabbed the phone off the base on the wall. Before I could click it on, it rang.

"Hello?"

"What's up, Chica?"

"Nothing much."

"So how did it go with the dresses today?"

"We're working on it. I tried on a few. Got a few ideas of what I might want."

"That's good."

"Yep."

A moment went by before either of us said anything. My mind was somewhere else.

"What's going on with you? You're pretty quiet. Something happen?"

"I was just thinking." I sat on the sofa near the window and looked out. I noticed the truck pull off to go around back to bring in the new furniture. I got up and walked to my bedroom so I could continue being nosey.

"Asia, it's me you're dealing with. You know I like details."

I knew Linda would continue to push until I told her something.

"It's really nothing. I just met my new neighbor, is all."

"Uh oh."

"Uh oh, what?"

"Girl, the brother must be…"

"Don't make me curse you. I'm about to get married, so the thought never crossed my mind."

"Now did I say anything about you wanting him? No, I did not."

"But you and that *uh oh*."

"Hell, let me know what he looks like. Maybe we could make something happen. And from the way you're not saying much about him, I can tell he's definitely good-looking."

I smiled and walked closer to the window as I heard Ray walk out and give the guys directions where to put what.

"I have to be honest, brother man is definitely fine."

"Redbone, chocolate?"

"Deep chocolate, girl."

"Umm. The blacker the berry…"

"I was thinking how much he looks like one of my favorite actors."

"Who, Morris or Lem?"

"You act like you know me." We both laughed.

"I do know you."

"Yes, you do. Lem, girl. A whole lot like him."

"Umm, sounds really nice to me. Is he single?"

"You know, I didn't ask him."

"Girl, you know those are things you have to know. Just because you're getting married doesn't mean you get amnesia and forget how the game is played. Especially when you have friends who are still single."

"I only talked to the man all of five or ten minutes. What was I supposed to do, pull out a probe light?"

"Yes."

"You're crazy." I moved back from the window when I noticed Ray looking up at me.

"What are you up to tonight?"

"Nothing really. Johnny called and cancelled out on me. He's working on another case and Yani and Alex are taking the kids out. So that leaves me and the TV. What about you?"

"Derrick is supposed to take me to Ruby Tuesday. But you know how that goes."

"Girl, stop trying to act like you're not into that man."

"I'm not acting."

"You now Derrick is going to be your baby's daddy."

She and Derrick had being doing the off-and-on thing for almost three years. While I couldn't understand why she continued to wait for him, she did. No matter how many times she threatened to leave him alone for good, he would somehow ease back in there. Brina and I had long since stopped trying to figure out why she continued to deal with him. We all knew how it was when we had a man who could really lay down the dick. Letting go of him means letting go of it and it's hard to let go of it.

"Whatever. Well, I guess I need to get dressed if I'm going somewhere."

"Linda, you know you need to quit. You and I both know you're going. You don't have to put up a front for me."

"I'm not putting up a front."

My other line beeped.

"You go and have a good time. Let me see who this is."

"Okay. See you at church tomorrow?"

"Of course. Bye."

I clicked over.

"Hello?"

"Hey, Baby. Guess what?"

"You're going to make it after all?"

"No. Actually, I'm calling to let you know I have to go down to Virginia tonight."

"Virginia? For what?"

"It has to do with a case I'm working on."

An instant flashback of Hayden popped into my head. I leaned back on the bed and was quiet.

"Believe me, if I didn't have to go I wouldn't."

"I wasn't thinking anything."

"Yes, you were. Look, I've got to go. They're expecting us to be there by a certain time and we have to drive. I called to let you know so you wouldn't be worried. I'm going to be gone for at least two days."

"Okay," I said reluctantly.

"Oh, how did the dress thing go today?"

The dress thing? That's about as much as it had meant to me. Why did I want it to mean any more to him? At least he'd asked.

"It went good."

"You have your dress?"

"Not quite. I have an idea of the dress I want."

"An idea of a dress. Okay."

"Have you looked into the tuxedos yet?" I decided to shift the ball into his court. See where he was with his planning.

"I haven't had the time, but I'll get to it."

"Jeanette said something about FUBU having really nice tuxedos."

"FUBU? You trying to break my boys' pockets?"

"She said they're not expensive. You want me to see if she has a hookup or something."

"Do that. Baby, let me get going. I love you. I'll try and give you a call tomorrow, as soon as I get a chance."

"Love you, too. Be safe."

"I will."

I clicked the phone off and leaned deeper into my pillows. I keep reminding myself I knew what he did for a living when I met him. The only question is would I be okay being a cop's wife?

❖❖❖

After browsing the wall of new releases at Blockbuster, I picked up my dinner from my favorite Chinese restaurant up on the corner from me. The smell of fried rice and ribs wafted up through the bag and into my nose as I locked my car.

"Two times in one day, after more than a month of nothing. I'd say it was kismet."

I turned and smiled when I spotted Ray who looked to be headed out somewhere.

"Now how odd is that?"

"Looks like you're having a night in."

"Yeah. Dinner in one hand and entertainment in the other," I said, holding each bag up as proof.

"I'm on my way to Nell's. You want to join me?"

I looked down at the bags in my hands and mentally weighed my options.

"You can put it in the fridge and eat it tomorrow for lunch."

"I don't know."

"Aww, come on. I'm meeting up with a few friends of mine. They're having a really good spoken word set tonight."

"But I'm not dressed and…"

"It can't take you that long to put something on. And it doesn't have to be fancy. I promise, if you don't enjoy yourself within the first hour, I'll bring you home. Fair?"

He looked so sincere. I would call Johnny and let him know what I was doing and if he didn't have a problem with it, I was going.

"I wouldn't want to put you out. I mean, you'd have to leave because of me."

"If it makes you feel better, you can drive yourself. I know you women in New York are wary of being too friendly too fast."

"Okay, you pulled my arm hard enough. Cab fare is a fair enough deal. Give me twenty minutes and I'll be down."

"Cool."

I ran up the stairs and put the food and movies away before running into my bedroom and grabbing something out my closet to wear. Not wanting to send the wrong messages to him, I threw on a pair of blue jeans and a crisp white collar shirt. My blue jean heels gave it a classy but casual look.

I ran into the bathroom and tightened my ponytail up. Added a couple of sprays of deodorant to make sure I was fresh for the rest of the night.

I buttoned up my shirt and fastened the bell cuffs. The last thing to get was the bag to match it. I pulled the blue jean bag from the top of my closet—a real sistah has a bag to go with everything. I put the necessities in it—driver's license, credit card, and a few dollars just in case. I finished checking everything and grabbed the phone. I dialed Johnny's cell, but got his voicemail. I left him a quick message letting him know I had gone out and he could reach me on my cell if he needed me. I hung up and headed down to Ray's from the door in my kitchen, which was a staircase that led down to the basement and the other apartments. I took my time on the steep steps. I'd had a slip once before and it wasn't pretty. As soon as I lifted my hand to knock he opened the door.

"Wow! If this is what twenty minutes of preparation looks like, I wonder what an actual hour would be like."

"I told you I would only need twenty minutes." I was close to blushing.

"I know, but usually women take a long time to get dressed."

"See, that's what sets me apart from other women. I'm not one for standing around trying to figure out what to wear. I usually have it paired up so I can just grab it and go."

"You need to enlighten some of your sisters then. 'Cause there's nothing worse than waiting for a woman to get dressed."

"Now don't act like men don't take a long time. There are some brothas out there who can give the sistahs a run for their money."

"True, true. Come in for a minute. Let me finish up something and then we can roll." He opened the door wide to allow my entrance.

I was amazed at the transformation the place had taken. While it screamed *Bachelor Pad*, the dark brown furniture and wood and metal tables gave it a modern look. Throughout were beautiful paintings. A massive-sized mirror trimmed in the same wood and metal as the tables sat above the sofa. Over in the dining area was a stainless steel, rectangular-shaped table large enough to seat six. Even the wood on the floors had been changed to match the furniture.

"Did you have someone come in and do this for you?" I asked, pointing to the faux tangerine-colored walls.

"Nope. I did it all myself."

"Wait a minute. You mean to tell me that you…" I pointed to him. "Did this?" I swept my hand around the room.

"Yes. I picked out the furniture. The paint colors. I even did the floors myself. Want to see something?" He motioned for me to follow him into the kitchen.

I was blown away as he revealed the beautifully tiled countertops and maple and glass cabinets. The package was completed with stainless steel appliances.

"You put in a dishwasher?" I walked over and admired the one kitchen appliance I was missing in my apartment.

"Umm hmm. I did all of this."

"Are you some sort of handyman?"

He laughed. "Not by trade. My father owns a construction company. He basically buys properties, fixes them up, and then resells them for a nice profit. I was trained from the time I could hold a wrench how to fix or build most anything. Especially in a house. While I didn't choose to join him in the business, I still love to do the work. Plus it makes you feel good when you see your finished work and people tell you how much they like what you've done." He beamed with pride at the way I was carrying on over the work.

I still couldn't believe this was the same apartment I'd walked into a little more than a couple of months ago.

"I'm a bit jealous." I scanned the room again and then followed him out into the living room.

"There's no need to be. I bet your place can rival…"

"Don't even go there. The linoleum floors are rubbed up in numerous spots. And we won't even talk about the cabinets. I can guarantee they're the original ones from when the house was built. Even though you haven't showed me, I bet your bathroom puts mine to shame. The soap dish I've been meaning to put back on the wall has a permanent stain on the side of the tub now where it's been sitting for more than six months." I laughed and he joined me.

"You have to let me come take a look and tell you what you can do."

"You mean what I can *afford* to do. I've been here for quite a few years, but I'm not crazy about fixing up someone else's property."

"See, you have to look at it as your enjoyment. You've been here long enough to enjoy any upgrades you would've made to the place had you done it when you first moved in. Plus, it gives you negotiating power."

"How so?"

"When the Brands saw the work I was doing to their place, they were glad to give me a break on the rent. I saved them a load of money and time. Now when I move, they'll be able to get much more than I'm giving them."

"If I had your skills, maybe I would entertain the idea. But seeing I would have to pay someone to do the work, now we're talking a whole different ballgame."

"Maybe we can work something out. I can help you out. Do the bulk of the hard work, but still teach you a few things in the process."

"We'll talk about it." I glanced around one last time before we walked out. Out the corner of my eye I saw a beautiful fireplace.

"How'd you pull this off? There's no chimney on this building."

"It's not real." He smiled.

"Is that a Charles Bibbs?" I walked over to get a closer look at the beautiful piece of artwork hanging above the fireplace.

"Yes. It's…"

"'The Red Umbrella.' I'm a big fan."

"You know your Charles Bibbs."

"And a few other artists. I have a girlfriend who's not quite struggling, but she's still trying to get her name out there."

"What's her name? I might know her."

"Jilley Boyte."

"I've heard of her. You're right. A few years ago you could get a Boyte for a couple hundred. Now… you're forking over no less than five hundred."

"And that's unframed."

"You have to get a brotha the hookup." He winked at me and grabbed his keys. He held the door open for me.

"Ready for a good time?" he asked as he glanced over at me.

"Lead the way, my newfound friend."

CHAPTER 16

YANI

"Girl, he's so adorable," I said to Carmen.

"How's Jay with him now?"

"He's much better. Dr. DeVaughn has really helped us."

"Well, that's good. From the pictures you emailed me, Corey is as cute as he can be."

"Did I tell you I was thinking about taking him to the agent? I've had so many people come up to me and say how cute he is and how he should be a model or something." I smiled as I thought about the upcoming meeting I'd set up with Sunni. She'd been representing Nat since we moved to New York. Nat worked more now than she'd ever done when we were in Florida.

"How's Alex?"

"He's fine. Been working a lot. Did I tell you Corey's teacher said he is the smartest one in his group? He's doing so well. I came home early today so I could take him to see a play tonight."

"What play?"

"'The Lion King.' Girl, I had a time finding those tickets, but he wanted to go so bad. So I had Alex pull a few strings. He's so excited!"

"Who? Alex?"

"Girl, no. Corey. Alex isn't going." I laughed. I got Corey's clothes to wear out of his closet and placed them on the bed.

"Are you taking Nat and Jay?"

"They wouldn't want to go. You know they're at that age where they prefer to stay in the house or just do their own thing."

"Did you at least ask them?"

"Why? It would only be a waste of time. Besides, Alex only got two tickets." I walked up to my bedroom.

"Yani, do you hear yourself?" she asked. She sounded as if she was upset.

"What are you talking about?"

"Have you realized all you've talked about since we got on the phone is Corey?"

"Well, it's hard not to. I mean, I'm doing so much with him."

"That's what I'm talking about. It sounds like all you're doing is with or for him now. You've been Corey this and Corey that. How does Alex feel about this?"

"He loves Corey. Why would he have a problem with the baby?"

"Speaking of baby, have you guys been trying? You know the doctor said there was a *possibility* you could still have one."

"We've been so busy lately, I can't tell you the last time we had sex."

"Yani! That's not good. You guys are still newlyweds. Y'all should still be wearing out that new bedroom furniture."

"We've both been busy. That's all." I started trying to think of the last time Alex and I had been together. As of late, Corey wanted to watch TV in our room and would end up falling asleep. The doctor warned me he would likely cling to me since I represented the mother figure.

"Yani? Did you hear me?"

"What?"

"I was suggesting maybe you should do something nice for you and Alex. You know, make reservations at one of your favorite restaurants. Have an afternoon rendezvous. Just a few months ago you were telling me about an afternoon delight you'd slipped off to have with him. Go get a room and messenger the key over to him. Have lunch waiting in the room when he gets there. That would really be nice."

"Aren't you the romantic one?" I asked with a hint of sarcasm in my voice. I was really starting to get irritated with her.

"Girl, you do remember you have to work at a marriage? Like anything else, neglect it and you'll pay in the end."

"Yes I remember, but between running my business, my household, and taking Corey to different appointments he has, it's hard to just up and do something. "

"Once again it's about Corey. I'm trying to be a good girlfriend and tell you nicely, but I think I need to go Asia on you and curse you out so I can get through to you. Yani, you're *fucking up*," she said in a harsh tone.

At first I didn't respond. What the hell did she know about what I was doing? She didn't know what I was going through trying to make sure this baby wouldn't go through any more trauma than he'd already experienced in his short life span. Hadn't he suffered enough?

"Look, you're my best friend. I just want to make sure you're happy and you stay happy," she continued. "Maybe taking on this baby was more than you bargained for. I honestly don't think you've thought about the kids or Alex's feelings when you decided to take this on. And maybe you should…"

Click!

By this time I was furious. After I disconnected our call I flung the cordless across the room where it landed against a wall. My hands began to shake. I couldn't believe Carmen had the audacity to even talk to me that way about this subject. Sure, Corey took up a lot of my time, but he needed it!

The phone rang. I knew it was her, but couldn't bring myself to answer it. I was in no mood to get into a debate about something that wasn't debatable. She could leave a message. Anyway it was time to start getting ready. Carmen had totally fucked up my mood.

I was about to walk out the room when it hit me…

I wonder if Alex called and talked to Bryce?

Before my better judgment could kick in I was racing to retrieve the phone from where it landed.

"If he has a problem with something he should talk to me before throwing our business out in the street." I punched in the numbers so hard the phone almost fell to the floor. I could feel my adrenaline kick up a notch. Before the first ring registered Asia opened the door.

"What's up?" she said as she plopped down on the bed.

I hung up the phone and walked over to the window. I took a deep breath before saying anything.

"Yani?"

"I'm just so…" I closed my eyes and took another deep breath trying to calm down.

Asia approached me and turned me around. Before I knew it tears were sliding down my face.

"Girl, what's wrong with you?"

My anger had been taken over by another emotion—hurt.

"Carmen called and started saying all these things…"

"What things?"

"About Corey… And me and Alex. Asia, what am I supposed to do?" I was in full throttle cry mode.

"Wait a minute. You need to get yourself together so I can understand what's going on." She grabbed my hand and led me over to the sitting area of the bedroom.

"Now, what's going on?"

"Carmen called and you know, I was telling her about what's going on. So, I told her about all the things I've been doing with Corey and then she accuses me of putting Corey before everyone else. Saying I'm jeopardizing my marriage and what not. So, I hung up on her."

"You hung up on Carmen?" Asia looked as if I'd just slapped her.

"Yes. It's obvious Alex must've called Bryce and now she's calling me. You know how she is. Always has to stick her nose in places…"

"Remember, she's your best friend. So don't say anything you're going to regret later."

"I know she's my best friend, but sometimes best friends get on your nerves."

"So you're so furious now you were about to call Alex until I walked in, right?"

I turned away from her.

"You mean you were going to blast the man out while he's at his place of business?"

"It's not like I was doing it in person, like that bitch Taylor used to do."

"You can't call her out. You're pretty damn close." She swept a stray curl behind my ear and got up to grab the box of tissues off the dresser.

"Here. Clean yourself up. I can't believe you're all ready to accuse him of something you're not even sure he's done. Yani, do you know you're like an open book to Carmen? Do you want the honest truth?" She glanced at me out the corner of her eye.

"You're going to give it to me whether I want it or not."

"I'm trying to be nice about it."

"What's the honest truth, Asia?"

"You do spend a lot of time doting on that boy. And I can say this because I've seen you with him. How you act and talk to him. By your own admission, he's sleeping in your bed with you. You didn't allow your two to sleep with you, but all of a sudden it's not a bad thing." She took the first two fingers on both hands and pumped them to make sure I knew she was quoting words which had come directly from me.

"Nat and Jay hadn't experienced the things…"

"Don't you dare go there," she snapped, surprising me. I turned my head to look at her. "Have you forgotten their daddy pulled a Houdini? Jay was what? Pretty much the same age as this child. Don't start on what they didn't go through."

"But they still had me."

"Who voted you to be the mother savior for this child? Did you even check and see if Dede in fact had any friends who would've taken him? She had to be here visiting with someone. Or is there something else motivating you?" She looked at me curiously.

"And what would that be?"

"Hey, he looks a helluva lot like Jarrin," she said as she stared at me in what seemed like a stance of defiance. Her hand nestled on her hip, one leg slightly in front of the other. I was too stunned to really say anything. This time I couldn't disconnect the call like I'd done earlier with Carmen. This face-to-face confrontation had gone even deeper.

"You know…" I carefully picked my words of response. "I can't believe you would think that would even be a factor. Do you think I've forgotten what Jarrin did to me? To my children? The hell he put me and Alex through barely a year ago?"

"But for some reason you're allowing him to reach from his grave and put his hand right back in the mix."

"Asia…"

"No Yani, you listen to me. You need to check yourself. Don't think because Alex hasn't said anything this isn't bothering him. With the way you've been acting, he doesn't have to say anything for me to know it." She strutted out the door.

I sat there for a moment and thought about what she'd said. Had I done all the things she was saying? I shook my head and stood up.

"She's crazy, too. I'm just doing what anyone else in my shoes would do. Right?" I continued to get dressed. Corey's bus would be pulling up to the house soon to drop him off.

You need to talk to Dr. DeVaughn and see what he has to say about this.

CHAPTER 17

ASIA

I decided to take full advantage of the beautiful summer afternoon. Usually we were in what they call the "dog days" of summer. Today was one of the few days we were blessed with weather that allowed us to actually go outside and enjoy being there. I was no different from anyone else who was at the park trying to enjoy this rare moment.

With my face buried deep into a book, I was pleasantly surprised when I heard the familiar voice of someone I hadn't seen in close to a year.

"Is anyone sitting here?"

I looked up into the face of my past.

"Actually, no. You're more than welcome to sit here if you like."

I pulled my bag over and self-consciously tugged down the legs of my cut-off shorts and ran my hand over my ponytail.

"Still beautiful as ever. How's life treating you?

"I'm still here. What about you? Is fatherhood and marriage everything you wanted?"

"Same ole' Asia. Straight for the gut."

"Any reason I should change?"

He smiled as he took a seat next to me. "No reason at all."

I placed the book in my bag. "So, are you going to answer my question?"

"Truth?"

"Nothing else."

He looked at me and something went through me. The familiarity of the passion he and I had once shared hit me. I caught a sudden chill, then shook it off.

"Things didn't work out as planned."

"Really? I'm sorry to hear that." I tried to hide the slight delight I felt at hearing his misery.

"I thought we were being truthful."

"I'm being truthful, Hayden. I never wished you any ill will. I've always wanted nothing but happiness for you." Now that *was* the truth.

"Then why wouldn't you take me back?"

I was caught off guard by his bluntness. More like I wasn't expecting it.

"I wasn't your happiness…"

"Yes, you were. You were led by your anger and couldn't see it at the time."

I crossed my arms over my chest. Suddenly the bareback halter felt like nothing more than a handkerchief.

"So you're divorced, separated?"

"It was an annulment. Didn't last a good month. Talk about wasn't meant to be."

"What about the baby?" I at least hoped he was decent enough to be a good father.

"She miscarried."

I gasped. "I'm so sorry…"

"Don't be. Like I said, it wasn't meant to be. After she miscarried we realized the only thing keeping us together was the fact we were going to be parents. So, we decided to cut our losses." He shrugged his shoulders and looked out at the kids playing in the park. An emptiness settled in his eyes for a moment, then passed.

"What about you? Still with the detective?"

"Yep." I decided to give him a minimal amount of info. Wasn't like he was invited to the wedding.

"Is he treating you good?"

"Yes, Hayden. I have to say he's treating me very good."

"Unlike some people?"

"I didn't say that."

"You were thinking it."

"No, I wasn't." Hell yes, I was.

He reached over and grabbed my hand. I didn't stop him. We would always have a connection. This we both knew.

We sat there for a few minutes. Holding hands. Not a word was passed between us.

"What brought you out here?"

"I was riding by and had the most beautiful vision…"

"I see you're still full of it."

"I'm being honest. Every time I ride this way I always look to see if I see you." I looked at him and laughed.

"We haven't seen each other in about nine months and you want me to believe you just happen to spot me sitting in the park as you were riding by?"

"I'm telling you the truth."

"Bullshit."

"Now that's the Asia I know." We both laughed.

"How's your sister and her family?"

"Don't ask." I crossed my arms again. This time out of frustration. Just thinking about Yani and her petty drama pissed me off.

"Don't tell me they've broken up."

"No. They're still together—barely. Just some more Jarrin shit in the middle of things again."

"Wait, I thought homeboy was dead. Didn't the police kill him…"

"Yes. This time it's a child of his. If I hadn't seen the little boy's mother die with my own two eyes, I'd swear she was pulling some kind of scam scheme on my sister. But for some reason my sister has taken on the role of mother for Jarrin's four-year-old son."

"Wait, this kid is basically an orphan and you're mad with her for that?"

"No. I'm mad with her because she has allowed her efforts of mothering this little boy to consume her life and it is now affecting her marriage."

"Oh."

He draped his arm behind the bench and slid into a comfortable position. I cut my eyes at him. He was still sexy as hell. Johnny was more bulk than Hayden. Hayden was hella fine and the way his clothes fit him made him ultra sexy.

Girl, what is up with you? You are not sitting here thinking like this about this man. Don't forget what he put you through.

But it wasn't his fault. He was confused.

Whose side are you on?

My inner thoughts battled one another. Good versus evil.

"You okay?" Hayden draped his arm over my bare shoulder.

"I'm fine."

"Looks like you were deep in thought."

"Just thinking about Yani, is all." I wasn't about to let him know he was having any kind of effect on me. I was allowed to be cordial, but that was as far as this thing was going.

"What do you have planned for the rest of the day?"

"Nothing. I was planning on finishing this book and then going home and find a good chick flick on Lifetime."

"Where's the detective?"

"Working."

"What do you say to having lunch with an old friend?" He looked at me with pleading eyes.

"Lunch and only lunch?"

"Nothing else. We can go and grab a slice from Ray's or your favorite."

"Calientes?"

"You feel like riding to the Village?"

It's just two friends having lunch. It's not like I'm going to his place. We'll be out in the open with other people.

"I might need to change."

"You look fine to me." He looked me over with approval.

"No, I think I need to put on something a little less revealing." I got up and grabbed my bag.

"Did you drive over?"

"You know I never drive to the park. It's only what? A five-minute walk from my place."

"Then your chariot awaits you." He pulled out his keys and stood. He extended his elbow to me.

I threw my bag on my shoulder.

"Lead the way."

Lunch between friends is all it was…

CHAPTER 18

ALEX

After another session with Dr. DeVaughn I found myself standing across the street from my former place of residence.

"Damn, I miss this," I said to myself. The noise of the city had been a constant to me all my life, growing up in Harlem.

I looked down at the set of keys I kept locked in my desk at the office. It had taken me too long to acquire this dream for me to give it up that easily. My initial plan was to keep my place on Park Avenue as a weekend getaway for me and Yani. Once the kids graduated and went off to college we could move in permanently. Sell the house in Brooklyn and enjoy the full benefits of living in New York City. Lately, I had begun to miss this place more and more. This was the first time I'd come with the keys.

I slowly crossed the street and made my way toward the building. It had been a little over a year since I'd been here. I walked into the lobby and looked around. Nothing had changed. The marble tile was buffed to a high shine. The elevators beckoned me to jump in for a ride. A ride up to my past.

"Mr. Chance?"

I looked up into the face of Mike, the doorman who had greeted me every evening numerous times before.

"Hey, Mike. How are you?"

"Can't complain, Mr. Chance. And yourself? How's life in Brooklyn? The family?"

I smiled. He was always on his best behavior. Inquisitive without being outright nosey.

"It's good. They're good."

"I've been making sure maintenance takes good care of your place. The cleaning lady comes in once a week."

"That's good, Mike. I think I'm going to go up and have a look around."

"You go right ahead, Mr. Chance. Take all the time you need." He walked over and punched the up button to summon an elevator.

I looked around the lobby and smiled as a few memories came to mind. One of them being the first day I moved in. I can't tell you how proud I was of that accomplishment. Mike had been the first face that greeted me.

"Here you go, Mr. Chance. Do you need me to get anything for you?" He held open the elevator doors.

"No, Mike. I'm good." I gave him a nod and stepped into the elevator.

On the ride up I stared at the numbers as they lit up as I passed the floors. The ding let me know I'd reached my floor. Slowly I stepped out. Walked the short distance across the hall even slower. I fingered the keys that were now in my pocket as I stood in front of my door.

Go ahead and open it. You know you want to. If only for an hour, go in. Sit on the balcony and watch the city. Listen to the soothing sounds.

I pulled the key out and inserted it into the lock and turned. The click of the lock calmed me. The gush of air hit me in the face as I opened the heavy door. My sanctuary. Like an old familiar friend, it welcomed me. The mirrored wall with the table at the end of it. The glass bowl I used to throw my keys in. The beautiful marble tile I had shipped in from Italy. It all was there, just like I left it. Except for a few pieces of art, everything was still in its place.

I walked into the bedroom and looked at the nicely made bed. I walked over and pulled the heavy curtains back. The late afternoon sun came pouring in. I pulled open the balcony doors and looked out at the park. People rushing by down below. Others in the park walking, jogging, or engaged in some sort of physical activity. The noise. Oh, it was so heavenly. Even the honking horns were a welcome sound. All of it soothing to my frayed emotions.

"How I miss this."

I would never be away this long again. I took a seat on the chair and looked at my watch. Two-thirty.

Just an hour. That's all I need.

❖❖❖

I was awakened by the insistent ringing of my cell phone. I reached out for it without opening my eyes.

"Yeah?"

"Alex? Where are you? You left here to go to your appointment with Dr. DeVaughn…"

"Yani?"

"Were you expecting someone else? It's almost ten o'clock. You could've at least called and said you weren't going to make it. I ended up taking the kids without you."

My eyes flew open. I scanned the room and looked down at my watch. Nine forty-seven."

Damn.

"Are you sleeping?"

"No, Baby. I stopped by to see Mike and we got to talking."

"Well, you could've called. I was worried about you."

"Really?"

"What do you mean really?"

"Look, I'm sorry. I'll make it up to you guys."

"Are you on your way home?"

I sat up on the edge of the bed and scanned the room. I had slept a good seven hours. The best sleep I'd had in months.

"Since you've taken the kids to get something to eat I'm going to hang here with Mike a lil' longer. That okay with you?"

Had to give her the courtesy of shooting me down. If she insisted, I would head back to Brooklyn. For the first time I actually dreaded making that drive.

"Sure. No problem. I'll get the boys ready for bed."

"Where's Nat?"

"She's staying over Lucia's. She's babysitting Torian tonight."

"Oh."

I ran my hand over my face and tried my best to stifle a yawn.

"What time are you coming?"

"I don't know. It'll be late so don't wait up."

Silence on the other end of the phone. I should've felt guilty and jumped in my car and sped home as fast as I could, but I didn't.

"I guess I'll see you when you get here then."

"Okay."

"Bye."

"Bye." I disconnected the call and lay back on the goose down pillows. Flat on my back, I spread my arms and legs out.

"A whole bed to myself!" I yelled out. Smiling as I thought of how I had to fight for space in my own bed at home. For those who don't know, little children are some of the worse sleepers. Corey sleeps like a clock. He starts out at twelve. By the second hour he's working his way to three. By midnight he's at six. And when morning comes, he's working his way back from nine. I'd been to the chiropractor twice in one month to work out the kinks in my back from the pounding his little feet had put on me.

"Better let Mike know I'm using him as an alibi." I said his name into the mic piece of my cell phone. It promptly dialed his number.

"Speak."

"What's up, man?"

"Nothing much. About to get up in this lil' piece..."

"Spare me the details. I need a solid from you."

"Name it."

"If it comes up, I was chilling with you tonight."

"Wait a minute. Sounds like you getting into a lil' something yourself."

"It's not like that. I lost track of time."

"Lost track of time? That means you've already gotten into..."

"I'm not cheating on my wife," I said nice and clear for him.

"You told her you were with me and you're not."

"Man, just do me this favor. Okay?"

"You know I got your back."

"Thanks. Oh, and don't forget to cover it up."

"A playa like me has stocks in all the condom companies." We both laughed.

"I'll check you later."

"All right. And don't stay out too late. I don't need no friction when I come over to visit."

"I hear you."

I walked back out on the balcony. The cool breeze greeted me. A blaring horn, lights from nearby buildings, and constant flow of cars delighted my senses. Even the smell was inviting. I dreaded going home.

"What are you thinking about, Alex?" The thought of spending the entire night danced around in my head. I'd tell her I fell asleep. We'd had too much to drink and I decided to stay at Mike's to be safe.

I was only doing what Dr. DeVaughn had suggested.

"Stop sacrificing yourself for the sake of peace."

Tonight I would do just that. I stripped down to my boxer briefs and walked into the kitchen.

"Damn, I need to get something to eat." My stomach reacted to my outburst. I hadn't eaten since earlier before going to see Dr. DeVaughn.

I strolled over to the drawer where I used to keep the menus.

"Please let there be at least one menu in here." I pulled open the drawer and was pleasantly surprised to find the stack of menus I'd accumulated over the years.

"Let's see." I thumbed through them and settled on a Thai restaurant that wasn't too far and had pretty fast delivery.

I was going to have a one-man slumber party tonight.

"Damn, I should've left the stereo system." I made a mental note to get another one.

I made my way into the living room and sat on the only piece of furniture that remained in there. A tan leather lounger Taylor had picked out on one of her shopping excursions.

"Now there's a name I haven't said in a long time." And I didn't have any plans to linger there. She was the last person I needed to conjure up. Our last encounter was a bit odd. Cordial, but odd. I guess the fact that Yani was with me added to it. She was nice enough. Even gave Taylor a comment on her outfit. But ended it with an off-the-rack comment. I knew that rattled Taylor's cage. She was quick to let you know she didn't shop on any other street but Madison and Fifth. If the name on the sign outside wasn't recognized worldwide, she didn't grace the door.

"Enough of that." I sat back in the chair and put my feet up on the ottoman. *Better be careful. I could really get used to this.* Now that thought scared me.

CHAPTER 19

ASIA

Another Friday night ritual with the girls found us at the Sugar Bar. It was Yani's turn to pick the spot and she always went above and beyond.

"Have you gotten your passport back, Brina?"

"Yes, Linda. I got it back three days ago."

"I'm only making sure. Wouldn't want you to go all the way to Miami only to be turned away because your credentials aren't in order." Linda took a sip of her drink.

"Girl, there's no way I'm going to miss out on this trip. I can't wait to get on that boat and unwind."

"Stay away from the staff. Those guys are usually looking for a way to get a green card."

"Are you insinuating that I'm some kind of slut, Linda?" Brina asked in a prim and proper voice. Her hand placed on her chest for emphasis of her virtue being at stake.

"That statement was meant for everybody."

"Bullshit. Everyone else has a man. So that leaves me and you."

We all laughed.

"She's got a point." I looked at Linda.

"Enough of that. What's going on with everyone? How was your week? What did you guys do over the weekend?" Yani looked around the table.

"I didn't do much over the weekend. Just cleaned out my closets and helped my mom put some things away. What about you, Linda? Did you go out with Derrick?"

"Let's not be catty. It's not becoming."

"I'm not paying her any mind, Yani. And for your information, yes, Derrick and I did go out last weekend and the weekend before."

"Touché." I held my glass up to Linda. She held hers up to Brina.

"What about you, Asia? What did you do this weekend?" I wasn't sure if I wanted to share the fact that I'd gone to lunch with my ex-fiancé while my fiancé was working. But they are my girls and I wanted to get some feedback about it.

"I ran into Hayden Saturday afternoon."

The three of them seemed to sit up straighter and leaned in toward me. I took my time. Sipped off my drink. Took the stirrer and swirled the contents around and took another sip.

"Now that you have our attention, would you mind giving the details?" It was Yani's turn to play nosey.

"I was at the park near my house reading a book and he walked up. We talked. I found out he wasn't married anymore. He's not a father."

"What happened?"

"Let her finish, Linda," Brina snapped.

"She had a miscarriage and they ended up having the marriage annulled."

"Are you sure about that? Did he show you some proof?"

"Yes, Yani. He always walks around with it in his wallet." I rolled my eyes at her.

"Don't get snippy with me. Remember how he led you on the last time. Burning the candle on both ends."

"We're friends. Nothing more. We went out and grabbed a quick bite to eat and I was back home before ten."

"You did what? Where was Johnny?"

"Where else? Working."

"Did you tell him about your friendly lunch?"

"Yani, let her finish."

"She's my sister, Brina. So stay out of this."

"Did you tell him you're about to get married?"

"No. It wasn't important."

Yani put her drink down and stared at me in disbelief. Linda and Brina sat motionless looking between me and Yani. Patiently waiting for what would come next.

"It wasn't important?!"

"Keep your voice down, Yani. This isn't the time or the place…"

"No, it wasn't. All we had was some fun conversation and lunch at Calientes. Nothing more," I said through my teeth, which were shut tight to keep me from screaming on her.

"And what did Johnny say about this friendly lunch?"

"Nothing, because he doesn't know about it. And that's the way I'd like to keep it." I glared at all of them with a threatening stare.

"Girl, you don't have to worry about me saying anything. I say do your thing."

"Brina!"

"What? You don't agree with me, Linda?"

"I'm not saying I don't, but we shouldn't be encouraging her. She is engaged."

"You two have completely lost your minds. Have we all forgotten the lies he told?"

"People change, Yani. Besides, he was in a situation…"

"There's no situation that can excuse him from the lies he was telling."

"Damn, Yani. You'd think he did it to you instead of Asia. What's with you?"

She dug in her purse for her wallet and pulled out five twenties and placed them on the table.

"Evidently I'm the only one who has a problem. So I think I'll leave now." She went to grab her suit jacket from the back of the chair. I stopped her.

"You have some nerve. Here you are raising the son of your dead ex-husband. The child of a woman who stole your man from you. And you sit here being judgmental? You actually thought about going back to a man who left you even though you had a better man. I think you need to look in the mirror and check yourself." She tried to pull out of my grip. I grabbed her arm tighter and stared at her.

"Fine. You go right ahead and mess up your good thing."

"You mean, like you're doing?"

"You don't know what the fuck you're talking about!"

"Yani…" Linda looked around at the nearby tables.

"Where was your husband Saturday night, Yani? Did he sleep at home with you?"

"That… that was something I told you…"

I let go of her arm. I knew I was wrong, but I had to hurt her like she was doing me.

She'd called me close to tears around midnight. She went on about how Alex had stood her and the kids up. How when she called him it sounded like she'd woken him up. She was all up in arms about him lying about being with his trifling ass friend, Mike. How she felt he was with someone else. I calmed her down enough to get off the phone and go to bed. The next morning I got an early morning call letting me know Alex hadn't made it home and her asking me what to do.

"Look, ladies. Let's start over. It seems all of us have had pretty hectic weeks. Let's not let this ruin our night. Please," Linda begged.

I stopped the waitress and ordered another drink. Yani sat there staring down at the table not saying a word.

"I'm sorry, Yani. I didn't mean…"

"It's okay. I'm sorry, too." She never looked at me.

For the first time since we'd started girl's night out, we all left early.

"What's going on with you guys?" Linda asked as we walked to my car.

"Nothing."

"Don't tell me nothing. You're sneaking around with Hayden and…"

"I'm not sneaking around. We just went out. We're friends. How many times am I going to have to tell you that?"

She put her hands up. "Hey, I don't have a problem with it. I thought you and Hayden were the perfect couple."

"Linda, he'll always have a special place in my heart. I…" I paused for a minute. Linda was my closest friend next to my sister. I had to be honest with her.

"Linda, I'm so confused."

"You want to go somewhere and talk?"

I nodded my head yes. We walked back to my car in silence. I hit the alarm to unlock the doors.

"Why don't we go back to my place?"

And that's where we went. Once at Linda's she put in a CD and lit the plethora of candles she had in her living room. Linda was all about setting the mood.

"Okay," she said as she took a seat on the sofa next to me. "What's going on?"

I didn't know exactly where to start so I just opened my mouth and let it fall out at will.

I told her how I was unsure of my engagement to Johnny. How I wasn't sure being married to him was what I wanted. While I know I loved him, I didn't feel like I was *in* love with him. And yes, there is a difference.

"When I saw Hayden, it was like being in a familiar place. It felt good. As bad as I didn't want it to, it did." I leaned my head back against the sofa and sighed heavily.

"Have you talked to him since you saw him?"

"Twice. He sent flowers to my office. A potted plant. Said it stood for a new beginning."

"Are you thinking about getting back with him?"

"No. Right now I only want to be friends. If anyone knows me, Hayden does."

"That's the comfort you were talking about." She grabbed my hand and squeezed it.

"Like an old pair of shoes, girl."

"You know I've got your back, but you need to straighten things out with your sister. I'm not used to you guys going off like that. And I think you really hurt her tonight."

I sighed again and rolled my eyes up to the ceiling.

"You guys don't know Yani. She can be very stubborn. I'm tired of her shit. First she practically pushes the man away and when he goes for a breather, she gets upset."

"I don't think she means it in a malicious way. Her heart is in the right place."

"Of course. Her heart is always in the right place, but at what expense?"

Linda got up and went into her bedroom. I looked at the TV across the room. The 36-inch was a Christmas gift from me, Brina, and Cheryl two years ago. When Derrick moved out he took everything that was his. So we got together and replaced the 27-inch piece of crap with a state-of-the-art Sony. It was our way of showing him we would make sure she was fine without him.

I got up and browsed through the bookshelf in the corner. We were all avid readers. Linda and I read across the board. Black and white authors. Brina, on the other hand, let it be known that she was one of those people who looked at the pictures on the back.

"If they ain't black, the book goes back," was her motto.

"I heard Lolita Files is coming out with a new book."

"*A Child of God*. Yeah, I'm trying to get an advanced copy of it. My friend who works over at Simon and Schuster is supposed to be hooking me up. She says it's her best one yet." I slid the copy of *Sugar* by Bernice McFadden back into place.

"Did you enjoy that book or what?"

"Girl, it was so good. I know she's coming out with a sequel. She has to." I walked back over to the black leather sofa and sat down. I grabbed the glass of wine and took a sip.

"Blackberry Merlot?" I held up the glass.

"Arbor Mist. You know I like ghetto wine. If it ain't sweet, I don't want it."

I laughed at her. I remembered our days in college when we thought we were doing something drinking Boone's Farm. Strawberry Hill was our flavor of choice. Nice and affordable.

"What's so funny?" Linda came and sat down next to me. The bottle of Arbor Mist in her hand. She refilled our glasses and sat the bottle on the glass coffee table.

"Thinking about something from the past."

"So… are you going to see Hayden again?" She tucked her leg underneath her and pulled the throw pillow to her chest.

I shrugged my shoulders and took a sip of my wine.

"Okay, your shoulders work." She looked at me.

"I don't know."

"Okay, then put it like this. Do you want to see him again?"

Did I want to? My heart was screaming, "HELL YES!" My head, on the other hand, was slowly processing all of it.

"Girl, I'm not sure of anything right now. I can't wait to go on this cruise and kick back. Get a chance to clear my head."

"Two more weeks and we're out. I hope you and Yani patch things up by then."

"We'll be fine by tomorrow. We've never been able to not talk to each other for more than twenty-four hours."

"Good, 'cause I hate traveling with funky acting people. I like when everyone is enjoying themselves."

"Here's to good times to come." I held up my glass and waited for her to touch it with hers. We both took a nice long sip.

"Tell me something,"

"What?"

"Who's going to keep the little boy while she's gone?"

"I'm guessing Alex."

"Damn. He's almost too good to be true sometimes."

"That's why I'm trying to warn her. Men like him don't come around every day. She needs to check herself before he forgets his way home more often."

❖❖❖

I inserted the key in my door. The ride from Queens gave me time to think about what was going on in my life. On one hand I was engaged to a man who loved me. But he had a dangerous job that I was always going to come second to. On the other hand was the man I had loved longer and harder than any other man—besides my daddy—and I wasn't sure if anything more than friendship was in store for us. But this man had hurt me before and I wasn't sure if he would do it again.

Girl, what are you trippin' about? Hayden pops up and now you're really screwed up.

"Asia." I turned and saw Ray at the bottom of the stairs. "How was your week?"

"Hey, Ray. It was interesting, if nothing else. How about yours?"

I placed my purse in the chair on the porch and walked midway down the steps.

"I can't complain. You in for the night?"

"Yeah. I'm just getting back from hanging with my girlfriends. Looks like you're about to hit the town though. Anywhere exciting?"

"Actually I'm having a get-together at my place. I walked around here to put something in my car." He pointed to the black Navigator parked two doors up.

"Why didn't you park in the back?"

"I let my company park back there so they wouldn't take up all the spaces around here."

"That was considerate of you."

"Would you like to join us? It's pretty much the same crew from the other night. They asked about you."

"I really shouldn't. It's…"

"Only for a little while. We're sitting around kicking it *Love Jones* style."

I smiled. "Anyone ever tell you you're persistent?"

"All the time. But in this world you have to be if you want to get ahead." He flashed me his beautiful smile.

"Let me go inside and put my purse up."

"Want me to come up and wait for you? That way you don't have to walk around back by yourself."

"Sure. Come on up."

I walked back up the stairs and grabbed my bag from the chair. I left the door open for him.

"Give me a minute to freshen up, Ray."

"Take your time."

I put my purse in my room and then went into the bathroom. I checked myself out in the mirror. Freshened up my lip gloss and tightened up my ponytail. After placing eye drops in each eye to keep my contacts from drying out, I rinsed my mouth with a little mouthwash. Flashed a quick smile in the mirror to check and make sure I didn't have any food or something else lodged in my teeth.

"Okay," I said as I walked back into the living room where I found Ray having a look at the multitude of pictures placed throughout the living room and down the hall.

"Your place isn't as bad as you claimed."

"We'll address that another time." I grabbed my keys off the table and went to the door in the hall that led down to his place.

"You know, I always forget about this door."

"I don't. It's much quicker than walking up the block, around the corner, and then back down the block again."

"You have a point."

He led the way into his place. The conversation was in full swing.

"Look who I found," he announced as we walked in.

"Hey, Asia." Felicia waved me over.

She and I had clicked from our initial meeting the weekend before. Felicia was the girlfriend of Ray's best friend, Ephraim. They'd been together for three years, the two of them living under one roof, and he still hadn't asked her to marry him. She was going through her nesting period. Only twenty-four, her innocent smile was infectious. She talked nonstop about how she was ready to be a mother. I wanted to tell her she had more than enough time for that. What she needed to do was get out and enjoy herself more rather than sit up waiting for him. But who was I to tell her how to handle her man?

Felicia was the youngest of the group. Everyone else was in their thirties or banging on the door to get in. I'd kicked the door in two years ago and loved it.

"What's the topic now?" Ray asked. He pointed to a bottle of wine and held up an empty glass for me as I sat down next to Felicia on the sofa.

I thought about the three glasses I had at Linda's and the two martinis I had at the club. Even though I didn't have to go far to get home, I knew I was at my limit. I shook my head and mouthed "no thank you" to him. I looked around the room at the party of eight, myself and Ray included. They were a lively group.

"Relationships. What else."

"Umm, the heavy stuff already." Ray sat in a chair next to me.

"Asia, you're engaged. At what moment did you know you were really ready to make the commitment to be with this one person for the rest of your life?"

I scanned the room as all eyes fell on me.

Maybe I should've taken that drink.

"I don't know if I'm qualified to answer this."

"Girl, go ahead. Represent for the ladies," Felicia edged me on. I knew she was counting on me to say the right words. Words she could bring up in a conversation with Ephraim after they were back at their respective place. Maybe even during the drive home.

"Well, first let me say this is not the first time I've been engaged. The first time I was in my early twenties and was madly in love."

"What happened then?" This time Selwyn spoke up. He was the poet of the group. He performed at the spoken word set the weekend before and brought the house to their feet with his work.

"We were too young, I guess. I mean, we were trying to get established in our careers and didn't really have the time needed to nourish a marriage."

"What's different this time?" It was Ray's turn.

"Why are you guys putting me on the spot?" I laughed nervously. I sat for a moment and thought about it. What was different this time?

"I'm older. I'm established in my career. He asked me three times." This got a laugh out of everyone.

"Three times? Brother really wants you then."

I smiled at Selwyn.

"I have a question, Asia. Please don't take this the wrong way. We're all friends here."

"Kira, get to the point," Felicia called out.

"Why isn't he with you now? I've met you twice and neither time was he with you."

I looked at her and gave her a big smile.

"He's a homicide detective. So his work keeps him busy. Besides, tonight is a night I normally spend with my sister and a few of my girlfriends. We called it an early night. So that's why I'm here."

"And we're glad to have you here with us," Ray said to ease the uncomfortable tension that seemed to hover in the room.

"That we are," Selwyn added as Felicia and Ephraim decided to second and third it.

"Are you planning to have any kids?" Felicia eased in another question that would make for good conversation later on.

"I want kids, yes. But if I don't have any, it's no big deal. I have a niece and nephew that I love like my own."

"See, Fe-Fe baby, every woman is not listening to their biological clock."
Ephraim kissed her on the cheek.

"I didn't say I didn't want any. Sometimes I wish I would've had a baby
when I was younger. I look at my sister and she's not quite in her forties,
but her kids are teens now. She still has time to enjoy her life once they're
out the house and on their own."

Felicia winked at me.

Good save.

The night went on with friendly banter and debates. When I looked at
my watch I couldn't believe it was after three in the morning.

"Well, people. I have once again enjoyed my time with you, but I need to
get upstairs and get some rest."

"We're going to follow your lead." Ephraim stretched and stood up. He
gave Felicia a hand up. Everyone else followed suit.

"Come with me to walk them out and I'll see you to your door." Ray
placed his hand on my back and guided me toward everyone else.

After giving out smooches and promises to do it again, ten minutes later
Ray was following me up the narrow steep steps. We walked quietly past the
Brands' door and up to mine.

"I really enjoyed myself. Thanks for inviting me."

"Sorry about Kira. I think she and Felicia are working on some kind of
conspiracy to make you the poster child for their cause." We both laughed.

"I do what I can to help the ladies."

"Your man back from Virginia?"

"Yeah. He got back the other day. He usually spends Fridays at his place
though. Most times I stay over there also, but I decided to come home
tonight."

"Well, I'm glad you did. I enjoyed your company tonight."

"You say that like I was the only one there." I smiled nervously. That mag-
netic attraction was working overtime. I found myself slipping into first-
date mode. Wondering whether or not he was going to kiss me or even try.

"You weren't, but it's nice to add someone new to the mix." He smiled back.
An awkward moment of silence passed between us.

"Well…" He cleared his throat. "I'm going to get back downstairs and let you get some rest. If you get up at a decent hour, you're more than welcome to breakfast."

"What's on the menu?"

"What do you like?"

He was as smooth as butter.

"Hmm… French toast, bacon, grits. And I'm not talking about regular grits either. I'm talking about some good *Southern* grits. Where you cook them for at least a half an hour. Pack'em with butter and salt for taste." I added a lil' Southern drawl in the last part.

"I keep forgetting you're not a *real* New Yorker."

"Real? That depends on what you consider real. No, I wasn't born here, but I've been here for more than a decade. I walk the walk and talk the talk. Furthermore, I was meant to be here. And, baby, it doesn't get any realer than that." My New York accent was prominent in each word I spoke. I didn't notice I'd inched my face closer to his with each point I made.

"I stand corrected."

I could feel his alcohol-tinged breath in my face. He stood two steps below me.

Time to go in now. Say goodnight.

"Well, let me get in here and get some rest or I'm going to miss breakfast, brunch, and maybe lunch."

He laughed at my rhyming skills.

"Okay, Asia. I'll leave the door unlocked in case you change your mind. You know, wake up in time for that Southern breakfast." His tone was low and sexy.

"Goodnight, Raymond." I gave him a smile.

"Goodnight."

I walked into my place and closed the door. I leaned against it for a minute. I couldn't believe the obvious flirting we were doing.

Girl, you're seriously playing with fire.

It was bad enough Hayden had been invading my thoughts all week. Now Ray would invade them tonight.

CHAPTER 20

ALEX

I walked out of the condo and across the street to the park. I'd been spending any spare time I got there. Earlier during the week I'd gone to the market to get some food, in case I ended up sleeping overnight like the last time.

Yani had been acting strange for a couple of weeks. I was shocked when I came home Friday night and found her in bed. That was the one night she was sure to be out until at least one or two in the morning. It was after midnight, so I didn't bother waking her. I changed into my bed clothes and went downstairs and slept that night. With Corey in my spot, there was no sense in my moving everyone around.

Yani was leaving for the cruise Monday and Corey would be my responsibility for five days. While we hadn't discussed it, I knew she was nervous about it. While I may have had my problems with the whole situation, I would never do anything to hurt him.

It was after eight o'clock and time for me to head home. I had a feeling she was becoming suspicious, but she hadn't said anything and neither would I. I was enjoying my small window of peace too much to care. Being in the city made me feel alive and sparked my enthusiasm for my work. It seemed to push my ambitions further.

It was late August. The end of summer was near. People were out everywhere trying to get in as much outdoor time as they could before the bitter cold of winter made its way on the scene. Myself included.

I found myself driving in the opposite direction of Brooklyn. It had been a minute since I'd been by the old neighborhood to check on my mom. The area was undergoing visible changes, but her building looked the same. Rundown and in need of a good scrubbing to get rid of the years of ambitions from the different graffiti artists who lived somewhere in the neighborhood. I'd tried on numerous occasions to get her to move. Even went as far as buying her a nice place on the East Side. A neighboring address to the Jeffersons, but she wasn't having it.

"Why would I want to leave the place I grew up? My friends are here, not over there in bourgeoisyville."

It was a lost cause so I stopped fighting the battle and did the next best thing and paid to have her apartment fixed up. Now that was something she liked.

I parked my car in front of the building and got out. Looked up and down the block as I walked in. The usual suspects were out. The corner dwellers with brown paper bags to disguise their choice of liquid poison and the hip-hop heads dressed in their baggy gear.

I walked up the two flights to her apartment and rang the bell.

I could hear her slippers as she dragged her feet across the floor until she reached the door. She looked out the peephole.

"Alex?" She undid the numerous locks.

"You and this prison. See, if you would move…"

"Don't start with me. You just got here." She reached up and kissed me on the cheek and waited for me to walk by her. She looked out in the hall. "Where's Yani?"

"Home, I guess."

"You guess? Oh, Alex…"

"Don't start with me. Remember, I just got here." I sat on the noisy, plastic-covered couch. There were some things that weren't going to change. Thankfully I had on long pants and didn't have to worry about it sticking to the backs of my legs.

"Don't you tell me what not to do. I'm the mother here." She mumbled a few choice words in Spanish and sat down in her favorite chair.

"I was at the office and decided to come and see you. Is that a crime?"

"No, but you should've called your wife and let her know."

"Anyway. How are you?"

"I'm good. You remember Alejandra from upstairs in 5B?"

"Mrs. Cruz?"

"Yes. She's in the hospital. Heart trouble." She shook her head and made that face most older people make when sickness hits too close to home.

"I'm sorry to hear that. How are Roberto and Juan taking it?"

"Please, Roberto, that bum. He's in and out of jail so much that no one can keep track anymore. Juan is a good boy to his mother. He's the one that sees about her. But you know he's gay?"

"Ma, that's not nice."

"It's the truth. I saw it with my own eyes. We always knew he had those, you know, ways about him since he was a little boy. Poor Alejandra tried to prevent it. At least he's a good son to her though." She turned her attention back to her favorite Spanish soap. They had to be the most violent shows on TV, but they were good.

"How's Lucia? I heard Natalia was babysitting for her the other night."

"Yes, she went on a date or something. I try and stay out of it." She threw her hands up and laid them back in her lap.

I leaned forward and placed my arms on my legs, letting my head drop.

"What's wrong, Alex?"

I looked up at her. She was still watching the TV.

"Nothing."

"Don't nothing me. I know something is wrong. I knew it from the moment you walked in. So, are you going to tell me or do I have to nag you to death about it?"

I laughed and sat back.

"Really, Ma, it's nothing."

"I guess I'll call mi nuera and find out from her…"

"You don't need to call anyone. Leave Yani alone."

"Seems like you're doing a good job of that yourself." She glanced over at me.

"I didn't come here to be attacked and accused. I think I'm going to leave."

"Leave then. You don't want to hear the truth, then leave." Once again she went into a tirade of choice words in her native tongue.

"So you want me to leave? Your only son? You barely see me, but you send me off without a second thought." I placed my hand over my heart, pretending I was wounded by her gruffness.

"You suggested it; not me."

She patted the spot next to her. I got up and went to her. I slowly sat down.

"Now tell me what's bothering my *mejo*." She pulled my head on her shoulder and I let it all out.

"Ah, I don't know why you're paying somebody to tell you what you already know. You need to talk to Yani, Alex. Nothing is going to be resolved by keeping secrets." She took my palm and rubbed it with her hand, then turned it over and looked at it.

"Things will work out. You'll see."

"I hope so, Ma."

"Now, you get home to your wife. It's my bedtime." She got up and turned the television off.

I kissed her and headed for the door.

"You have to go through the bad to get to the good, *mejo*. Remember that and you'll be okay."

"I will."

❖❖❖

I pulled up to the house and sat in my car for a few minutes. I had to stop dreading coming home.

It'll be better tomorrow.

I got out and went in. The first floor was dark except for the light in the foyer. I walked into the kitchen. A note was stuck to the fridge.

We tried to wait for you. I put your food in the oven if you want something. If not, put it in the fridge so it won't spoil. Yani.

I looked in the oven and found a T-bone steak, baked potato, and asparagus tips.

I was going to have to kiss ass big time behind this. T-bones were for special occasions. It meant she'd fired up the grill and I was the grill man in the house. Yani didn't eat steak unless it was cooked on the grill.

I put the covered plate in the fridge and went upstairs. Stopped on the second floor to say goodnight to the kids. Jay was already asleep. I kissed him on the head and eased back out. I walked down to Nat's room and knocked.

"Yes?"

"Can I come in?"

"Sure." She was under the covers watching TV.

"What's up?"

"Nothing." She looked at me. "Is something bothering you, Daddy?"

"No, I'm good. Is your mom sleep?"

"I don't know. She wasn't when I went up there, but that was twenty minutes ago."

I shooked my head and looked around her room. Everything was neatly put away.

"Where's Corey?"

"Now he's sleeping."

"With your mom?"

"Daddy, go upstairs and talk to Mommy. I don't think I'll have the answers you need." She yawned.

"Goodnight, princess." I kissed her on the forehead.

"Goodnight, Daddy." She pulled the covers up and snuggled in.

I slowly made my way up the stairs. I anticipated the familiar scene that would greet me. Yani snuggled up with Corey. He slept right up under her. I was surprised when I opened the door and found her stretched out on the chaise.

"Hey, Baby," she said.

"Where's Corey?" I looked over at the bed. It was neatly made. I walked into the closet and took off my shoes.

"Downstairs in his room." She placed the magazine in the rack and sat up.

I peeled my shirt off and tossed it in the hamper. My pants and socks followed.

"Alex." She got up and walked over to me.

I continued to get my things so I could take a shower.

"Yeah?"

She waited a minute before saying anything. "I think we need to talk."

"Let me take a shower first. I stopped by my mom's on the way home and I was out running around today." I grabbed my robe from the hook and walked into the bathroom.

I stood under the water for a minute. I'd finished bathing five minutes earlier, but I was stalling for time. I knew Yani was patiently sitting waiting for me to enter the room so we could discuss what was bothering her. The same thing that had been bothering me for a while. I finally decided to face the music. It had been a long time coming and we needed to get this out in the open, but I'd hoped to be able to put this off until she came back from her trip.

I cracked the door open slowly and stuck my head out. Just as I predicted she was sitting on the chair looking out the window. I walked into my closet and put my things away. After taking a deep breath I walked back into the room.

"You see something out there?"

"I was just looking at the street. You ever notice how quiet it is out here?" She sighed.

Oh, I've noticed. "Well, it is considered to be America's first suburb." A well-known fact about the Brooklyn Heights area.

"Yeah, I remember reading that somewhere." She moved from the window and walked over to where I was putting on my shirt. She stopped right in front of me. We stared at each other for a moment.

"Are you happy with me, Alex?"

I finished pulling my shirt down and stared at her before saying anything.

"Honestly, Yani, I'm not sure. I'm not happy about things you're doing." I walked around her and went to the bed. I pulled back the covers and fluffed my pillows. I was willing to prolong this for a little while longer. I hadn't quite figured out exactly what I was going to do or say.

"What things are you not happy with?" She was standing on my side of the bed right behind me.

"Yani, can we do this another time? I'm really tired and I have an important meeting in the morning."

"What if I don't want to wait?" Her voice had taken on a sound of authority. Her hand sat firmly on her hip. The black woman's battle stance was taken.

I had to bring this situation back to non-hostile territory.

"Look, Baby, I told you, I'm tired. The only thing I want to do right now is climb into bed and go to sleep. I promise, when you get back from your cruise, we'll talk all you want."

With a look of frustration on her face, she stormed out the room. As bad as I wanted to, I couldn't bring myself to get out of bed again. I decided to give her the time she needed alone. When she was tired she'd come back.

I fluffed the pillow and sunk my head into it.

I'll deal with this later.

I could hear her slamming things around downstairs. I turned over on my back and took a deep breath. My hands buried behind my head underneath the pillow. I stared at the ceiling and wondered what was happening to my life. It had been close to a fairytale only a few months ago and it was now turning into one of those ongoing storylines that were overused on the soaps.

"You have to go through the bad to get to the good, mejo. Remember that and you'll be okay."

I tried to find comfort in those words, but wondered how long I was going to be on this road of bad.

CHAPTER 21

ASIA

Now, it doesn't get any better than this. Beautiful weather. Food for days. Nonstop parties. Best of all, I was with my girls. I looked over on both sides of me. Linda to my left, Brina to my right and Lucia on the other side of her. It was the last day of the cruise and we were scheduled to be at sea all day today. We'd done our share of the three D's—drinking, dining, and dancing.

"Next time you chicas do this, you have to let me know. I haven't had this much fun in forever." Lucia reached for her drink on the table at her side.

We'd been lounging by the pool for over an hour. Taking in the different characters as they passed by. The amount of spandex we'd seen over the weekend should've been outlawed. The amount of extra skin that bulged and poured from the spandex wearers was another story.

"I wonder where Carmen and Yani are."

The waiter brought over the next round of drinks. Linda reached over and signed the tab.

"Knowing Yani, poor Carmen is somewhere listening to her sob story. I don't know why she came. She hasn't been out of her room other than to eat." I adjusted my shades.

My sister had been a huge party pooper during this trip. The phone bill in her cabin was going to be astronomical. She called home three times a day to check on the kids. So she said.

"The sad thing is Carmen has had to miss out on things because she's had to play nursemaid to Yani."

"You wouldn't do that for me, Asia?" Brina looked at me.

"Girl, you all know I love you, but I'm not going to be miserable and ruin my trip because of some drama you're going through. Especially if it's drama you're causing and it's something you can deal with when we get back."

"What's going on with my brother and your sister? They're madly in love with each other, but for some reason they can't seem to get it together."

"You have to talk to them, Lucia. I've decided to stay out of their business. Especially after I was informed that I needed to mind my own business. When I get a husband and some kids, then I can have a say."

"You guys are going through it like that?" asked Linda.

"I'm not going through anything. She doesn't have to worry about me sticking my nose into any more of her business. I've got my own life to deal with."

"I haven't talked to Alex lately, but I will when I get back." Lucia readjusted the straps of her bikini top after applying suntan lotion.

"I'm telling you to stay out of it. It's not worth the aggravation." I took a long sip of the cold, red and white, slushy drink in the souvenir glass.

"I don't know what that means when it comes to my brother." Lucia laughed.

"You don't think you should check on her, Asia? She did say she felt like she was seasick."

"She has Carmen. What am I supposed to do? Help her hold her head over the toilet?"

"You know you're cold sometimes," Brina said to me.

Linda looked down at her watch. "Well, ladies, I'm going to go to the cabin and take my shower so I can get ready for the show later tonight." She gathered the towel she had in the chair underneath her along with the book she'd tried to read in between us talking.

"I'm coming, too." Brina got up.

"I guess we all should go then." Lucia looked over at me.

"I'm coming," I said and sat up on the lounger. I adjusted the red sarong around my waist that went with the blue and red bikini I had on. The roaming eyes from the male passengers made me a little uncomfortable. Brina, on the other hand, was basking in all the attention that was being thrown her way. And with the barely there one-piece she had on she was commanding it.

"I'll meet you ladies in a minute," Brina said as the bronzed Adonis from the night before walked toward her smiling.

"Chica, you are bad," said Lucia.

"You don't know the half of it." Brina winked at her and waved us off.

"Can you believe Cheryl called me the day before we left?" Lucia and I followed Linda inside the ship through the sliding glass doors. We'd spent the better part of the first two days of being on board getting familiar with the ins and outs of the ship. Meaning, finding all the bars and eating areas. We spent the majority of our time lounging out by the pool people watching. And oh what sights you see. An array of different nationalities. From the passengers to the people in the crew, it was possible to cover every inch of the globe.

"What did she say?"

"Some lame ass excuse why she couldn't come. I told her it was too late anyway." Linda dug around in her purse for the room key as we descended the two flights of stairs that would take us down to the Empress deck.

"He's really got her nose wide open."

"And some," Linda added.

We reached the cabin. I stood behind her as she opened the door. The cabin steward walked by offering a friendly hello. We smiled and acknowledged him. I'd caught a few of the other passengers talking to him as if he was beneath them, but the elderly Asian man told them he didn't handle their cabins even though he was at a door directly across the hall from them. I wanted to high-five him for handling them in a just way.

The cool air rushed out and greeted us as we pushed our way into the cabin. Linda flung the straw hat from her head onto the vanity.

"Whew. Girl, I'm going to have to get my edges touched up when we get back after all of this sweating."

"Stop tripping. You know it's hot as hell in New York right now."

"We're really breaking you in, Lucia. She's talking shit and all now." We laughed at her.

"I thought this was a part of the initiation into the group?"

"You just passed then." Linda hugged her. I plopped down on the bed.

Lind opened the closet and pulled out her outfit.

"Asia?"

"Yes, Linda?" I rolled over and looked at her.

"You haven't said much about the wedding. What's going on with that?"

I rolled my eyes up at the ceiling and reached for the TV remote. "Nothing."

"Wait a minute." Lucia walked over to me and took the remote from my hand. "Now that I'm initiated and all. What the hell is going on? You changed your mind about marrying JJ?" She was now sitting on the bed staring at me with disbelief in her eyes.

"We're still engaged."

"Girl, JJ is…" Before she go into detail, I cut her off.

"I know, but I don't know if I'm ready to make that step, is all. Before you ask, yes. I love him. But I don't know if I love him enough. Something is missing for me. I'm not sure if he's the person I want to spend the rest of my life with." I sat up.

"I wish I had that problem. Here I am trying to get a decent man and you have that and more."

"Don't we all, Lucia? But Asia's biggest problem is she's been dipping into another…"

"I haven't dipped in anything. I've just been enjoying going out when Johnny can't."

"You're cheating?!" Lucia's eyes became as big as saucers.

"No! I've gone out with my new neighbor. And it wasn't a date. I just hung out with him and a few of his friends. Nothing more." I looked over at Linda who was giving me a look that said she wasn't buying it.

"What about Hayden?"

"You went out with Hayden?! I thought he was married."

"He was, but he's not any more. And I met him for lunch."

"Is that why you're unsure of what you want to do with JJ?"

"No, that has nothing to do with it." I flipped through the channels on the TV.

"Well, whatever it is, you need to figure it out soon. You have this man expecting you to marry him. And stop being so judgmental of Yani when you don't have your own house in order."

"Whatever, Linda." Yani's situation was different than mine. She'd already made the decision of what she wanted when she married Alex. I, on the other hand, was still too scared to cross that line. I wondered what Linda and everyone else would think if they knew Dede had a brother who was living in Atlanta and Yani knew it, but had yet to share that information with Alex.

So, whose house was in worse shape?

CHAPTER 22

YANI

I gave Carmen a tight hug. "Thanks for everything, girl. I would've been a wreck without you."

"What are girlfriends for? You make sure you do what we discussed."

"I will. As soon as I get back."

The attendant took my bags and placed them underneath the plane. I'd stayed a few days more than the others. I still had some unfinished business to attend to.

"This bag is pretty heavy, Mrs. Chance." He patted the black duffle bag.

"Just a bag of books." I gave him a friendly smile and winked at Carmen. She'd held on to the money until I was ready to come and get it. Thanks to being able to fly on a private jet, I didn't have to worry about the prying eyes of airport security.

"Tell Alex and the kids hello." Carmen waved as I headed up the steps onto the plane.

"I will. And thank Bryce again for me. Love you!"

"Love you, too!" She walked through the doors that said office.

❖❖❖

"Mommy!" the kids yelled as I opened the door.

"Hey, boys." I hugged Jay and scooped Corey up in my arms.

"Where were you? I was looking all over for you." His little face was animated as he threw his arms up to show me how much he'd looked.

"I had to go on a trip." I smiled. "Jay, can you get Mommy's bags?" I walked into the parlor and placed my keys in the glass bowl.

"What did you do on your trip?" Corey's eyes were filled with concern.

"I got to see my best friend. I also went on a cruise on a big boat called a ship."

"Did you bring us back anything?" Jay asked.

"Do I ever go anywhere and not? I've got you." I winked at him and kissed his forehead. His smile stretched wider across his face.

"Where's Daddy and Nat?" I looked through the mail on the table.

"Nat should be here soon. She was over at Kayla's house. I'm not sure about Daddy. He was gone when we got up this morning." Jay shrugged his shoulders and took the stairs to my bedroom so he could put down the two bags he was carrying.

"Has he at least called?" I stopped looking at the mail and concentrated on what Jay was saying.

"Not today."

"It's almost three o'clock. Have you eaten anything? How long has Natalia been gone?"

"I don't know, but I got me and Corey something to eat."

"Jay made me a sandwich, Mommy."

"He did? Did you eat it all?" He nodded his head and smiled. "You ate a whole sandwich?" He nodded his head again. "You're such a big boy." I hugged him and squeezed him tight.

"Place the bags there." I pointed to the spot near the chaise. I was paying close attention to the letter addressed to me from the name I'd seen on the private investigator's paperwork.

"What did you get me?" Jay was about to unzip the duffel bag.

"Not that one!" I startled both of them. Jay's hand was frozen on the zipper.

"It's the bag right there." I pointed to the red suitcase. "Bring it here." I placed the letters on the table and opened the bag.

"Here, this is for you." I handed a bag to Jay. "This one is for Nat." I placed that bag on the floor next to the luggage.

"Did you get me something, too?" Corey asked with wide-eyed anticipation.

"I sure did. Yours is right here." I handed him his bag. His smile was full beam.

While the kids opened their gifts, I took the duffel bag and placed it in my closet. Wouldn't want to have to explain what that was about.

"Jay, can you take your brother downstairs so I can change? Soon as I get situated I'll be down."

Jay took Corey by the hand and walked out. I picked up the letter and stared at the name in the top left corner. *Cornell Nelson.* My hands shook as I debated on what to do. I wondered how he'd gotten my information. I took a deep breath and tore open the letter. I couldn't believe what I was reading. When Johnny wasn't able to find any real information on Dede, I'd hired a private investigator to look deeper into her background.

Dear Mrs. Chance,

My name is Cornell Nelson and I was given your information by someone who recently told me you could help me find my sister Deborah. I would like to talk to you as soon as I can. Dede told me she was coming to New York to visit you when we last talked, but I haven't heard anything else from her since. Could you please call me?

I looked the letter over three times before folding it and placing it in my pocket. I knew about Dede's brother and the story of how they'd been placed into the system. Being that he was younger he was adopted without any problems, but she hadn't had such luck. She'd gone through the system until she was old enough to be on her own. Dede was three years his senior. At the age of ten when they were taken into the system, she did her best to take care of him. When the family who adopted Cornell wanted him and not her, Dede told him it was best and she'd always keep in touch. A promise she was unable to keep once she was shifted from one foster care home to another. Jarrin had indeed been her knight-in-shining-armor.

The phone rang, jolting me from the daydream.

"Hello?"

"Oh, you're home. Why didn't you call and let me know when you were going to get in?"

"I don't know. I guess I wanted to surprise you. But seeing that you're not here, the surprise is on me."

Alex let out a deep breath. "You know…"

"Yeah, I know. You had to go to the office. That's also why I didn't call you." We were both quiet for a moment. "You know the boys were home by themselves?"

"No. I thought Nat was there with them."

"Did you at least call to check on them?" I was becoming impatient with him.

"I'm just…"

"Jay said he hasn't seen you at all today. I'm starting to think you didn't come home at all last night."

"Look, I'm on my way. Can we not start this? You're just getting back from your trip and I'm too tired to argue."

"I wasn't…"

"Yes, you were and you have a right to. I apologize for leaving the boys. We'll talk about it when I get there."

"I guess." I was trying to hold on to my anger, but I thought about what Carmen and I had talked about and was losing the battle. "I'll see you when you get here," I half-cooed.

I clicked the phone off and patted my pocket. I would deal with this later. Right now I had to get ready for something else.

I unpacked the rest of my bags and placed the gifts for Nat in her room and the ones for Alex on the bed.

I picked up the phone and checked the messages and then called Nat to find out why she wasn't home. She reminded me she had asked if it was okay for her to go over to her friend's house long before I decided to spend the extra days down in Florida. After settling that, I began to get ready for my plans for later.

Carmen, I hope this works.

CHAPTER 23

ALEX

I'd made a mistake and had fallen asleep the night before and didn't make it back to Brooklyn. I knew I was going to have to discuss with Yani what was bothering me. She wasn't going to continue pretending to be deaf, blind, and dumb to my actions. While I wasn't cheating on her with someone else, I knew I wasn't being honest about my whereabouts.

There was no question of whether or not I loved my wife. I loved her more than life itself, but I was unhappy about the situation she continued to force upon me. While I thought what she was doing for Corey was admirable and I went along with it, I could no longer deny my feelings for wanting to try for a child of my own with her. She was too wrapped up in him to see she was ruining things between us. Mike's comments were really affecting my thinking. I was taking care of a child I shouldn't be.

I walked through the front door prepared to defend my actions, but what I found was something totally different. The aroma of frying chicken greeted me. The melodic sounds of Jill Scott blasted through the sound system as she sung about the way her man loved her.

I walked into the kitchen to see what else would be accompanying the chicken. I was pleasantly delighted when I saw the pan of macaroni and cheese, a pot of cabbage flavored with bacon, and a pan of twelve blueberry muffins rising in the oven. All the fixings of a Sunday dinner were on the stove.

Yani slipped behind me and wrapped her arms around my waist, startling me at first.

"Hey, Baby," she said.

"Hey, yourself. You're throwing down in here. What's the occasion?"

"Just thought I'd make a real Sunday dinner. It's been a really long time since we've had one."

I pulled her arms from around me and brought her in front of me. Her tan was beautiful. Her hair was beautiful. She was beautiful. She kissed me long and hard. The anger I came in armed with was pushed to the back of mind.

"Umm…" Her moans were matching mine. "Now that was really nice."

"How was your trip?" I lightly stroked her back with my hand.

"I was sick almost the whole time."

"You didn't take anything for it?"

"I popped a few of those pills, but they didn't help much. How about you? What did you do while I was gone?" She kissed me softly on the lips.

"Nothing exciting."

"Ready to eat?" she asked as she removed the last pieces of chicken from the pan.

Was I ever? My mouth had been watering just from smelling it. I smiled wide and kissed her harder than she'd done me. She smiled and motioned for me to pull the plates from the cabinets.

❖❖❖

"I'll take that over eating out any night," I called to her. She was in the bathroom starting the water for a shower.

"Wanna join me?" she asked. Her bare leg teased me from behind the towel she was holding tightly around her body. A sexy "come hither" look was on her face. A look I hadn't seen in months.

"You don't have to ask me twice." I followed her, removing my clothing along the way.

The steam from the heat of the water had begun to fill the room. I could smell the scented candles she'd placed in different places throughout the room. She turned off the lights as she walked in behind me. The flickering lights from the candles and the steam rising in the room gave off a romantic feel. I was fully aroused at this point.

"I'm going to soap you from head to toe. Wash your back, your hair…"

I grabbed her and pulled her into me, flinging the towel to the floor. The feel of her skin against mine had me on fire.

"Baby, you can do whatever you want to me," was my response.

She took my hand and led me into the shower. The heat of the water mingled with that of her touch. As promised, she soaped me up, down, and in between. I returned the gesture. I could feel the tension wash away with every stroke.

"I love you, Alex," she whispered in my ear as I pulled her down onto me.

"I love you, too, Baby. More than you'll ever know."

She straddled my lap as I sat on the seat in the shower—an added feature she requested. The first plunge was heavenly. My toes curled at the sensation of entering her warm wetness. I could feel her pulsating vaginal muscles as she pulled me deeper into her. It had been so long since we'd had sex I was afraid I wouldn't be able to control myself.

"You missed me, Baby?" she moaned in my ear.

"Umm, hmm. You missed me?"

"Can't you tell?" She leaned in and kissed me hard and deep. "My body has been craving you."

I placed my hands on her hips to help guide her up and down on me.

"I have something I want us to try."

I got excited just from the mention of something new. Like an eager puppy wanting to please its master, dripping wet, I obediently followed her into the bedroom. Obeyed when she ordered me to lie down on the bed. Watched with baited anticipation as she walked into her closet and retrieved a box and returned with a seductive smile on her face.

"What you got there?"

"I thought I'd see what all the hype was about, so I made a lil' visit to an adult toy store. While there, the sales lady talked me into a few buys. She said it would bring us to a new level of intimacy." She winked at me as she pulled out a bottle of clear liquid lubricant. The next item nearly made me bounce up from the bed.

"Yani... Baby... I hope you're not expecting to use that on me!"

"No, Baby. I'm expecting you to use it on me." The neon pink plastic was the shape of a perfect dick. Veins and all.

"You see this." She pointed to what seemed to be a shape of an animal protruding from the base of the shaft of the rubber dick above an electronic box that looked as if I would need to read the instructions to turn it on. "This is a rabbit."

"A rabbit?"

"Yes, a rabbit. Between you, the rabbit, and the pearls." She pointed to the four rows of pearls inside the vibrator near the top of the shaft beneath the head. "I should be on cloud nine in no time."

Hey, I've always been game to try different things. She's my wife so I didn't have to worry about this showing up in a tabloid at a later date.

In the spirit of things, I put my hesitation away and obeyed her requests.

"You have to use the lubricant or it might chafe me." She opened her legs inviting me to come play.

I picked up the lubricant and read the label. *Umm, sensual lubricant. Heightens stimulation.* Sounded good to me.

"You only need a couple of drops."

I dropped enough in my hand to lubricate the toy and her. The rubbing alone was turning her on like crazy. Watching and feeling her move against my hand caused my dick to come to attention like a new recruit trying to impress the drill sergeant. Feeling as if it was an added extension instead of an actual piece of my flesh. I reached down and began to stroke it while I stroked her.

"Now put it in so the rabbit will sit on my clit," she instructed me.

And being the good and obedient husband I am, I obliged her. Ever so slowly I inserted the vibrator exactly the way she asked. The ears of the rabbit rested on her clit waiting to stimulate her at a speed I was basically incapable of doing. I looked at the box and hit the on button and the dick came to life. Gyrating in a circular motion, the pearls danced against the saturated walls of her sweet pussy. Her head lolled back as she moaned in a way I had yet to hear.

"Hit the other button, Baby. Turn on the rabbit," she begged. Her hips were moving in rhythm with the movements of the plastic dick.

I looked down at the box and hit the second on button. The light was at the bottom and had a ways to go until reaching full throttle. I continued to hit the button until the light was all the way to the top, at which time Yani clamped her legs shut around my hand. Her body began to convulse and I couldn't get enough of it.

"Oh… my… God!" she practically yelled through clenched teeth. "Ooh, Baby… Ooh, Baby," she whimpered as her movements deepened.

I grabbed my dick and began to rub it. The shit she was doing was turning me the hell on! But it was nothing compared to what she did next. I was kneeling at her side watching the show when she reached out and pulled me closer and turned on her side. She moved my hand and slid me into her warm, inviting mouth and began to suck me off with an intensity I'd never experienced in my life. When she finally climaxed her legs clamped tightly around my wrist and hand, her jaws pulling in with everything she had, I could feel a tremble come from deep within her. Suddenly my hand being held captive was soaked with her juices. I threw my head back and let loose the nut I'd been trying my hardest to hold on to.

"Ugh, Baby… I'm sorry," I said as I loaded her mouth with my juices. She'd never allowed me to stay in her mouth. The feeling was so overwhelming I thought I would cry. My chest heaved up and down as I tried to regain my composure. For the next five minutes we both struggled to fight off the nonstop wave of tremors of pleasure. I was finally able to dislodge myself from the vise grip hold of her jaws. I handed her a towel which she deposited the contents of her mouth into.

"I, I… I can't believe…" I took a deep breath.

"That was incredible! No wonder why Asia is always bragging about this thing!" She rolled over. The squirming vibrator slipped out onto the bed churning out movements.

"Is that who took you to get this?" I was still trying to catch my breath.

"No. Carmen suggested I do something different." Yani groped around between her legs until she grabbed the wiggly toy and turned it off.

"This was definitely something different. Damn! I can't believe you let me cum…"

"I know." Her faced balled up as if it was disgusting. "And I loved it. The sounds coming out of you… Look at my leg!"

I looked down and saw it uncontrollably jumping.

"Baby, I have never come that hard before."

"Do I get my turn now?" I reached out and pulled her close to me.

"Give me one second." She bound from the bed headed to the bathroom.

Regardless of how good it felt, I knew she was going to clean her mouth. I laughed at the thought. A minute later she rejoined me in the bed. She kissed me, shoving her tongue deep into my mouth.

"Now. That's much better."

I rolled her over on her back and took my time making love to her well into the wee hours of the morning.

As I lay holding her in my arms, I thought about how right everything felt at that moment. I looked down at her peaceful sleeping face.

If I could just get you to understand. It could be like this always.

But life didn't always give us what we wanted.

CHAPTER 24

YANI

Things between Alex and I had started to look up. He'd started coming home at a decent hour. Always looking for a rendezvous with the rabbit. In order to accommodate my husband, I began to put Corey down to sleep in the bed that had been placed into Jay's room for him. Jay was his security blanket at night. What could be better? I was having great sex with my husband and everything was in order. Or so I thought. There's always that something lurking around the corner waiting to pounce when you least expect it...

❖❖❖

After a long day in the office, I rushed home to prepare a meal for dinner and get the kids off to bed early so I could seduce Alex as soon as he walked into the door. The surprise was on me when I pulled up and his truck was already out front.

"Baby," I called out as I walked into the house. There was no answer. I placed my briefcase in the parlor and undid the buttons on my suit jacket. I placed my keys in the bowl and picked up the mail on the table and walked into the kitchen. I scanned through the envelopes as I searched the lower part of the house for Alex. After coming up with nothing, I started up the stairs. From the moment I opened the room door I knew something wasn't right. The icy reception was the first sign. The next one was the look on Alex's face.

"What's wrong, honey? I rushed home so I could cook…"

"Who's Cornell Nelson, Yani?"

I stopped in mid-step. I could feel the shock registering on my face as I tried to think of a way to answer him without making this seem as bad as he was taking it.

"I'm waiting." His words were ice cold, like the look in his eyes.

I noticed the opened letter in his lap.

"You opened my mail?" I asked incredulously.

"No, I opened *my* mail. This time he addressed the letter to me. The man said he's written you twice with no answer. So, now do you want to tell me who Cornell Nelson is?" With a face of stone he sat on the chair in the sitting area and waited.

Seeing no use in lying, I told him everything I knew about Dede's brother—the same things he'd added into his letter to him, plus a few things I'd learned from the private investigator. When I finished I looked up at Alex and waited. Waited for his screams of anger, but was surprised when he began to laugh. A laugh laced with anger and disgust.

"Here I am beating myself up because this baby doesn't have anyone. Alex, you're being unreasonable about this situation. You can do it, Alex. You can raise the child of a man who has brought nothing but hurt to you and the ones you love. Man up, Alex. Stop thinking about yourself. Stop thinking about the fact that your wife seems to be more into raising her dead ex's child than trying to make another one with you. Dumb ass me. Being miserable as hell living out here in the suburbs just to make my *wife* happy and forsaking my own happiness."

"What are you talking about, Alex?" I was confused by his constant babble.

"Yes, Yani. I prefer to live in the city. I've been craving it so much that I've been spending time in my apartment. The one I lived in when I met you. The one I'd worked hard to attain my whole life, but was willing to give up to make you happy."

"I never asked you to give up your place. Remember, this," I threw my hand out and waved it around, "was your idea. Your doing." I was becoming heated with each word.

"You're right. It was. So, I guess it won't bother you when I undo it?" He was now standing coming toward me. The look on his face frightened me. I slowly backpedaled a bit, but was determined to stand my ground with him. I'd been meek at one time in my life and all it had gotten me was a broken heart.

"Undo it how?" I spat at him.

"I'm selling it," he said nastily.

"You can't sell our house. The kids are in school and have their friends…"

"Like you always say, they'll adjust." He threw the letter at me and tried to walk out.

"Where are you going? You can't walk out on me without hearing me out." I tugged at his arm.

"I'm not in the mood to listen. Not right now." He pried my hands from his arm and pushed me away.

I was stunned. In all the time we'd been together Alex had never displayed any sort of violent behavior toward me, but I knew from the look on his face he was mad enough to hurt me if I didn't leave well enough alone. So, I decided to give him a chance to cool down and stepped to the side. Allowed him to grab his cell phone and two-way from the dresser and walk out.

He just needs a little time to think things out, Yani. You've got to give him time.

That was three days ago. I was now on the verge of being a mess.

While I still managed to get up every morning and get the kids ready, drop them off, and go into the office, I was falling apart from the inside out. By Friday Asia was in my face questioning me.

"What the hell is going on with you? You're sitting in the meetings, but you're not there." I brought my attention away from the window and looked at her. She was six inches from my face.

As hard as I fought, it was no use. The tears I'd been holding back came out full throttle. Asia closed the door to my office as I collapsed on the floor. She rushed back over to me and knelt down in front of me. Her hands reached for mine.

"What the hell is going on with you? What happened?"

I looked at her exposed knees, which were just below my line of vision.

The black skirt and houndstooth-patterned blouse were my point of focus. If I could just think about that and nothing else I could get myself together.

"Yani, talk to me. You have to tell me what's going on so I can help you." She continued to prod.

I wanted to tell her to hush. Just let everything go quiet so I could concentrate on her knees, her black skirt, and the houndstooth-patterned blouse.

"Is it one of the kids, or Alex?"

My eyes traveled back to her face and the tears came harder. Just the mention of his name was enough to send me over the edge.

"It's Alex. What happened? You're not eating and obviously not sleeping. Did you guys have a fight or something?"

As I tried to go back to looking at her knees and clothing she moved. She sat down on the floor next to me and rubbed my back. I tried to open my mouth to tell her what had happened. How my husband had threatened to sell our house. How he'd walked out and hadn't called. But I couldn't get my mouth to cooperate.

"Yani, you've got to talk to me." I knew she was growing impatient with me.

"I... I..." The hiccups came. I'd been crying so hard I could barely catch my breath.

"Calm down. Let me call Linda and tell her we're not going to be able to make it tonight."

A sense of panic set in. I'd promised myself I was going to be strong. Me, the one who'd kept going when one man had walked out on me. I wasn't about to change things up because of another one. The thought of having two men walk out on me sent me into another tizzy fit of cries. Was it something about me that pushed them out the door?

"I'll be right back." Asia got up and walked over to my desk and picked up the phone.

I shook my head no until I could get my mouth to work.

"Don't... don't call. I'll... be okay," I hiccuped out.

"Girl, please. Your ass is a mess. You're in no shape to go out drinking or anything else. Just relax." She continued to punch in numbers. I could hear remnants of her phone conversations as they floated over to me.

"She really needs us. Tonight…" I knew that meant she was calling out the cavalry.

I forced myself to stand and walked over to the phone and placed my finger over the button to disconnect the call.

"What are you…"

"I can't do this, Asia. Not tonight… Not… right now." I took the receiver from her hand; placed it back in place.

"You need…"

I held up my hand and silenced her, then took enough deep breaths to calm myself down.

"I need to sort things out. I did something I shouldn't have and now I have to figure out how to make it right. Or if I can make it right."

"What are you saying?"

"I'm saying I need you to see about the kids for me this weekend." I straightened myself up.

"And where are you planning on going?"

"To a place where I can figure this whole thing out. I love Alex, but I may have pushed too hard and too far this time."

"I'll come over and…"

I placed my hand on hers and looked at her. Although she'd been pretty pissed with me for the past couple of weeks, I knew she always had my back no matter what.

"It's going to be okay, Asia." I hugged her. I grabbed the tissues off my desk and cleaned my face. After reapplying my lipstick, I grabbed my things and prepared to leave.

"Yani, you can't leave and not tell me what's going on."

"I'll call you and let you know where I am. I'll be home Sunday at the latest. I promise you, this too shall pass."

As I walked out of the office and made my way down to the train station, I knew exactly what I had to do. The thing I should've done from the beginning.

CHAPTER 25

ASIA

"I'm telling you, Linda, she grabbed her things and walked out like the entire thing had never happened."

I was sitting in the media room of Yani's house watching TV. It was now Saturday night and I still hadn't heard anything from Yani. I'd called Alex the night before to see what he would tell me about what was going on. He told me he would call me back and I was still waiting on that call.

"I don't know what to do. She came home and grabbed a few things and took Corey with her."

"You don't think she'd do anything to hurt herself or him?"

"While I know she's going through some deep shit, I don't think she's suicidal." I flipped through the channels, looking for something to help take my mind off of the drama in the Chance household.

"You should call around and see if she caught a flight somewhere. If you have her credit card..." Right then the phone beeped deep and long.

"Let me call you back. I'll see if I can find her statements."

"Okay. Call me back."

"I will." The phone beeped again. I hurried and clicked over.

"Hello?"

"Asia."

"Alex? Where are you?"

"In the city. What's going on there?"

"You tell me. I've been here since yesterday and you haven't bothered to grace the front door. Yani had what seemed like a nervous breakdown for all of ten or fifteen minutes and then she asked me to watch the kids. Next thing I knew she was gone and she hasn't called."

"Gone where?"

"I don't know! You need to tell me what's going on, and right now!"

"You need to talk to your sister. This is all on her." He was trying his best to brush me off, but I wasn't having it. Not for a second time.

"No, brother-in-law. You're going to tell me; whether you like it or not. So start talking."

He blew out a frustrated sigh.

"Look, all I know is I'm sick of Jarrin being in our lives. He's done nothing but cause drama and shit since the day he resurfaced."

"What are you talking about? Jarrin is dead." I knew where he was going, but I had to get him to see how silly they were both being.

"That he may be, but his ghost is still living in our house. What was he like? Why is it she can't seem to let go?"

I had to think about Jarrin. There were two Jarrin Millers I'd come to know. The one I'd loved in the beginning and the one I'd grown to hate.

"Have you asked Yani this?"

"No. I don't think she's going to be as honest as you."

Me and my mouth. I knew one day it would get me wedged into a situation I didn't know how to deal with.

"Well, at first Jarrin was a good guy. He really loved my sister. They'd been through the fire and back with one another."

"Through the fire?"

"Yes. Between him being an only child who was spoiled beyond belief by his overprotective, meddling ass mother, and the admiration of all the disrespectful girls who wanted to be with him, Yani caught hell from all sides. Every side except him. Regardless of what his mother said or how many girls came to him promising to do things my sister wasn't, wouldn't, or couldn't, he stayed true to her. That's why when all of the shit went down with him disappearing and all, it was such a shock to everyone. He'd never done anything but love her and the children; up until the day he left. At least it seemed to be that way to everyone.

"Alex, you have to understand, Yani feels for Corey. She's always had a soft spot for less fortunate…"

"Did she tell you she found out Dede has a brother?"

So the cat was out of the bag. I was silent for a moment. No, she hadn't told me, but I'd found out when I mistakenly opened some correspondence from the private investigator she'd hired.

"No. How did you find out?"

"He sent me a letter. The damn man got tired of begging her to contact him so he contacted me. Hoping I would be the next best source of helping him find his sister.

"Asia, it was like someone had reached inside my chest again and snatched a chunk of it off. Here she is telling me Dede was an orphan and she didn't have any family."

"But you offered to keep the baby."

"Yeah, because he didn't have anyone else. I didn't expect her to give him to the state or anything like that. I'm not that heartless."

"Did she say why she didn't tell you?"

"I didn't give her a chance. You just don't know how tense things have been in that house since all of this has happened. And I would be able to deal with it if she was different about the whole situation. She's almost forgotten about the other inhabitants of the house when it comes to Corey."

"Alex, he's a baby. He's gone through a lot. She only wants to make sure he's okay." I was trying my best to get him to see that Yani wasn't doing it intentionally.

"And I want the same thing, but it should be an equal thing. Asia, I want us to have a baby, but she's so wrapped up in this boy, she doesn't have the time needed for us to accomplish that."

"I thought things were better between you guys."

He laughed slightly. "They have been since she got back from the cruise, but that's because Carmen told her she needed to get her act together. If Carmen hadn't said anything I wonder how things would've been."

"Look, trust me when I tell you my sister loves you. There's no question of whether she loves Nat and Jay, and she also loves that little boy. You have to agree, there's something infectious about him. Even I'm hooked on the lil' bugger." I laughed a little, trying to lighten the mood, but to no avail.

"Yes, everyone is in love with Corey. Who just happens to be damn near the spitting image of his daddy."

"Is that what's wrong? You think she feels for him because he reminds her of Jarrin?" I laughed. "You couldn't be further from the truth. Alex, Yani has a good heart. She loves him because he's a baby. Because right now he needs her. And maybe, just maybe, because he's her answer from God when she asked Him to send her another baby. A baby she could love and shower with affection. One she could do all those things to with you. Maybe she wasn't specific enough, but she asked."

"Good try, Asia, but I'm not buying that. Yani is hooked on that baby because he's a link to her past. A link to someone she loved unconditionally. I'm starting to feel she'll never have that kind of love for me." The sadness in his voice tugged at my heart.

"I hope that's not the sound of defeat I hear. You've accomplished too much to not be willing to fight for something this important. And I'm not sure it's a fight or more of an understanding that needs to be reached." I shifted on the seat. Tucked my legs underneath me a bit and turned and looked at the picture of him and Yani during their happy times. The bright smiles of two people deeply in love with one another beamed at me. I wouldn't let myself believe that something this petty would be their downfall.

"Asia, I appreciate you being a good sister…"

"And a good sister-in-law."

"Yes. You are a *great* sister-in-law, but once again I find myself at a crossroad in my relationship because of your sister and her first husband. I'm not sure…"

"Alex, you knew this wouldn't be easy going in. Can't you remember the fight you were willing to wage in the beginning?"

"I'm trying. I'm really trying."

"Hey, let me get out of here. I was returning your call. Are the kids okay?"

"They're fine. Yani took Corey with her, wherever it is she went."

"See, once again he's her number one priority."

"Don't be that way. Look, as soon as she gets back I'll make sure she calls you."

"Don't go out of your way. As I've said many times before, I love Yani with all my heart, but at what cost? Maybe I'll give you a call tomorrow. Tell the kids I said hi and I'll give them a call later. Bye, Asia." The click on the other end signaled he was gone.

I placed the phone on the seat next to me and smoothed my ponytail with both of my hands. As if I wasn't going through enough drama of my own, I now had this to add to it.

A few nights ago was the first time in a couple of weeks Johnny had stayed over. Again I was awakened by the overwhelming sensation that I was drowning. The dreams had started coming more frequently over the past few months. Each time I was submersed in the ocean waiting for someone to come and save me. At first I thought that someone was Johnny, but more and more the face and figure began to change. While I wasn't quite sure who it was, I knew who it wasn't. I had finally made the choice to visit the woman Lucia had told me about. A good friend of the family is what she called her.

"She'll tell you exactly what's wrong without you even opening your mouth." Lucia had pulled out the little phone book she kept in her purse.

"I don't know, Lucia. I'm not too crazy about having someone…"

"You don't need somebody to tell you what you already know. What you need is for someone to tell you why." She found the number and scribbled it on another piece of paper I had strategically folded and placed deep inside my purse.

I went back and forth with myself as I looked at the piece of paper in my hand. I'd always been one who was afraid of people who claimed to be psychic or anything close to it. At this point, I was willing to do anything to make these dreams stop happening. The other night was the worst one yet and I don't think… No, I *know* I can't keep going through this.

I picked up the phone and dialed the number. I was shocked when the voice on the other end sounded as normal as mine. I was expecting music or maybe a long drawn-out message accompanied by creaky sounds and what not. The slightly older sounding voice said hello again.

"I'm sorry. I was given this number by my…"

"Lucia? Yes, she told me to expect a call. Can you come by later today? I have an opening."

I took a deep breath before setting everything up. I would leave Nat and Jay there while I went into the city. I didn't expect it to take any more than two hours at the most. I smiled as I thought about asking her to evaluate what was going on in their household also. *We all needed to stop the madness.*

❖❖❖

"So what did she have to say?" Linda and Brina had agreed to meet me at Wells—a restaurant well known for its fried chicken and waffles.

I ordered a sweet tea and waited for the waitress to leave.

"We're waiting," said Brina.

"She said the man in my dreams is trying to get me out of harm's way. Something about me being in a situation that's about to go bad or what not."

"Hunh?" Linda looked at me as if I was talking Chinese.

"She was able to tell me about the three men in my life and how I'm in the role of a puppeteer."

"A who?"

"A puppeteer, Brina. You know, the people who control the puppets." Linda looked at me and rolled her eyes upward.

"Oh, like on *Sesame Street?* Okay." She shook her head as if everything was just registering in her brain.

"Back to what you were saying, Asia." Linda waved Brina off.

"The puppeteer is trying to situate each of the men where there's no conflict or something like that."

"So the three men are Johnny, Hayden, and who?"

I'd only really talked to them about me meeting Ray and all, but never went into details about the attraction between us. I was confused enough without bringing them into the mix.

"I'm not sure, but maybe that man hasn't come along. Maybe he's the one who's trying to rescue me from drowning."

The waitress walked over with our drinks and informed us that our order would be up soon.

"Have you heard anything from Yani yet?" Linda placed the straw into her Sprite.

"Not since the day she left. Tomorrow is Monday, so hopefully whatever she had to do will be taken care of by then. I need to get back to my own place. But Alex called."

They both looked at me.

"Did he tell you what's going on?"

"He was kind of vague about his whereabouts, but he's pretty fed up with Yani and the way she is with Corey."

"But Corey's a baby who doesn't have anywhere to go."

Linda and I looked at each other.

"He found out about the uncle."

Linda's jaw almost hit the table. Her eyes bugged out of her head for a minute.

"Wait a minute. What uncle?" Brina looked between both of us, waiting for an answer. Brina was pretty much in the dark about certain things, but not out of spite. Whenever anything important was going down she was usually busy on a date or shopping.

"Did she tell him?"

"Nope."

"Then how…"

"Could one of you please answer my question? What uncle?"

"Dede has a brother."

Just as we were about to get deep into the conversation, the waitress appeared again. We all sat back in our chairs. Everyone seemed to be in their own thoughts as she placed our identical orders in front of us. Soon as she left Linda's mouth was working again.

"So how did Alex find out about the brother if Yani didn't tell him?"

"He wrote Alex a letter."

"I wonder how he got their information."

"He probably had Jarrin checked out and came up with Yani's information. I mean, anyone with an ounce of brain matter would know to do that."

We both stared at Brina as she buttered her waffles and situated her chicken on the plate.

"Miracles never cease to amaze me," Linda said as she continued to look at Brina.

"What?"

"If her brother had recently talked to her he would know she was married to Jarrin and probably a few more details about Yani. Brina, you're on to something," I said with my fork pointed at her.

My mind started rolling over different scenarios of what her brother more than likely knew. I needed to call Alex and find out exactly what the letter said, then, I would be able to figure out the man's angle. If he was genuine, or after something else. There was no telling how much his sister had shared with him.

CHAPTER 26

YANI

I sat at a table in the food court section of the CNN Center. I had no idea what the man I was waiting for looked like, but I had a feeling I would know him the second he walked up. Corey was at the park with Carmen while I felt this man out. She'd agreed to fly up as soon as I called her. I was so nervous that my leg began to shake involuntarily. I tried to take deep breaths so I would calm down, but nothing seemed to work.

I looked up and noticed a man entering from the doors near the Georgia Word Congress Center side. He seemed to be looking for someone. I was just about to throw my hand up to signal for him when his face registered he'd found his party. He quickly walked over to a group of other men who were seated near the doors for the Philips Arena.

As I watched him I noticed a man come in from that side. Something deep inside me told me it was him. I told him to look for me near the Waldenbooks store and he was headed that way. I balled my hands into tight fists and let them go a few times as I psyched myself up.

Stay calm. Everything is going to be okay, I said over and over in my head.

"Yani?" he asked as he approached me.

I stood to greet him. "Cornell?"

"Yes." He smiled and reached for my hand. An awkward moment passed.

"Please. Sit." I pointed to one of the three empty chairs at my table. He took the one directly across from me. I placed my purse in the one to my left and pulled it closer.

"I'm really glad you called me. I had a hell of a time getting your information. Dede called and told me she was going to New York and then I didn't hear anything from her."

"Would you like to get something to drink or to eat?" I was prolonging the inevitable. I hadn't asked him if he knew about his sister's death.

"No, I'm fine. So, you say you have Jay?"

It took a minute to register in my head he was talking about Corey.

"Yes." I picked up my cup of coffee and took a sip.

"Where is he?" He looked around as if he expected him to come from behind one of the columns or something.

"He's not here, but he's not far."

The look of confusion was expected. He stared at me, waiting for an answer as to why everything seemed so secretive.

I took a deep breath again and looked him in the face. The smile I had been wearing was now gone. In its place was a look of sympathy and sadness. I bit slightly on my bottom lip and tried to figure out how to give him the news about his sister and what had happened to her and Naya. How her youngest child had come about being with me.

"Mr. Nelson…"

"Cornell. Please. Call me Cornell."

I nodded at him. "Cornell…" I gathered up my strength again. "You said you haven't heard from Dede since right before she came to New York?"

He nodded his head yes. "She called and said she was going there to meet with you about the kids and some other things."

"You said you guys were split after the death of your mother?" I was prodding him for more information.

"Yes. We were placed in foster care and split up after I was adopted. She was never adopted and ended up leaving around the age of sixteen." He stared at me.

"When did you finally find each other? This year? Last year?"

"It was actually right before she got married. I was finally able to track her down in Florida back in '94. Toward the end of the year. This was right before she and Jarrin became seriously involved." The look in his eyes told me he knew the full Jarrin saga.

I shrugged my shoulders and gave him a slight smile.

"I tried to tell her not to get involved with him, but she was so in love. I apologize..."

"Hey, you didn't do it to me. Besides, it's over and done with now anyway." I tried to smile away my discomfort.

"Yani, I'm not sure if your questions are for closure or something else, but can you please tell me what's going on with my sister? I haven't heard from her in months and when I called her girlfriend she was supposedly staying with in New York, she told me that Dede had left out one day to meet you and never came back. Thinking she'd pulled another disappearing act, the friend didn't think anything of it. But I'm starting to think something is going on; especially since you have Jay with you." He looked at me, waiting for an answer.

I pulled in another deep breath and held it for a few seconds before releasing it. I nervously popped my fingers. *Stop beating around the bush and tell the man.*

"Cornell, I..." I swallowed hard. "I really don't know how to tell you this." I reached into my purse and pulled out the article that had covered the story about the accident and a copy of their obituaries and handed it to him. I watched as his eyes went from left to right reading. I knew he'd reached the part about the death of Naya when his composure changed. The more he read, the more his mouth parted.

"I was at the hospital with her. She... she never told me she had any family. She asked me to keep Corey."

His head popped up. "Corey?" His face looked as if he was offended by the name.

"We call him that because the boys—my son and Dede's son—both have their father's first name."

"And he answers to Corey?"

"Yes. He actually likes it."

The gentle demeanor he came in with was now replaced by what seemed to be a hint of distrust. As if I was trying to pull a fast one on him.

"Where is my nephew, Mrs. Chance?"

Mrs. Chance? A few minutes ago we were on a first-name basis with one another.

"Mr. Nelson." I could play that game also. "I'm not sure if you're who you say you are, so I'm not about to take a chance. You can tell me all the stories you want, but I need some concrete proof..."

"Jay, or Corey," he said dryly, "has a birthmark on his right leg." He rattled off his birthday, place of birth, and the day he was born. He told me about Dede and Jarrin being on the run and about them running into me in Florida last year. He also knew about Jarrin's death. "I think I should be the skeptical one here, Mrs. Chance. Seems like every time there's some contact made with you, people turn up dead." He stared directly in my eyes.

Although his words hurt, I was not about to give him the satisfaction of seeing how much. I stood up and grabbed my bag. "Mr. Nelson, you have my information and I have yours. You'll be getting a call from my lawyer." I was about to storm off when he stopped me.

"This is a battle you can't win. In case you're wondering what I do for a living, I'm a lawyer. One of the top lawyers in Atlanta." He pulled out his wallet and handed me his card. "So maybe you need to rethink this a bit. I'd hate for your adoring public to know about your baby-snatching scandal. You know, how you blamed your ex-husband, who happened to get killed during an ordeal with you, for the loss of your baby after he shot you."

I couldn't believe the Jekyll and Hyde he'd pulled on me.

"Good day, Mr. Nelson." I walked away from him and hurried for the bathroom so I could call Carmen and tell her to go straight to the hotel with Corey. If he wanted to see him, he was going to have to bring the authorities.

Before dialing her number, I thought about his words about people dying when dealing with me. Would he really make it seem like I had caused Dede's and Nya's deaths? But how? I was nowhere near the area when she had the accident.

But she did have an accident where she was the only car. Now that would seem a bit suspicious to any jury.

I walked out of the bathroom and looked for Cornell. I turned from left to right until I had completed a circle. My heart began to race as panic set in. The last thing I wanted was for this to get ugly. Without thinking about whether or not I was being followed, I rushed out the building, headed toward Marietta Street and dashed across the street into Centennial Park. Carmen was coming out of the little shop on the grounds of the park. She'd gone in to buy Corey an ice cream cone and her something to drink. She immediately noticed the panic on my face.

"What happened?"

"Come on, let's get back to the room."

"Mommy, Auntie Carmen got me some chocolate ice cream. Chocolate is my favorite." He licked at the ice cream that was leaking down the sides of the cone before it touched his hand.

"That was nice of Auntie Carmen. Looks like it's really good." I stooped down with a napkin I got from Carmen and wiped his mouth. I stood back up and looked at Carmen. "Let's go."

"Jay?" a male voice said.

Corey continued to lick his cone until Cornell called him a second time.

"Jay, do you remember me?"

He looked at Cornell as he continued to lick the ice cream. His face lit up as he smiled.

"Uncle Cornell," he blurted out.

My heart sank deep into my stomach. I swallowed hard to keep the food I'd eaten earlier from rushing back up my throat.

"Hey, big boy. How are you?"

"Good. See my ice cream, Uncle Cornell. Auntie Carmen got it for me while Mommy went to find something over there." He held the cone out for an inspection as he pointed toward the CNN building.

"Mommy?" Cornell looked at me.

"Umm hmm," Corey said. "My real mommy is gone to heaven to sleep. So now Yani is my mommy."

"Don't you want to come to my house and see Nadine and Brandon?" He was now in a stooping position, allowing him to stare directly into Corey's eyes. Corey looked up at me, as if asking permission. I gave him a reassuring smile.

"Can Mommy come, too?" He looked back at Cornell.

"Maybe next time Mommy can go."

"No. If I can't go, neither can he." Trying my best to remain cordial toward Cornell, I spoke in a nice even tone. As smart as Corey was, he would be able to tell if something was wrong and I didn't want him to become upset.

Cornell shot me a nasty glance and looked back at Corey who was now working on the edges of his cone.

"Jay…"

"Corey…"

"His name is Jay. I don't know why…"

"No, Uncle Cornell, my name is Corey also. Corey is my number two name. My big brother's name is Jay, too. So I like being Corey." From the mouths of babes is all that came to my mind. I had to keep myself from bursting into a fit of laughter as I marveled at the handling of the situation by a four-year-old.

Cornell stood back up and looked at me. "Can I speak to you over here?" He looked at Carmen. "Privately?"

I took a few steps away and then turned to face him.

"I'm confused about all of this. How it was possible for you to handle my sister's affairs without her next of kin being contacted. If I found you, you definitely could've found me."

"You knew about me and where to look for me. When I talked to Dede she led me to believe she didn't have any family."

"If you think I'm going to let you simply take my sister's child and keep him as your own, you need to think again. Just because you were once married to Jarrin doesn't give you the rights to his children as well." He was so close in my face I could see the outline of his contacts.

"You know, Cornell…" I got a step closer into his face. "I didn't volunteer for this. Didn't sign up somewhere saying, hey, bring me the illegitimate child of my dead husband so I can raise him. I could've just as easily let the state step in and take him, but I knew I wouldn't be able to live with a decision like that. A tragedy happened and I dealt with it. And I think I'm doing a damn good job at it. So if you think your threat has me shaking in my boots, then *you* need to think again."

He stepped back an inch and straightened his blazer and ran his hand over the back of his close-cut head. The scowl from his face slowly disappeared and formed a smile that was traced with a hint of humor.

"Lady, this is far from over." He walked around me and went to tell Corey goodbye.

Once he walked away Carmen and I stood there silently for a moment. I had to figure out what I was going to do. I knew he had more legal claim than me, but I couldn't see myself walking away from him at this point. He'd become a big part of my life. I didn't know what I was going to do.

CHAPTER 27

ASIA

Yani was back from wherever it was she'd slipped away to, but something about her had changed. Things had become a bit strained between us. While I did feel guilty for my part in it, I wasn't at the point where I wanted to apologize either. I had enough craziness going on in my life without adding hers to it. Besides, she hadn't asked for my opinion anyway. In my eyes what she was dealing with seemed cut and dry. She needed to let go of one thing to keep all the other things in her life. I know it may sound cruel, but it's true. She stood to lose much more if she continued to fight this Cornell Nelson guy. Dede's brother wasn't backing down. He'd come at her full force. The petition for a custody hearing was at the office before we stepped foot into the lobby that Monday morning with a backup copy delivered to her house. Uncle Cornell was coming with the big guns drawn and his fingers on the triggers.

As much as Alex didn't want to get involved, he found himself in the middle of it. *Again.* Working to get Yani in contact with one of the best child custody lawyers New York had to offer. One who had connections with judges and politicians. The only problem; Cornell had filed everything in the courts down in Atlanta. Meaning, unless Yani's lawyer was affiliated with anyone down there, she was up you know which creek, and the paddle had fallen in before she'd pushed away from the bank good.

None of my problems had changed either. I was still dealing with the pressing question of my impending nuptials, the fact that Hayden had showed back up in my life professing his undeniable love for me, and this strong attraction I was feeling toward Raymond. I was all screwed up.

Johnny had begun to realize I'd been putting him off whenever he wanted to talk about the wedding and setting a date. Either it was something at work, something with my friends, or something with whatever popped into my head. He'd even started to spend less time at my place. It had been more than two weeks since he'd last slept over.

Hayden, on the other hand, was in full pursuit. I'd been honest and told him Johnny and I were engaged, but he didn't let that stop him. If anything, it made him more aggressive.

"Asia, you and I are soul mates. You can't deny that."

I held the phone without saying anything. It was the truth. Even after all he'd put me through, there was something about him that made my heart skip a beat whenever I saw or talked to him. But there was no sharing of this pie, so he would have to wait and see what happened.

The more I talked to Hayden, the more I nitpicked with Johnny. It seemed I found fault in things that wouldn't have bothered me before. From the way he kissed me to the way he walked. Everything seemed to bother me.

Then there was Raymond. Seemed like every time I opened my door I would see him. I wasn't complaining. Ray was a nice distraction from the craziness my life had become.

The spoken word sets he invited me to were relaxing and enjoyable. I loved hanging with him and his friends. We went to an open mic set one night and I was shocked when Ray went on stage. His rendition of Johnny Gill's "There You Go" had me speechless and damn near breathless. When he came back to the table I didn't know what to say. I enjoyed it so much that I went home and looked through my CD collection for my *Boomerang* soundtrack and hadn't stopped playing it since.

It was Friday evening and I was looking forward to chilling with my girls. I expected Yani to opt out since she had so much going on, but she surprised me when she showed up in my office asking if I was ready to go. It was ladies choice this week. Meaning we all agreed on the one place we enjoyed the most—Metronome. It was always the perfect place to unwind and get your groove on before the night was through. When Cheryl was a regular part of our group, we had a real good hookup. The guy on the door was a good friend of hers. He always made sure we were treated like royalty.

Good ole' Cheryl. She knew someone, no matter where we went.

I walked in the door and made my way over to the stairs. I knew they'd be in our favorite booth—right where we had a bird's eye view of everything that happened downstairs. I slid in across from Linda.

"Heard from Brina?"

"She said she was on her way. How about Yani?"

"She should be here any minute."

Linda shook her head. "You two still walking around here mad with each other?"

"I'm not mad with anybody." I searched through my bag for some money to pay for the drink I was headed to the bar to get.

"Then why didn't you come with her? That's what you usually do." She gave me an evil look.

"What?" I glanced back at her.

"You need to quit tripping, Asia. That's your sister. What would you do if something were to happen to her? Both of you are being silly about nothing."

"I'm not being silly." I sucked my teeth and rolled my eyes at her and slid out the booth.

"You want something from the bar?" I looked down at Linda.

"You buying?"

"I wouldn't have asked if I wasn't."

"I've got the drinks tonight," Yani said. She waved her platinum Amex card at one of the passing waitresses.

She'd snuck up so quietly behind me I knew she'd probably heard the conversation between me and Linda.

"So, what's up, chicas?" She pulled off her jacket and sat down. I slid in next to Linda.

The waitress she'd summoned over was hovering over us waiting for our orders. Once we'd all given them she left with the promise to return shortly.

"So how was everyone's week?" Yani asked.

"Mine was good. I can't complain."

"What about you, Asia? Anything exciting or new happen?"

"Nope. Nothing at all." I looked around the room and then down on the dance floor. It was still early so the place was practically empty. I reported to Linda and Yani that Brina was headed our way. We all watched as she climbed the stairs and came over to sit with us.

"Hey, ladies," she said in a joyful voice.

"Work must have been really good today," Yani said as she made room for her to sit.

"Yes, I must admit today was a good one, but work is over and I don't want to see or talk about it until Monday morning."

"Where's Lucia? She told me she was coming."

Lucia had stayed true to her word and had become an official member of girls' night out.

"I guess she'll be here in a minute. I haven't talked to her today. What about you, Yani?" I asked.

Yani shook her head.

"Uh, there she is right there." Linda pointed out to where she'd just walked through the door.

"Is Alex back at home?" I asked quickly, trying to get an answer before Lucia reached us.

Yani gave me a wicked look and then smiled. "Not yet. He's still living in the city in his old place." She shrugged her shoulders and smiled an uneasy smile.

"Girl, you better get your shit together and get your man back in your bed before he slips into someone else's." I put on a big smile for Lucia, who was now stooping to kiss me on the cheek.

"Hello, chicas!" She continued to make the rounds to the other three.

Yani and Brina slid over to make room for her.

"Now we can get this party started. My girl is here." Brina slapped Lucia a high-five.

The waitress walked over with the first round of drinks and then took our appetizer order. Yani handed her the credit card she'd waved at her earlier and ordered her to start a tab. From that point on she kept the drinks flowing.

"Asia?" I looked up and smiled, then got up and gave him a hug.

"What are you doing here?"

"We try to get here at least once a month on Fridays." He looked around me at the table.

"Oh, where are my manners? Ray, this is everyone. Everyone, this is my neighbor, Ray."

Ray flashed them his brilliant smile as he shook their hands and tried to log to memory the names they were throwing at him.

"Yani? Oh, so you're the big sister. It's nice to finally meet you," he said when he got around to shaking her hand.

"I would say the same here, but since my sister has omitted to tell me anything about you, I guess I can't." Yani shook his hand and then looked at me.

"I did tell you I had a new neighbor." I rolled my eyes at her and then looked back at Ray.

"Oh yeah, you did mention you had a new neighbor. You just forgot to mention how neighborly you two had become." She smiled and then took a sip of her drink.

"Well, I'll let you ladies get back to your food and conversation. Asia, are we still on for Tuesday? Shakira wants to know if you'll be there."

"Tell her I'll be there."

"Good. Maybe I'll see you tomorrow. I'm cooking French toast in the morning. You know the back door is always open." He smiled slyly and kissed me on the cheek and left.

I watched as he walked back over to a group of guys. I guessed they were friends of his from work since none of them seemed familiar.

"Umm, the back door is always open?" Brina asked.

"You need to explain, baby sis. You've got a man leaving his door unlocked for you and you're engaged to get married. Shame on it all."

"Shame on nothing. She's not dead. Fine as that man is... Girl, I'd be at that back door every day." We all laughed at Lucia.

"You didn't tell me the man was fine," Linda said.

"Wait a minute. Linda knows about him and we're just now finding out? Foul," Yani said. "You know that's foul as hell. You could've at least..."

"She mentioned the man looked like someone, is all. It's not like we've been gossiping about him or something. So stop trippin'."

Just then the music got louder. I smiled as Ray looked up at me. He knew the song they were playing was one of my favorites and signaled for me to join him on the floor.

"While you bitches sit here trying to get all in my business, I'll be back." I stood up and went downstairs and met him in the middle of the floor. We smiled at each other as we fell into step. Dancing and swaying to Koffee Brown singing about the after party. We were having a good time as one song after another came and went. The DJ had gone back a few years on the R&B charts and brought damn near everyone out on the dance floor when the opening rifts of Frankie Beverly and Maze's "Before I Let Go" came through the speakers. At that point everyone was singing and dancing.

Ray leaned in to talk into my ear.

"You seem to really be feeling this one." He leaned back and smiled at me. He knew the drama that consisted in my life. The whole Hayden saga. He'd been the one I'd gone to for moral support and advice when Hayden made it known he was looking for more than friendship from me. I had my girls and all, but this time I wanted a man's point of view. Wondered what he would do if he were in the same situation.

Ray had proven himself to be a true friend at that point. Telling me to take my time, but to listen to my heart. The part of my heart that was speaking the loudest would be the way to go.

"Now who doesn't like Frankie?" Just then the DJ put on Cheryl Lynn singing her hit "Encore." The crowd went crazy again. The DJ was getting mad props for being able to work the thirty-something crowd. Then he decided to slow it down. I guess the owner had sent word to him the crowd was thin around the bar.

"Whew. Now that was a workout." I smiled at him and fanned myself.

"I didn't know you could move like that. I have to tell everybody how you showed out on the dance floor." He placed his hand at the small of my back and guided me over to the stairs. We laughed as we made our way back up to the table where I'd left everyone.

"If it isn't the dancing queen." Yani had clearly run up a nice tab since I'd left the table.

"Maybe you should go out there and give it a try. Work off some of the unnecessary stress in your life. Maybe sweat out some of the liquor you've consumed while you're at it."

I turned around to thank Ray before my sister had a chance to say something else embarrassing.

"Thanks for walking me back up here. I know your friends are probably looking for you."

"Yeah. We should do this again. See you at home?"

I nodded my head yes and smiled. He kissed me on the side of my face, an inch away from my lips. I could feel my face turning red as my smile broadened. He then said goodnight to everyone and left.

"See you at home? Sounds to me like he wants to be more than your neighbor."

"I have to agree with you there, Yani. All these other women in here and he's danced with Asia all night. Seems to me, someone is working overtime in the men's department."

"Like you can talk, Brina. You change men like you change your drawls." I intentionally said the word in Southern dialect.

"And since I'm single, I can do it like that."

"I'm not married yet, so I can work it like that too, boo."

"Hey, hey. We're here to have a good time. No fussing. Yani, you need to stop sitting over there feeling sorry for yourself. Get your ass up and go over and tell my brother to get his ass home. That's all you have to do. Asia, you go right ahead and enjoy yourself. Once you get married then you worry about it, but until then, have fun. Men do it all the time." Lucia picked her drink up and held it up.

"Here, here." Linda clinked her glass and then drained hers.

"Hey, ladies!"

We all stopped talking to look at the body standing at the end of our table. Cheryl had put on a few pounds, dreaded up her hair, and changed her style of dress. We were all shocked into silence by her presence.

"How are you guys?"

Brina was the first one to speak.

"We're good. How about you? You look fine."

"I'm good. I felt the need to get out tonight and, since the email said you guys would be here, I decided to join you."

I glanced down at my watch. It was a few minutes to ten and we'd been here since six.

"I know I'm a little late, but better late than never, right?" She nervously hunched her shoulders and searched our faces for some kind of reassurance.

Once I got a closer look at her, I could see in her face something wasn't right. Her eyes were slightly puffy and her skin had a blanched look. Even though she'd broken one of the cardinal rules of friendship—don't put your friends down for a man—we all knew she needed us and proceeded to gather our things.

An hour later we all sat in Cheryl's apartment listening to the details of a love gone wrong. How she'd changed things to please him, but in the end it wasn't enough. How she'd wanted to kill him when she'd walked into her place and found him embracing another man.

Another woman was bad enough, but when you lose your man to another man, I guess it sort of does something to you. Cheryl looked as if someone had sucked the life out from behind her eyes. The only person I knew who smiled more than Cheryl was the Gerber baby and that's because it was a picture. Her smile had been replaced by fear and doubt and a week's worth of tears.

"Don't worry about it. He's not the only fish in the sea. Get your reel out the closet and head back down to the lake, girl."

We all laughed at Brina's euphemism. Her polite way of telling Cheryl to get back into the game of living.

One by one we all said goodnight and made promises to check in on her. Even Lucia pledged to do her part after giving Cheryl a big hug. Cheryl promised not to be a stranger.

I sat in bed hours later thinking about the horror of what Cheryl was going through. How embarrassed she must have felt to tell us.

Since Johnny was on a working streak I was home alone. Which was fine with me. I don't think I would've been up to being intimate with him after what we'd discovered tonight. Not that I was questioning his manhood or anything. It's just the thought of something like that. It makes you begin to question all men.

I could hear the closing of a car door from out back through my open window. I crept over to the window and watched as Ray walked into his apartment. I thought about his open door and got up and slipped on a pair of jeans underneath my night shirt. I slowly made my way down the back stairs until I reached his door. I softly knocked on the door. I could hear him shuffling around in the kitchen so I knocked a little harder.

He opened the door and stood aside so I could come in.

"I saw your car out front. Everything okay?"

I walked by him and headed straight for the living room and sat on the sofa.

"What's wrong?"

"Just needed to talk."

"Which one is it? Hayden or Johnny?" He came and sat down next to me.

"Neither one actually. This has to do with someone else."

"You want something to drink first? Maybe a cup of coffee or tea?"

"What kind of tea do you have?" I asked as I got up to follow him into the kitchen.

"Regular and green," he said from behind the cabinet door.

"Regular is good for now." I reached into the cabinet and grabbed two mugs while he put water in the kettle he kept on his stove, more for decoration than anything else.

"So what happened between the club and home that has you this deep in thought?" He placed the kettle on the stove and turned on the eye beneath it.

"A friend of ours came in. It's been months, almost a year, since we last saw her."

"A year? Why so long?"

"She got a man."

"Oh, so she put her girls down for him and now that things aren't as blissful as they once were with her and homeboy, she's looking to you guys for comfort."

"Yep. The classic case. But it's the circumstances behind the unblissfulness that has me going."

"Do tell," he said and hopped up on the counter.

"She caught him with another man. Well, not actually having sex or anything, but if she had waited a few more minutes, no telling what she would've walked in on. And they were at her place. Can you believe that?" I looked at him to gauge his reaction. He gave off a slight laugh and shook his head.

"I tell you. There are so many brothers out here pretending. Pretending to like women when they know they'd rather be with a man. Sneaking around to do their nasty deeds. And that shit is nasty. To give a woman false hope is truly nasty."

"How can a man lay down with a woman and then lay down with a man?" I was leaning against the counter. My arms were folded across my chest.

"Unfortunately there are men out here who think it's cool to do that. I say they ought to make up their minds."

"Do you believe in people being bisexual?"

"I believe people use that word because they feel they have to fit into a group. So being bisexual is better than being classified as gay to them. But the way I see it, if you sleep with someone of the same sex, your ass is gay. Nothing in between."

The kettle began to whistle. I placed the tea bags in the mugs and waited for him to pour the water. As we waited for the bags to brew a little I asked him another question.

"Have you ever thought 'bout being with another man?"

"I don't swing that way. I love pussy too much. There's nothing about a man that arouses me."

"I hope I didn't offend you with that."

"You didn't. You need some answers and it's only a question. I'm secure in my sexuality so nothing you ask will offend me. I'm here to answer anything you may want to ask." He finished dunking his tea bag and placed it in the sink. I did the same. After adding a few spoons of sugar we went back into the living room. It was late, but I wasn't ready to go to sleep.

"TV or CDs?" He pointed at the remotes on the table in front of us.

"Is Maxwell in rotation?"

"Urban Hang Suite?" He got up to look.

"You know it." I smiled as he turned on the CD player. He had a state-of-the-art sound system on the wall. The ones you see in the Sharper Image.

I began to sway as the "Til the Cops Come Knockin'" began to play.

"I've got to stop hanging with you so much. You're starting to know me too well." I smiled as he came back and sat down.

"That's what friends do. They spend time with each other so they can get to know one another." He looked at me over the rim of his cup and took a slow sip of the steaming liquid.

I swung my feet up on the sofa and tucked them underneath me and looked at him and smiled.

"Have I ever told you how happy I am you moved here, Ray?"

"I don't think I remember you saying that to me."

"Ray, I'm so happy you moved to East 82nd Street. Thanks for always keeping your back door open for me." I laughed a little and took a sip of my tea.

"Did you catch flak from your girls for that one?"

"They had a little to say, but whatever. They're just jealous they don't have a man friend to talk to."

"Yeah, a man friend." He smiled.

We talked until the tea and Maxwell were done. Made promises to hook up at some point during the weekend.

I walked into the house to a ringing telephone. I took a deep breath, knowing it was either Johnny or Hayden on the other end. I answered through a yawn.

"Hello?"

"Did I wake you?"

"Umm," I said as I stretched and climbed into my bed. I looked at the clock on the night stand. It was close to four.

"I'm sorry. I called you earlier, but didn't get an answer."

"It's Friday, Hayden. I go out with my friends on Friday."

"Oh, yeah. Sorry, Baby. Go back to sleep. I'll call you later."

"Okay."

I clicked the phone off and slid deeper under my covers. I didn't check the caller ID or the answering machine. Right now, the only thing I cared about was getting some sleep. Whatever and whoever would have to wait until tomorrow. Or rather later on today.

CHAPTER 28

ALEX

"I can't believe you let what jar head over here said bother you enough to make you leave your wife. Have you lost your damn mind?" Ed was sitting on the edge of the chair in the den as Mike leaned back against the plush sofa I'd put in to replace the one that had gone over to the house.

"Jar head? Man, your head is three times the size of mine, so I don't know who you have the right to talk about."

"I'm also three times the man you are. Every single part of me."

"Fuck you, niggah."

"Man, that didn't have anything to do with it. I told you I'm not feeling the suburban life at all."

"That's right. That man has a right to want to live where he wants to live. Besides, as long as we've known him all he could talk about was getting a place on Park Avenue. Living across the street from Central Park and shit. You telling me because he got married he has to give that dream up? Told ya'll marriage is bad for your health. It kills your dreams and all."

"Marriage hasn't killed any dreams for Alex. He's lived that dream already. Now he's on to the next one."

The Jets game played in the background as we all debated over what *I* needed to do. Ed was definitely pro-marriage. He and Jen had been going strong for more than fifteen years. So he had a good track record to plead his case. While Mike, on the other hand, had nothing concrete to support his argument other than smart remarks.

"It's more than the living situation causing a problem. Yani needs to get her shit straight and then we can talk." I took a swig from the bottle of beer and balanced it on my knee.

"Get *her* shit straight? Man, please. Marriage ain't easy. You have to work harder on it than any other thing you'll work on in your life. You're talking like you're supposed to walk into it and live happily ever after."

"See, more work. I work hard enough on my job. Then to come home and work on being with someone I'm supposed to be in love with. That's exactly why I'm still single."

"Niggah, you still single because ain't no woman out there foolish enough to try and deal with you and your shit on a regular. You know, you're a lost cause."

Mike flipped Ed off and took bite off one of the numerous hot wings on his plate.

"I'm willing to work on things, but she has to be willing to do her part."

"Alex, I never thought I'd see the day when you'd listen to something this dumb ass niggah here has to say."

"I'm not listening to him. I'm listening to me." I poked myself in the chest for added emphasis.

Ed shook his head. "Tell me something, what have you solved by moving out the house? Has she given the baby over to this man? Has she been running behind you more? Is this the kind of existence you want?"

I left out the room and went into the kitchen. He was right. Nothing had changed. Yani hadn't come by or even called me. It was almost as if I'd been gone on a business trip for the past week.

Ed walked into the kitchen and stood next to me.

"I'm telling you this because you're my boy and we go way back like that. The first years are the hardest in a marriage. If you can make it through them…"

"I know. I know. But this first year has been harder than anything I've ever done. Seems like I'm always the one doing the compromising in this relationship. Man, I'm so tired of playing second fiddle to this cat. I thought once he was dead that would be end of it. If this is the kind of work needed to be put in, then I don't have it in me." I opened the fridge and pulled out another beer.

"I know at times it can seem like it's an uphill battle, but isn't that what life is? Everything you've ever wanted you've had to fight for. Getting out of the old neighborhood. Getting your feet in the door on a set. Even opening your own company was a battle. But you were willing to fight until you couldn't anymore for all of those things. You have to have that same determination about your marriage. Believe me, there's no more worthy opponent in the world than love." He slapped me on the back and walked out.

I knew something had to give, but I wasn't sure I was willing to be the one giving in just yet.

CHAPTER 29

ASIA

"I'm not moving to Brooklyn and that's that!" Johnny stormed off into the bathroom. Two minutes later I could hear the shower running. An indication he wouldn't be staying for the rest of the night. This behavior had become a common occurrence over the past few weeks. We'd argue about setting a date for the wedding and about who was going to give up their place and move in with the other one. I wasn't leaving Brooklyn and Harlem was the place he wanted to be. And at this point there was no in-between.

I snatched my robe from the hook behind the door and threw it on. I was vexed beyond the norm this evening. I could've gone out and done something I would've enjoyed, but no. He had some free down time from his all-consuming job and I decided to cancel my other plans to spend time with him.

I plopped down on the couch and grabbed the remote.

"I don't know what makes him think I want to move there. Hmph, he can hold his breath waiting on that shit." I flipped through the channels. It was only a few minutes after ten. The water in the bathroom went off. My eyes were focused on the TV screen. I had to do something to divert my attention, because my mind was screaming for me to go over to the door and let him have it the moment he opened it.

I settled on watching *Comic View*— a rerun I'd seen twice before. Needless to say, my mind wasn't into it, but my eyes were focused.

This argument about who was moving where had begun to affect our sex life. Affect it; hell it had stopped it all together. We were approaching a month and a half of celibacy. The only time Johnny and I went without touching each other before all this marriage stuff was... never! And as mad as I was at the moment, we could make another two months!

My leg began to bounce involuntarily. A clear sign I was about to blow up if I didn't figure out a way to let off some steam. I scanned the room in search of something to punch, throw, kick, or break.

Now you're being stupid. You don't break up your own shit over a man.

The dreams had started to happen again. Whenever I had to deal with any dumb shit with Johnny, my head got messed up and I would start to have those crazy ass dreams again. The one a few nights ago was bad enough to cause me to fall out the bed as I struggled to keep my head above water.

The click of the lock and waft of steam in the air preceded Johnny as he emerged from the bathroom. No sex at all, but he still felt the need to wash his ass.

"We feel better now?" I asked nastily.

He turned his head quickly as if I'd scared him. "Yep." He continued down the hall to the bedroom without another word.

Knowing I would say something I would regret in the long run, I got up and went out to sit on the porch. The cool breeze was a welcome relief from the heat that was boiling inside the apartment and me. I looked up at the sky and began to question my decisions in life.

If I had just been patient with Hayden from the get-go, maybe things would be different. We'd probably be married with a kid or two...

Stop second-guessing yourself. Things happen for a reason.

Johnny opened the bar door breaking me away from my thoughts. "I'll check you later. Maybe by then you'll calm down enough so we can have this discussion like two adults." He leaned in to kiss me, only to be given the side of my face. He stopped and looked at me, then slightly chuckled without his lips touching me at all. He stared at me for a few seconds before jogging off down the stairs and down the street to where he'd parked his car.

"An adult conversation? Oh, I'll show him how adult I am." What an oxymoronic thing to say with what I had on my mind.

❖❖❖

Just as he'd said a million times recently, the place was still in the same spot. Nothing about him had changed. His address and phone numbers were still the same.

"Why are you here?" I asked myself as I placed my finger on his doorbell. "There's no turning back from here," I thought out loud as I pressed down hard. I was ready to take this trip down memory lane. It had been a long time coming.

After a minute of waiting, I turned to leave and he opened the door. I turned back to face him. A few wisps of hair sneaked from the opened top buttons of his shirt. The smile in his eyes let me know he was pleased to see me. There was something there that said he knew why I was here.

"I hope I'm not disturbing you. You know it's unlike me to pop up unannounced, but..."

"You don't need an excuse. Come in." He stepped aside to let me pass. I hesitated a moment before finally walking in.

I scanned the room for any kind of changes. Anything that would give me a hint of the woman who had stopped our second chance. Any hints she had once made this her home. But there were none. Not even a picture in a frame. Everything was just as I remembered it when I last visited almost a year ago. The beautiful painting of the little black girl and boy he'd bought from Jilley the night we met was still in its place on the living room wall. The black leather furniture that screamed "bachelor" hadn't been touched. Not even the eggshell paint had been changed.

"Looking for something?"

I turned and looked at him. He reached out his hand and lightly stroked my cheek. There was no surprise when my body reacted to him. His scent. His touch. They brought something out in me I thought was long gone.

I had to be crazy, but something made me feel, at that moment, that was exactly where I was supposed to be.

"Why?" I whispered.

"Maybe because this is how it's supposed to be."

"But I have Johnny, and…" Hayden placed his finger to my lips to silence me.

"Right now you have me and I've got you and that's all that matters." He pulled me into him and kissed me and I melted like butter.

I didn't care about anything but what was happening at that very moment. I wanted Hayden to make love to me. Everything that ever went wrong between us was forgiven with one kiss.

He caressed me and traced his finger over my neck until he reached the base of my neck and released my hair.

"I haven't seen you with your hair this long since we first met." He ran his fingers through it as he lightly massaged my scalp.

"Asia, do you know how much I love you?"

"Hayden, make love to me. No questions, no regrets." I grabbed his hand and led him to the bedroom where I began the undressing process. With each button that was undone, my heart beat faster and louder. After we were completely nude, we faced each other. An old familiar feeling came over me, causing me to think back to our first sexual encounter. There was never any type of clumsy, uneasy feeling between us. It was if being nude in front of one another was the most natural thing in the world.

He pulled me to him, molded my body into his. His hand traveled the length of my back in rhythmic motions. I wanted this more than anything. Gone were any thoughts of Johnny or the ring I'd left on my nightstand. Maybe there would be regrets in the morning or even a few days after, but right then I wanted to feel Hayden inside me. His hands on every inch of my body. His lips on all my kissable places. And that's exactly what I got. He made love to me until neither of us could lift our heads. We were exhausted.

I strolled out of his place six-thirty that morning feeling as if I'd been totally and completely satisfied.

Things were definitely different now.

CHAPTER 30

I had missed the past two Fridays with the girls. Feeling a bit guilty about skipping out on them, I thought it would be a nice gesture to take them with me to an album release party. I received an invitation three weeks earlier inviting me to share in the celebration of the debut solo project of M.V. Atkins. They had sent over a demo a few months earlier and I couldn't wait to hear the rest of what she had to offer.

I'd been there about thirty minutes before I spotted Brina and Cheryl. I guess they'd worked on fixing Cheryl's spirits by bringing her back into the fold. She looked much better than the last time I'd seen her. I made my way across the room to greet them when I ran into Linda and Lucia.

"Hey, stranger." Linda hugged me.

I turned to Lucia and hugged her extra tight. "Hey, yourself."

"Why haven't you called me? You know Mama is not happy with Alex right now and neither am I."

"I don't want to talk about that tonight. Tonight, I just want to dance, have a few drinks, and spend time with my girls. Speaking of which, Brina and Cheryl are..." I pointed and was surprised when Asia walked in with Hayden. I looked at Linda, who had spotted them at the same time. She shrugged her shoulders.

Asia and I had gone about avoiding each other as best as we could in the office for the past few weeks. My sister was stubborn and I was feeling the same. I hadn't attempted to make up with Alex yet either.

We all made our way to the center of the room. I hugged Brina and Cheryl as Asia hugged the other two.

"Hello, Hayden. Now you're the last person I expected to see here." I looked at Asia and then gave Hayden a hug.

"Well, I was hoping to see you, Yani. Still looking good, I see. Where's your husband?"

At first I thought he was trying to be malicious with that remark until I noticed Asia jerk his hand and shake her head.

"Seeing that you haven't been briefed, Alex is…"

"Right over there." Lucia pointed to the door.

Like always, my husband walked in and his presence seemed to brighten the room. Looking as if he'd been ripped from the pages of a high fashion magazine, Alex commanded the attention of everyone without saying a word. I watched with a twinge of jealousy as he was approached by a female guest. Always the gentleman, Alex softly grabbed her hand and flashed his Hollywood smile.

"Aren't you going to go say hello, Yani?" Asia said as she nudged me with her elbow.

"No, I'm going to the bar to get a drink. Anyone want to join me?" Lucia looped her arm in mine and walked off with me.

"Have you even talked to him since he left?"

"Once or twice. He asked me about coming to visit him, but I'm not about to turn our marriage into occurrences of glorified booty calls." I shrugged my shoulders.

"My brother loves you, crazy woman." She laughed a little.

"Well, he sure has a strange way of showing it."

"Let's get you a Cosmo and me a White Russian. Maybe it'll help loosen you up a bit."

We patiently waited until we were granted the attention of one of the three bartenders and ordered our drinks. An up-tempo cut from the CD was playing in the background as people arrived and began to mingle amongst themselves.

I placed a couple of dollars in the tip cup as the bartender handed us our drinks. I gave him a gracious smile along with a thank you when I felt someone approach me from behind.

His familiar scent invaded my space before he ever said a word. I closed my eyes and braced myself as he leaned in close to my ear and said in a low voice, "So now I'm the invisible man?"

The hairs on my arms stood at attention from his closeness. I took a couple of deep breaths before turning around. His arms were planted firmly on the bar on both sides of me. I was missing him something terrible and I knew it was showing, no matter how much I didn't want to admit it.

"You looked busy when I saw you." I tucked my hair behind my right ear.

"I like your haircut. I always thought a bob would look really nice on you." He reached out and stroked my hair.

"Thanks. I've had it for about two weeks now." I took a slow sip of my drink and glanced around him in search of Lucia who had slipped away without saying a word.

"They've got a VIP room..."

"It's probably going to be as crowded as this room soon."

Without another word, he grabbed my hand and led me away from the bar until we reached a hallway. We walked to the very last door at the end of the hall. He knocked on it and listened for an answer before trying it.

"This is their office, Alex. You can't go busting..."

"I want to talk to you alone for a minute." The look on his face told me he was serious and the sooner we got this over with the better.

I walked over to the opposite side of the room. My arms crossed defiantly over my chest. As soon as he closed the door he was on me.

"Why haven't you returned any of my calls?"

"What calls?"

"Yani, don't play games with me. You know I called."

"Twice."

"This week."

"By the time I get home I'm beat. Between the kids, the business, and this court battle... I don't know if I'm coming or going lately; especially since I'm once again doing it alone."

"Alone? That's your choice..."

"I beg to differ with you, Mr. Chance. You're the one who left. I don't remember telling or asking you to leave."

He opened his mouth to say something, but didn't. I turned my back to him so he couldn't see the emotional turmoil brewing inside of me. Alex slowly came up behind me and slid his arms around my waist. He leaned in and kissed my neck.

"Baby, I miss you." His nose buried in my hair, he took a deep breath.

"I miss you, too, but the door has always been open, Alex. All of a sudden our living situation became more than you could stand. How do you think that makes me feel?"

"I know, Baby. I needed a change. And you weren't hearing anything I was saying."

"About what?"

"Let's not get into this here. For tonight, let's act as if the past few weeks never happened."

"Never happened?" I pulled his arms from around me and turned to face him. My hands were on my hips and my neck was in position. I opened my mouth to give him a piece of my mind only to have the words smothered out by his lips followed by his probing tongue as he slid it into my mouth.

I could feel the onset of his erection as he began to grind his midsection into me. As much as I wanted to hike my dress up and push everything on the desk to the floor, I pulled away. I was angry with him and he wasn't about to get off that easy.

"This doesn't make it better."

He ran his hand over his head and then over his face. "I know, I know. I'm tired of being at odds with you over this shit. Damn it, Yani. I miss you. I miss the kids."

"Then come home, Alex. It's plain and simple."

"But it's not. We still have some things we need to work out."

"Then let's work them out! The kids and I miss you, but we can't work on anything if you're not there. We need you. I need you."

His struggle was evident, but I still wasn't hearing it. In my eyes he had abandoned me. I know I contributed to some of the friction, but he left. So he needed to be the one to make it right.

"Look, let's go back out there and enjoy ourselves and then we can talk about this later. Deal?"

I nodded my head in agreement.

He pulled me into an embrace and kissed me again. This time it was soft and slow. The kind I liked.

"One more thing before we go."

I looked up at him.

"What's Asia doing here with Hayden?"

"Your guess is as good as mine. She and I haven't been seeing eye-to-eye lately. If it wasn't necessary for us to talk with each other in the office about business, I don't think we'd be talking at all."

Alex shook his head. "Damn, Baby, you mad with everybody now?"

The incredulous expression on my face told him volumes. "Me?!"

"Okay, okay. I don't know the entire story, but it seems like your shit list is growing."

"I'm going to forget you said that for now. But later on…" I gave him a knowing look, which said it definitely wouldn't be forgotten.

The night rolled along at an even pace. The guest of honor blessed us with her vocal skills and received a standing ovation for a set that was clearly on its way to reaching platinum status. Alex and I played our parts. He'd call me over to introduce me to someone and I'd play the part of the loving, happily married wife and then go back to whatever I was doing and he would do the same when I called him.

I'd been paying close attention to Ms. Asia and Hayden. The lovey-dovey act they were portraying had me wondering where my sister's head was. Was this the same man she swore she'd never give the time of day to ever again? I guess it didn't apply to nighttime then.

I was downing my third Cosmo when Alex came over to the table.

"Do you have any plans after you leave here?"

"Nope."

"Did you drive or ride with someone?"

"I caught a cab from the office."

He pulled me to my feet and grabbed my bag off the table.

"Goodnight, ladies," he said. They all responded likewise as they watched him lead me to the door and out to the street.

"Where are we going?"

"Have you ever felt unsafe with me?"

"No, I just…"

"Then trust me. You're in good hands." He kissed me softly on the lips. I smiled and enjoyed the feeling that lingered from his kiss and the effects of the alcohol.

A short cab ride later we were pulling up in front of his building. I waited on the sidewalk as he paid the driver, then followed him into the lobby. The doorman greeted us with the tip of his hat as he walked over to help the woman entering behind us. We rode in silence up the elevator to what was his former, but now present living quarters. He unlocked the door and waited for me to enter.

"You want something to drink?" he asked nervously and rightly so. I'd avoided coming over there since he'd left. It was definitely the alcohol that had me making unwise decisions that night.

"I think I've had enough to drink for one night."

I scanned the room. He'd done a bit of redecorating. Gone were the heavy curtains and deep, dark-colored walls. The place kind of had a South Beach feel to it with the light-colored walls and large, white baseboards. The new curtains drew your attention to the windows and the beautiful view. The entire apartment seemed to be more open and airy.

"I did a few changes."

"I can see." I walked over to the window and glanced down at the park. The New York City backdrop was beautiful. The lights from the various buildings and street lamps from the park. A smile crossed my face. Alex slid up behind me.

"See, Baby. It's beautiful here. You're close to shopping. The kids would be attending some of the best schools the city has to offer. Plus, you wouldn't have to worry about that long commute to the office."

"Why did you buy the house in Brooklyn if this is where you wanted to be?"

He was quiet for a moment. "I thought it would make the transition easier on the kids."

"And what has changed from then to now? They're used to being in

Brooklyn. They've made friends and they like their schools. Why change now?"

"Because I feel like I'm suffocating there. I'm losing my creative edge. I'm not thinking or functioning the same."

I turned around so I could look him in the eyes.

"Yani, there's something about the city that makes me tick. I'm not ticking anymore, Baby. Can you understand that?" He leaned in and placed his forehead against mine and closed his eyes. "I won't pressure you. But give me tonight. I miss you, Baby, and I want to make things right between us."

I placed my hands on both sides of his face and kissed him with all the passion I had. He would have tonight and then we'd talk tomorrow morning.

CHAPTER 31

ALEX

Waking up to Yani had made going out last night worth the hassle. I'd been avoiding events for the past few months, but once I ran into Drake and he told me they'd gotten back a confirmation from my wife about attending, I knew I had to be there.

I slowly eased out of the bed, trying not to wake her. I wanted to surprise her with breakfast, but remembered today was shopping day so the pickings in the kitchen were very slim. There had to be something in there I could whip up. The four strips of bacon and blueberry pancakes would have to do.

I carefully placed everything on the tray and took it back into the room and was surprised when she came out of the bathroom fully dressed.

"Are you leaving?"

"Oh, that's so sweet of you, but I really need to get home to the kids." She seemed distant. Not the same woman I'd made love to last night.

"The kids will be fine for another hour or two. You hired a sitter for last night?"

"No. Nat is looking after the boys for me. She's old enough to handle them."

"Exactly. So what's the rush?"

"I've been gone all night. I don't want Corey to wake up looking for me and…" She looked at me. Without a word I walked back into the kitchen and plopped the tray on the counter. The dishes rattled a bit. I quickly grabbed the plates and started scraping the contents into the trash.

"You could've still eaten, Alex."

"Fuck it. Go on and do you." I continued what I was doing.

"And what's that supposed to mean?"

"Exactly how it sounds." I placed the dishes in the sink and quickly brushed past her.

"Alex, right now my situation is volatile, with this hearing coming up and all. It's bad enough I stayed out all night." She came in the room behind me.

"You were with your fucking husband! What's so bad about that?"

She was thrown back by my outburst and stood stock still for a moment.

"I'll give you a call…"

"Tell me something, Yani. What was last night about? Huh? I mean, you come home with me and fuck my brains out all night and now you've got to run home before someone sees you?"

"Just because we had sex last night doesn't mean things have changed between us. You're the one that left, not me, Alex. Nothing has changed. The phone number, the locks. All of it is still the same. Don't think a lil' make-up sex makes it all better."

"For better or worse. For better or worse. When the hell are we going to get back to the better?! Seems like there's been nothing but worse since that motherfucker came out of hiding."

"Like I said, you're the one who left me *again*. I didn't leave you." She searched in her purse for her keys.

"Here I am thinking we'd get a chance to spend the day together and you're up and ready to bounce."

"I've got to see about the kids, Alex. Corey…"

"Have you listened to anything I've said?! His uncle wants him! Give him his sister's child and move on! Why do you have to hold on to shit forever?!" I shook my head and turned my back to her as I slid my shirt over my head. "I regret ever telling you to meet with that bitch. If I hadn't he would've been with his mother and we wouldn't be going through this shit."

"So you're saying we would be better off if he had died with his mother and sister?" She narrowed her eyes and they were now fixed on me.

"That's not what I meant…"

"Then exactly what is it that you meant? 'Cause that's what it sounds like to me."

"I give up." My hands raised above my head I walked into the living room.

"You do what the fuck you have to do and I'll do the same. I can't deal with this shit any more." I slightly bumped into her on my way to the door.

"Oh, so now you're trying to knock me down or something?"

I turned and looked at her. "If I was, you would be." I walked out the door and slammed it. Knowing she would more than likely be on my heels, I slid through the exit door for the stairs and jogged down four flights before coming back in to catch the elevator. I wasn't about to get into a screaming match with her, causing a scene for the neighbors. That shit went out with Taylor.

I was relieved when the elevator arrived on that floor as soon as I pushed the button to summon it. I got in with the other passengers and hurried out as soon as the doors opened in the lobby. Still being pushed along by my anger, I rushed across the street and into the park. I kept running until I reached the jogging trail. Running had always been the one thing that helped to clear my head and right now it needed clearing more than ever.

The conversation played over and over in my head. The way she kept saying *again*. As if leaving was what I was good at. I thought of the promises I'd made to everyone; especially the kids.

Promise you'll never leave or hurt her...

I began to think of what could've been done or said differently. No matter what I thought of now the damage was done. Words out of your mouth couldn't be taken back. Even if you apologized for saying them, the hurt would always be there.

I ran until I was exhausted. After collapsing on a bench for a quick rest, I got up and started making my way back home. I knew Yani would be long gone when I returned. Dripping with sweat, I jumped in the shower. The hot water was a welcoming friend. Thoughts of what I was going to do were still plaguing my mind. Was I ready to give up this uphill battle that was my marriage?

The phone began to ring. I took my time answering it.

"Yeah?"

"Hey, Alex. It's Carmen."

I closed my eyes and let out an exhausted gush of air. Yani had probably hit the speed dial on her cell phone as soon as I walked out.

"I'm not calling to start anything up. Just hear me out."

"I'm listening."

"I'm on your side. Yani has taken this thing with this baby too far. She should give him to his uncle before he becomes too attached to her and his leaving becomes a psychological problem for him to deal with. He's already lost his family and his uncle has more rights to him than Yani. On top of it, it's causing problems in your house. I don't want to see you guys going through this. You've been through enough as it is."

"Tell your girl this."

"I have been. Look, while I am on your side, you haven't made things easier either. Running away doesn't make things better."

"I didn't run away!"

"Leaving is running, Alex."

"Yo, Carmen..."

"No, hear me out, Alex. I know you feel you don't need to be preached to, but sometimes hearing things from someone who's looking at it from a distance helps."

"Speak your peace then."

She hesitated before talking. "I know how you may feel about living in the city and all, but you're a parent now. And as parents we sometimes have to forfeit our feelings and dreams for the betterment of our children."

"Living in the city would be better for the kids to me."

"How do you figure?"

Once again I explained about the school system in the area being better. How they'd be exposed to more cultural things being right in the city. How the benefits of growing up in the area would be good for them all around.

"Have either of you sat down and asked the kids what they wanted to do?"

"Carmen, when we were coming up, did we have a say in what choices our parents made? Hell no. Between the ages of four and six my parents moved us around a total of seven times. One of those times we went to another country. Ask what we thought? They never sat down and explained what was going on. My sister and I would come home from school and the house would be packed up again. And after all that, we still ended up back here in New York."

"But that was then. Our parents didn't know any better because it was all they knew."

I laughed. "When it comes to finances and stuff of that nature, yes, I'll go with all the excuses of our parents not knowing any better. As far as upbringing. These kids now are worse off than we ever were. If we, as parents, would instill some of the disciplinary actions our parents did to us on our kids, the rate of kids committing crimes would be down and a whole lot of other things would be better. Kids aren't even scared of their parents anymore." I stopped before I started to sound like I was preaching.

"Well, we all have different opinions on discipline."

"I guess you feel I don't have enough experience as a parent yet to give mine."

"I didn't say that."

"You didn't have to. Anyway, I'm about to get up out of here. I respect you calling and all, but you need to talk to your girl. She's out of control."

"Out of control? How so?"

"Give Asia a call and ask her. But yo', I do appreciate you reaching out. Tell Bryce I'll give him a holler later."

"Bye, Alex."

I clicked the phone off and walked away from the window. My clothes were laid out on the chaise in the bedroom. I hadn't seen the kids in a minute and decided it was time for me to keep my promise to them at least. If their mother wanted to act silly, let her. I wouldn't let her keep me from being a good daddy to them. After the fucked up job the first one did, they at least deserved that much.

CHAPTER 32

ASIA

I'd been avoiding Johnny which wasn't hard to do since he was involved in a new case. The whole situation was getting tired to me and caused me to get bold in my dealings with Hayden. I knew Yani and everyone were going to trip when they saw us together, but I was in my "*I don't give a damn*" mode.

Everything was going well right up until the moment we were leaving. Of all people for me to run into, she was the last one on my mind. I damn near didn't remember her, but she took care of that.

"Ah, isn't your name Asia?" She gave me a look that said she should've been a familiar face to me. Her head stuck out away from her shoulders and slanted to the side a bit.

Hayden had just walked off to get the car, planting a kiss on me before he did and I knew she saw it.

"Yes. And you would be?"

"Tonya."

I tried to remember where I'd met her before, but nothing was coming to me at the moment.

"You know, JJ's co-worker. From the picnic."

Yes, that bitch. I guess she expected me to get jittery and nervous, but my motto is, "never let the other bitch see you sweat."

"Oh yeah. Now I remember you. I guess you're working an off duty tonight. Makes me feel a bit safer with you on the job." She was damn near getting a view of all thirty-two as I gave her the biggest phony smile.

"I bet you do. Uh, where's JJ tonight? That didn't look like him I saw with you earlier, unless my eyes are going bad." She had a smirk on her face that said she had the dirt on me.

"While I'm not quite sure where he is this very moment, the last time I talked to him he was working. But I'll make sure to tell him I saw you and you said hello."

"Don't worry, I'll do it myself."

I saw Hayden at the corner and decided she wasn't about to get a peep at the tag so she could do a full report.

"Well, enjoy the rest of your night, Tanya."

"It's *Tonya*. Oh, and believe me, I will."

Without another glance I walked over and got in the car.

"Where to now?" Hayden asked.

I glanced out the window one last time to where Tonya stood with her cell phone to her ear. The expression on her face was one of victory as she excitedly talked to whoever she was sharing her find with.

"Let's go to your place." I knew mine would be out of the question.

❖❖❖

"What's up with you and Hayden?"

"Nothing."

"Looked like a whole lot more than nothing last night."

"What's up with you and Alex?"

"Alex is my husband, Asia. So, being with him isn't wrong. You're the one walking around here wearing a ring from the next man and hanging out with the ex-man."

"Now if that isn't the pot calling the kettle black."

She rolled her eyes. "Stop comparing me to you. My circumstances were much different than yours."

"Why are you so worried about who I'm fucking anyway?"

"Excuse me then. I don't want to see you get hurt, is all."

"I don't need you to worry about me. I think I've been taking care of myself just fine, long before you got here. What you need to worry about is getting back with *your* man. Out here trying to do the right thing by Jarrin still. That shit is so played out. I don't blame Alex for booking."

Yani got up and grabbed her coffee and her purse.

"When you're ready to talk like adults, give me a call." She walked out of the coffee shop, leaving me sitting at the table alone.

Fine then, I thought. I don't need her. Her shit smells worse than mine right now. And what is with everyone telling me when I want to talk like an adult?

I pulled my cell phone from my bag and dialed Hayden. I'd gone home long enough to take a shower and change and then was out the door again. Johnny had left a message on my voicemail asking me to give him a call. I turned my cell off last night as soon as I'd gotten in the car. I still wasn't ready to deal with him and whatever his Amazon ass girlfriend had told him.

"Hey, let's go for a ride today," I said as soon as Hayden answered.

I could hear the smile in his voice as he agreed. After telling him I'd be there in an hour, we hung up so he could get ready. My cell phone rang. I checked the caller ID and saw Johnny's name and number. I pushed the button to send it straight to voicemail. Today wouldn't be the day I was going to deal with it either.

The next call I made was to Ray.

"Speak to me, beautiful."

"Hey, Ray, it's Asia."

"I know."

"Can you do me a favor?"

"Sure. What's up?"

"Can you look out the window and tell me if Johnny's car is outside anywhere on the street."

"Uh-oh. Someone hiding out?"

"Something like that."

"Give me a few and I'll call you right back." We hung up and I walked out of the coffee shop. Book in hand, I made my way up the street to where I'd parked my car and prayed it would be ticketless when I got to it. It was Sunday so you could get away with parking situations a bit more than during the week, but there was always that one cop who took their job extremely serious regardless of what day it was.

Five minutes later my cell phone rang. It was Ray calling me back.

"No sign of the detective on the block, but I did see him late last night when I got in going up to your place."

"Damn," I said under my breath.

"Is there a spat brewing?"

"I'm not sure. Thanks though. I'll see you later."

"Hey, wait a minute. You need me to do anything? Give him a message if he comes back? Tell him you're gone out of town for the weekend or something?"

I smiled at the sweet gesture. "That's okay. I'll deal with it another day. Thanks for looking out though."

"Told you. I'm always looking out for your best interests."

"And now I see."

❖❖❖

The ride landed us in New Jersey. We were down to the last days of summer and this was a beautiful day to be outside. We walked along the boardwalk and talked.

"Did you enjoy yourself last night?"

"Last night was nice. Real nice," I said and smiled as I looked down at my feet. The nice breeze blowing in off the ocean felt so good, I wanted to find a chair and relax.

"Where are we going with this, Asia? Is this some kind of get back at Hayden scheme or do you see this really becoming something again?"

I stopped and looked at him and then back at the ocean. "I'll be honest, Hayden. At first you were the last person I wanted to see or talk to. You really hurt me."

"I know. I know. But that's in the past. I'm trying to make things right, but you're the one with another man's ring on your finger."

"I'm not wearing it now." I wiggled the fingers on my left hand in front of his face.

"You haven't returned it to him either. So you're in limbo. I don't want to share you, Asia." He grabbed my hand. "And I'm talking about this thing being serious between us."

We started walking again.

"Give me time, Hayden. I want the same thing, but you have to give me enough time to figure out how to break things off with Johnny without any hard feelings being felt between us."

"How much time do you need?"

"I don't know."

I looked back down the boardwalk at the row of hotels we'd passed and would have to pass again to get back to our room.

"If I were to ask you to run off to Vegas with me tonight and get married, what would you say?"

I was caught off guard by the question. I'd told Yani I would prefer to run off to Vegas and get married than deal with trying to put together a wedding to make everyone happy.

"Now you want to marry me again?"

"I've always wanted to marry you. Don't you know that? You've always been the one I wanted to spend the rest of my life with."

"I, I don't know if we're ready for all that." My shoulders went up and down.

"I love you, Asia. I've never stopped loving you."

"I love you, too, Hayden, but I don't think this is something we need to do. At least not right now."

He smiled at me. "Feel like Italian tonight?" he asked.

"Mark Anthony's?"

"Yep."

I looked down at the sundress I was wearing.

"They're used to tourists and you look really good in that."

"If we can get in there, sure."

After a hearty meal of risotto di arogosta, an Italian rice and lobster dish, Hayden and I went and tried our luck in the casino for a couple of hours before retiring to the suite he'd gotten a really good rate on for us.

"You must come here often," I teased as I slid the polo over his head.

"Remember, I travel quite a bit for work," he answered in between the hot, heavy kisses we were sharing.

In no time we were on each other. I couldn't get enough of him being inside of me. I wrapped my legs tightly around him and held him there.

"Stay right here," I pleaded as the tears rolled out the corners of my eyes and spilled onto the pillow.

"I'm not going anywhere, Baby," he panted as he held me close to him.

The tears represented both my pleasure and my pain. I was in love with two different men and had no clue as to what I was going to do about it.

CHAPTER 33

YANI

An entire week had passed since the blow-up with Alex. He'd come by the house the same day to get the kids, but I'd stayed upstairs avoiding him. I was a bit skeptical about him taking Corey after his comment, but Corey would've been heartbroken if I would've made him stay while the other two were allowed to go. The fact that Alex took him softened my heart a bit. I knew he meant well, but it seemed he was only thinking about himself lately.

It was Monday and a new week at the office. I'd managed to hook up with Drake over at All or Nothing Records to talk about us doing some promotional events for M.V. Atkins. Her CD was holding down the number one slot in my disc changer in the car, office, and home. Xposure definitely wanted to be on board this sure thing.

"Mrs. Chance?"

"Yes?"

"Cornell Nelson is on line two for you."

I took a deep breath to steady myself. "Put him through."

Cornell had come up Friday to get Corey for a visit that would last a week. Court ordered, I had no choice but to let him go.

"Hello, Cornell."

"Good morning, Yani."

"How's Corey?"

"Jay is fine. We're just getting back from visiting with my wife's family in Tennessee for the weekend. He had a really good time with the kids." We were both quiet for a moment.

"Can I speak to him?"

"I called you exactly for that reason." I cringed as he called him his full first name. I knew he was doing it to purposely irritate me.

"Jarrin, Ms. Yani is on the phone for you."

"Hi, Mommy Yani," happily came through the receiver.

"Hi, sweetie. How are you?"

"Okay. I was playing with my cousins and Uncle Cornell said he's taking us to a big park today." He continued to tell me all the details of his trip that his four-year-old memory could recall. He sounded so happy.

"So you're having a good time?"

"Umm, hmm." I knew his head was nodding up and down as he said it.

"That's good."

"Brandon is calling me. I'll talk to you later."

"Corey," I called out, but he was gone.

I could only imagine the smirk on Cornell's face as he watched Corey lay the phone down. I hung up.

There was a knock on my door.

"Yes?" Angie walked in with a folder in her hand.

"Good morning, Yani. I need you to sign these for me. I would've asked Asia, but she hasn't come in this morning."

"Don't worry about it." I reached out for the folder.

Angie hadn't looked up from the folder until I asked for it.

"Are you okay?"

"I'm fine. I had a sneezing attack right before you came in. I'll go over these and get them right back to you."

"Okay. Um, it's for the Carrolton account that Asia was working on. His event is next weekend and I needed to get them couriered over to him for final approval."

"I got it, Angie." The only reason she was still standing in my office trying to give the details was to see if she could get anything out of me about my sister.

Asia hadn't been in the office at all the week before. Johnny stopping by every other day to see her only piqued the interest of the gossipmongers. Angie being the biggest of them all.

"When Asia gets in, I'll let her know you took care of this for her."

She stood for a few seconds longer. I glanced up from the papers and gave her a questioning look. She finally got the hint and left. She couldn't be stupid enough to think I'd talk about my sister's business with her. Even though I didn't know what was going on myself I still wouldn't discuss it with her.

Around eleven Alan buzzed me to let me know Asia had arrived. I thanked him and hung up and called her.

"Yes?"

"I need to see you for a minute."

"Okay."

Our operation wasn't a big one—ten employees at the most. We'd down-sized the office in Florida. Other than Carmen there were two other girls who helped her handle that office. I offered those who were interested a chance to move to New York when I opened this office. Alan, who had been nothing more than an office helper, signed on and was promoted to my dutiful assistant.

"What's up?" Something about her seemed to glow.

"It's nice to see you. Now would you like to tell me what the hell is going on? Or should I tell you?"

"Tell me what?" She plopped down in the chair.

"Where should I start? Let's see." I placed my finger over my lip and pre-tended to be thinking. "You disappeared without a trace. No one knew where you were or how to reach you for an entire week. Then Johnny came by here almost every day looking for you. So, I'm thinking he's gotten whiff of your dealings with Hayden."

"Did he say anything when he came by?" The nonchalant look was replaced with the slightest of worry.

"Nothing to me. Just asked me to have you call him when you got in."

"Oh." She relaxed again.

"What's going on with you? Where have you been? I know we're disagree-ing right now, but damn, Asia, you're still my sister." I sat back in my chair and waited for her answer.

"We can talk about it later. Just know that I'm happy right now. Well, I will be."

"And who or what can we thank for your impending happiness?"

"You'll know everything Friday when we all get together."

"I have to wait an entire week to find out?"

"What's going on with you and Alex? Or is that subject still off limits?"

"Nothing is going on with me and Alex. Have I talked to him? No. So, there isn't much to tell." I folded my hands in front of me and looked at her.

"What's going on with your case?"

I thought about the short conversation I'd had with Corey earlier. "He's in Atlanta with his uncle." She could see the cloud of sadness in my eyes.

"Yani, I know you don't want to hear this, but he belongs with them. This guy is his uncle. The last living link to his mother. If something were to happen to you, I would fight anyone I had to tooth and nail to get Nat and Jay. So, my empathy is on his side. Maybe you should sit down and think about it that way."

I'd never thought about if something had happened to me how I would feel about someone keeping my kids away from my sister. It was a known fact she would be there. For the first time in months I was seeing how wrong I was.

I needed to make a call.

"Have these couriered over to Carrolton's office. Angie brought them in," I answered before she could ask. "Oh, and thanks."

"What are sisters for?" She winked at me.

"Now we need to get things on track. And by things, I mean everything." I got up and hugged her before she walked out the door.

Everything is going to be fine.

CHAPTER 34

ASIA

The morning was crisp and clear. One of those gorgeous end-of-summer days. The thought of playing hooky from the office even crossed my mind until Hayden reminded me I'd already missed an entire week.

"Didn't you tell me last night you had a few things you needed to take care of?"

"Yeah, you're right." I begrudgingly got out of bed and before I knew it, we were climbing on the train headed to lower Manhattan. Hayden worked in one of the many offices housed in the south tower of the World Trade Center.

"You know how much I love you?" he asked right before he turned to go up the escalator that would take him into the building.

"Umm. Yes, I do."

"I like the sound of that. Say those words to me again."

I smiled. "I do. I do. I do."

He gave me a long passionate kiss and then he was gone.

I walked into the Krispy Kreme to get a doughnut and a cup of coffee. It was still pretty early so I could pretty much take my time before heading to the office.

Things are going to be fine, I thought as I went over in my head what I was going to tell Johnny once I met with him later today. I'd been hiding out with Hayden long enough. It was time to deal with the situation and move on.

I heard what sounded like a screaming engine from a plane flying too low. "What the hell?" My coffee ended up on the sidewalk as I turned and watched in shocked amazement as a jet plane flew over me headed straight for the north tower of the World Trade Center. Everything seemed to be frozen in time as I watched the plane sail into the building and disappear. The explosion, followed by smoke and a flurry of paper, were the first evidence this was not a dream. The next was the glass and metal that rained down causing everyone to run for cover.

I ran as fast as I could to find shelter. People who had an eyewitness view were crying and hugging one another as others collapsed to their knees in disbelief. What had started out as a beautiful calm day was in the first stages of a living nightmare.

The first thing that finally registered in my head was to call Hayden. The street was beginning to fill with the evacuees from both buildings. I dialed the numbers as fast as my trembling fingers would dial. He picked up around the fourth ring.

"Asia?"

"A plane! It flew into the other building!"

"Okay, Baby. Calm down. We saw it. I think it was an accident."

"No, Hayden! It was aimed at the building!" I could hear a voice on the PA system in the background, but couldn't make out what it was saying.

"Oh my God!"

"What's wrong?"

"People are jumping!" As horrible as the scene was I couldn't turn my head. The gruesome sight and sound of imploding bodies after they hit the ground would forever be embedded into my brain.

I could hear the voices, but I couldn't focus on the faces of the people around me.

"They're telling us this building is secured and we should stay put. We're safer here than out there."

"Baby, you should leave," I pleaded with him.

"Stop worrying. They're saying it's okay. I'm looking at the television in the break room and even the news is saying it was an accident."

Just then my phone went out. I pushed the redial button until I was able to get him back on the line.

"What happened?" he asked as soon as he picked up.

"The phone went out. Hayden, I'm going to go across the street and wait for you to come down."

"Okay, I'll meet you over there."

"Hayden…" Another screaming engine caused me to look in the direction of the building he was in.

"I love you, Asia." The loud boom was followed by a huge ball of flames.

He'd shown me numerous times before exactly which floor he worked on and without counting, I knew the point of impact was in the area of that floor. My cell phone hit the sidewalk and shattered into pieces. I was still as a statue in the middle of what was pure chaos. I began to tremble. I couldn't believe what I'd just witnessed.

"Come on, lady. It's not safe here," I heard someone say and felt them pull me by my arm. People were crying and running for cover. I felt like I had on cement boots as I was dragged along. We headed north to Broadway and joined the crowd of onlookers. Time seemed to stand still as people stood outside their cars and on the sidewalks watching in horror as everything unfolded. The sound of sirens surrounded us. The police and firemen went one way while everyone else retreated in the other. My mind raced as I tried to figure out what to do next. The guy I'd been following continued on when I stopped so I was on my own.

"We're under attack!" someone screamed out.

Just then there was a deafening sound and a quake.

"It's going to fall!" The inevitable was unfolding before our eyes. A cracking noise pierced the air as the floors above the fire seemed to shift and sway. I felt as if I had on weighted boots as my heart sank and I watched the concrete avalanche along with the steel and glass that had held it all together tumble in on itself. An unidentified chorus of high-pitched screams filled the air. Fear was visible on the surrounding faces as the soot and dust raced through the narrow valley-like streets. Before we could react it was barreling down on us.

"Run! It's coming this way!"

I forgot about the three-inch heels I'd worn to be cute for Hayden that morning. My life seemed to flash before my eyes as everything went dark. The sound of shattering glass and screaming people were muffled out with the roar that bellowed through the buildings. I felt a hand pull me inside a door and down a hall.

"Oh, Hayden!" I cried out. I felt an arm go around my shoulder.

"Shhh. It's going to be okay." I looked over at the lady who comforted me. We looked as if we'd been dipped in a barrel of flour. People were helping each other all around me. White, black; it didn't matter. We were all people trying to survive this madness.

As the air started to clear we slowly emerged from the building. We forged on a little further but were forced to find cover a second time as the north tower fell. The great exodus out of the city began as everyone sought safety. And Manhattan was unsafe at that moment. People were crying everywhere and speculating about what had happened and what would happen. One thing we all knew for sure was this was no accident.

I walked in the throng of people headed across the Brooklyn Bridge. There were buses waiting to collect those of us who had made it safely across to take us to wherever it was we were headed. I sat on the bus in a complete daze, unable to bring myself to believe any of the morning's events. I prayed it was one of my crazy dreams—I'd wake up and it would be all over. This time it was for real. It was late evening when I reached Canarsie and I barely had the strength to climb the stairs. Mrs. Brand, who had been standing guard in her front door, came out and grabbed me in a tight hug. I collapsed into her and cried the tears I didn't have time to shed earlier.

"Oh, my Lord. You were down there? Come in here." She guided me into her apartment. "Thurman!" she yelled as she led me over to the sofa. Her robust frame supported mine as if I were a featherweight. "Thurman, this child has been hurt."

Mr. Brand rushed into the room.

"Asia?"

"Get her something to drink, Thurman."

"I'm okay," I said between sobs. "I need to get upstairs."

"Come on. We'll help you." They both stood on either side of me. My shoes were still clutched tightly in my hand. When they opened their door Ray was standing there ready to knock.

"I've got her," he quickly volunteered and moved in to collect me. I was relieved to see him and wrapped my arms around him and cried into his shoulder.

"I saw it. All of it."

"Come on. Let's get you upstairs and cleaned up."

"I need to call my sister. Please, Ray. I lost my phone and I need to call my sister." I was close to hysterics now. I'd been numb from the moment the plane hit Hayden's building. Not once had I thought to check on Yani and her family or any of my girlfriends and now I needed everyone accounted for more than ever.

"Okay, okay. Once we get upstairs I'll take care of everything."

Ray helped me up the stairs and pushed me off into the bathroom while he called Yani. I looked in the mirror and burst into tears. The layer of white dust had streaked down my cheeks from tears. My hair was in disarray. I broke down, slowly sinking in a heap to the floor. Hearing my cries, Ray came in and gathered me in his arms.

"It's going to be okay. I talked to your sister and she's coming right over. I'll run you some water and you can bathe and get all of this stuff off you." He rocked me back and forth. Brushing my hair away from my face.

At that point I thought things would never be okay again. My world had crumbled when that plane hit the south tower, but it was only the beginning.

CHAPTER 35

YANI

I was one of the millions of viewers glued to the television that morning. Fear raced through me as I watched the second plane slam into the south tower. I ran to get my phone and dialed Alex. I'd talked to him a few days earlier and remembered he'd said something about going to the World Trade Center, but I wasn't sure which day. It was hours before I was able to get him on the phone and by that time I knew just from the conversation it would be a long road ahead of us.

He was supposed to be at the meeting by 8:30 that morning, but he was running late. "My mother wouldn't let me get off the phone. She wanted me to promise I'd make things better with you." His voice sounded hollow and distant.

"Don't worry about it, Baby. Why don't you come here? I'd feel much better if you were here with us."

"But Ed..." He muffled a cry and my heart sank. I hadn't thought to ask if anyone else in his office was going to the meeting with him.

Ed was on time as usual. Trapped on the 107th floor of the north tower, he'd called to let Alex know how much he appreciated him not only being his friend, but his brother. No matter how Alex tried to reason with him to try and find a way to get out, Ed knew he wasn't going to make it and was okay with it since he'd gotten the same call from his wife right before.

Employed at a law firm, she was also trapped above the floors on fire and called to let him know how much she loved him and always would.

"He said there was nothing anyone could do. How thick the smoke was."

"Alex, Baby, come here to the house." I choked on my tears.

"I can't. They've shut down everything."

"You can get out. They're showing on the news, people coming across the bridges."

"I'll try."

"I need you right now, Alex. I'm afraid. The children are afraid."

There was a long pause before he promised to get there and hung up.

It would be three hours before he would arrive, but he was there. While he wasn't in much shape to protect us, I was glad he was safe and felt safer as I curled up in bed with him and cried.

Asia was a wreck by the time we made our way over to her. Without asking, Alex was up and in his shoes from the first mention of her name. Her neighbor had been nice enough to phone me and let me know she was asking for me and she was in pretty bad shape. She'd been an eyewitness to the whole thing from the moment it started. I took a deep breath before entering her room where she was curled into a tight ball staring at the wall. I sat on the side of the bed and rubbed her back.

"I'm here, sweetie."

Her body was racked with tears as she went into everything. I'd been bracing myself for the worst when she told me about Hayden.

"Yani, it was awful," she said as she described the chaos she'd experienced.

At a loss for words, I continued to stroke her back and listen. The phone rang.

"Hello?" I asked.

"Asia?!"

I instantly recognized Johnny's voice.

"No, it's Yani. Are you okay?"

"If you're asking if I'm hurt, I'm not, but I lost quite a few of my friends today."

"I'm sorry to hear that. We've all been touched by this unnecessary madness."

"Is your sister there? I've been trying to reach her on her cell."

"She lost it. She was there… by the Towers when it happened."

He sucked in a deep gush of air. "Is she okay?"

"Not really. She's an emotional wreck and she's got a few cuts and bruises."

I looked at the bandages Ray had placed over the minor scrapes she'd gotten on her arms.

"The phones are ringing off the hook here and I don't know when I'm going to be able to leave. Is she in the mood to talk?"

I knew she wouldn't be but wanted to at least give it a try. I pulled the phone away from my ear and leaned in and told her he was on the phone. She shook her head no and kept staring at the wall.

"Johnny, maybe you should try later. Right now she needs to get some sleep."

"No problem. Look, I need to get back to work anyway. Are things okay with you? Everyone accounted for?"

I listened to Alex flipping through the channels in the living room.

"Yeah. We're all fine."

"Well, be safe and I'll try her later."

After saying goodbye I hung up and went into the living room with Alex. He looked up as soon as I came down the hallway.

"Is she okay?" he asked full of concern.

"A few scrapes, but she's in good shape physically, but not mentally." I slid down on the sofa next to him and placed my head on his chest. Instinctively he draped his arm around me.

"How can people be so cruel? What did any of these people do to them?" I asked as we watched concerned family members, pictures in hand, trying to locate their loved ones. The loop of the plane hitting the south tower and the collapse of both towers played over and over.

"Nowhere is safe anymore," I said more to myself than anyone else.

❖❖❖

The next few days would prove to be crucial ones in the city of New York. People everywhere were preaching about getting back to normal, but what was normal anymore?

I'd coaxed Asia into coming home with me so we could look after her. Her fragile state-of-mind concerned me and I wondered if I should give Dr. DeVaughn a call.

"How are you feeling today?" I slid the tray of food on the nightstand. I was surprised to find her sitting up. For the past three days she'd done nothing more than cry and sleep.

She took a deep breath and shrugged her shoulders.

"Johnny's been calling you. He's busy with all that's going on, but he's concerned about you."

"I married him, Yani."

"Who? Johnny?" I thought the lack of nutrients was making her delusional.

"No." She looked up at me through tear-filled eyes. "Hayden. We snuck off to Vegas last week and got married. He asked me and it felt right."

I didn't know what to say. I wanted to ask her about her engagement to Johnny, but the extent of her grief had just gotten deeper. They'd finally gotten it right and now he was gone. I eased in closer to her and hugged her tightly.

"You'll get through this. I promise." I gently rocked her back and forth.

"Yani, I'm sorry for being such a bitch lately…"

"Shhh. We were both going through something, but none of that matters now. Nothing matters but getting you better. Getting everyone better." I thought about Alex and his restless nights. He hadn't been able to bring himself to go into the office. He'd gone over to the apartment yesterday to get a few things he needed.

"You need to eat something." I got up and grabbed the tray and placed it on the bed next to her.

"I'm not really hungry."

"Girl, if you don't eat something you're going to wither away to nothing and I can't have that."

"Mommy, Grandma's on the phone." Nat handed the cordless to me and kissed Asia on the cheek before leaving.

"Yes, Ma."

"Is she doing any better today?"

I looked at Asia. "Somewhat. She's sitting up. Now all I have to do is get her to eat."

"I know it doesn't seem safe, but I'll get there the best way I can, if you need me to."

"No, Ma. Right now we don't know what's going to happen next. You stay put. If we really need you, I'll give you a call."

"Do you think she feels like talking?"

I placed my hand over the mouthpiece. "Asia, Mama wants to talk to you." She slowly rolled her head in my direction and lifted her hand for the phone. While she answered with umm-hmms and unh-unhs, I got up to go check on my husband. I was surprised to find him up in our bedroom getting dressed.

"Where're you headed off to?"

He turned and looked at me and pulled his T-shirt over his head. "I'm going over to the city. I've been hiding out long enough." He continued to dress.

"You're not hiding out." I smiled, trying to make sense of what he was talking about. I'd been wondering since he'd gotten here when he would leave again.

"Yani, I need to go see."

"See what? A pile of rubble? Death? Destruction? That's the only thing down there. They're saying the air quality is so bad down there that people are getting sick."

"Baby, I'm a New Yorker and will always be a New Yorker. It's in me. I'm not going to be like everyone else walking around here, shell-shocked and shit. No one and nothing will ever keep me from *my* city." He looked me dead in the eyes.

"So you're leaving again?"

"I love you, Yani. With everything I have in me. I've never loved anyone the way I love you."

"But you love *your* city more."

"I didn't say that."

"You didn't have to." I walked out. I was too worn out to fight. Especially what seemed to be a losing battle. I loved Alex, but I was scared. I was scared enough to move the hell out of New York at that moment. Something I had been thinking about quite a bit lately.

CHAPTER 36

ASIA

I sat with Yani as her lawyer went over the settlement of the custody case. She'd called Cornell and told him she finally understood. All she asked was to be able to see Corey and have a small role in his life. Maybe get him for a week or so in the summer and be able to have him one of the major holidays. He'd agreed. Said he never had any hard feelings toward her. He simply wanted what he felt was his right by birth. Since every other right he was owed had been taken from him as a child, he wouldn't let another one go without a fight.

Yani had plane tickets for her and the kids to go to Atlanta to see Corey so she could take him his things. The kids were a little scared about flying, but Yani assured them they were safer now than before 9/11. With all the armed gunmen at the gates and the new check-in procedures, you couldn't get on with a pair of nail clippers, let alone a box cutter.

"You sure you don't want to come with me?"

"I'm sure. It's time for me to get my life back together."

"Have you talked to Hayden's family about a memorial service?" She finished placing the last piece of clothing in the luggage and zipped it closed.

"His mom said whatever I decided to do was fine with her."

"How did she take it about you guys running off, getting married, and not telling anyone?"

"She was happy. Said I was his one true love and she knew he was happy when he died."

Died. It still didn't sound real talking about Hayden in such a way. The finality of it was like a hard slap in the face each time I thought about it.

I went to his house the other day and expected him to be on the other side of the door when I opened it.

After weeks of lying around Yani's house I decided it was time to face my realities. I called Johnny and left a message asking him to meet me so we could talk. He told me he couldn't make any promises, but he'd try to make it over this evening.

He himself was dealing with a great loss. He'd known quite a few of the officers and firefighters who'd perished in the towers. One in particular, he'd been pretty close to him and his family. They'd gone to high school and then the academy together. He was godfather to his son. So, he'd been spending as much time as possible with his family to help ease their pain.

Knowing the grief I was going through over Hayden, I thought it was a noble gesture. It sure helped having Ray to talk to when I couldn't take it. He was the one person other than my sister who knew about me and Hayden being married.

"Is Alex going with you?"

She gave off a dry laugh. "He's too busy loving his city to care about what's going on with me." She came and sat on the bed next to me.

I grabbed her hand. "I know you're feeling shorted, but I understand how he feels, Yani. At first I wanted to run. I even thought about going back home and you know that's a stretch. But when I thought about it I asked myself, why was I running? I've been here too long to think about any other place as home. Am I scared? Hell yeah! I lived it. But I also know if it was my time to go, I would definitely be gone. I had too many close calls to know it wasn't time for me to leave this place. And before 9/11 I knew I was going to die here in New York, so why leave now?"

"Well, I've only lived here for a year. So, my love for the place isn't that deep."

"Is your love for Alex that deep?"

She looked at me. I could tell she was going to start misting up.

"I know it doesn't feel like it right now, but his love for you is deep enough to leave, but he would feel like a coward if he left now. Under different circumstances, he'd follow you to Kalamazoo. Go to him, Yani."

"I'm always the one that's going."

"So what? You stayed still and what did it get you? Not a damn thing. So get up off your ass—again—and go be with your husband. He's only trying to give you and these kids a good life."

"If life is so good across the bridge, why were you fighting Johnny tooth and nail about moving to Harlem?"

"Harlem and Park Avenue? There's no comparison. Besides, I wasn't fighting the move. I now know it was much deeper than that. I'm not a church-going person, but I do believe God has His hands in everything and things happen for reasons. I was meant to marry Hayden."

"But you said you loved Johnny."

"And I do—did. But I loved Hayden more. I loved him even when I didn't want to. The same way you feel about Alex. Tell me this, if Alex had made it to the meeting that morning, would you be sitting here with a heart full of regrets?"

She clasped her hands together and leaned into them. After a few tears and then a deep breath, she picked up the phone and dialed Alex.

I took that as my cue to leave. It was well after four and Johnny had promised to stop by around seven if he was able to.

At eight-fifteen I got the feeling he wasn't coming. In need of some friendly conversation, I walked down the backstairs two floors below me and tried Ray's door. True to his word, it was open. I called out to him.

"I'm coming out the shower, but make yourself comfortable!" he yelled out from the bathroom.

I walked into the living room and scanned over his CD collection. He had one pulled halfway out as if he was about to play it, but got pulled away to something else. I pulled it out and smiled when I saw Yolanda Adams. She was one of my favorite gospel singers. I went over the titles on the back, but one in particular stood out to me.

"In The Midst Of It All." I opened the CD and placed it in the player. As I listened to the lyrics of the song, I couldn't help but think this song was made especially for me. Lately I'd been through many trials. Some harder than others, but no matter how hard they were, I made it through. Losing

Hayden had been the hardest of all, but I knew I was going to make it through. Just like the song said, the Lord was there to keep me on that day and would do so on many others. He'd kept me in the midst of it all.

I thought about the pettiness I'd been going through with Yani the past month and how unimportant any of that stuff was now. Because in the midst of it all, my sister had been the one I wanted. The first person I'd asked for when I was about to come unglued. And without any type of hesitation she was there.

The more Yolanda sang, the more tears ran down my face. Unlike the tears I'd been shedding for the past month, these were tears of joy. I was unexplainably happy at that moment. It was as if all my sorrows had been washed away. I knew I would be fine again.

"You okay?" Ray asked when he found me in the middle of his living room crying and laughing. I'd almost forgotten I was at his place. The song had gone off and was on to the next one.

"You know, I think I am." I walked over and gave him a big hug. We held on to each other what seemed like an eternity.

"Good to have you back," he said as he stepped back to look at me.

"And it's good to be back."

CHAPTER 37

ALEX

I was sitting on the balcony looking out at the city when I was buzzed
from downstairs to let me know Yani was down in the lobby. I waited
for her to arrive on the elevator. When I saw her red eyes, I prepared
myself for the one thing I feared most.

"Look, it's really not…"

"Can I come in first?"

I stepped aside and let her in. She took three steps in, then spun on her
heels and faced me. The wringing motion she was doing with her hands
was a signal she was nervous, which also made me nervous.

"When are you leaving?" I asked without much feeling. I'd dreamed she
left the night before.

"We leave tomorrow, but…"

"Tomorrow? Damn, just like that? No fair warning?" My heart raced.

"Well, we promised him we'd come for a couple of days."

"What?" I asked confused.

"I'm going to Atlanta to take Cornell the rest of Corey's things and spend
a little time with him."

"You're going to Atlanta?"

"Yes. Where did you think I was going?"

"I thought… Never mind." I waved my hand at her.

"Alex, I love you. I don't want to fight anymore. If being in the city is
where you feel you need to be, then that's where I want to be, because being
with you is all that matters."

I looked at her, a bit confused by what was going on. Here I had been expecting her to come and tell me she was leaving, but she was doing exactly the opposite. I walked closer to her.

"I love you, too, Baby. And I was thinking that if you really want to stay in Brooklyn…"

She placed her finger to my mouth. "I've called an agent and the brownstone is on the market. This is where you need to be, so this…" She placed her hand on my chest. "…is where I want to be. Besides, I've done my research and I know the schools in the area *are* really good; like you said. There's plenty here for the kids to do. Outside those doors is a world of education, culture, and experiences they'll love us for in the long run."

I pulled her in my arms and gave her a long, deep kiss.

"I promise I'll make every day an adventure."

"You better."

I looked her in the eyes and then guided her by the hand into the living room. I sat down on the sofa and pulled her onto my lap. Her arms were around my neck and her head was against mine.

"You know, I thought about Ed and Jen. How they never had any kids. Now they're both gone and there's nothing to keep their bloodline going."

She sat up and looked at me.

"I know the possibility of us having a baby is slim to none, but there's still a chance it could happen. With all the madness going on in the world now I'm not sure I want to bring a child into it. But there's still that part of me who wants to hold a little someone with my blood running through him or her." I looked at her to gauge her reaction. Tears were forming in the corners of her eyes.

"There's nothing I would love to do more than give you a child. But what if we can't?"

I swiped the tears away. "Don't worry, Baby. It was just something I thought about."

"Legally Nat and Jay are yours."

"I know." I smiled and hugged her to me. Yeah, I knew I'd legally adopted them and they now had my name, but it wasn't the same.

"Hey." She sat up and turned my face to her. "If it's meant to be, then it'll happen."

"Well, can we at least get back to trying?" I nuzzled her neck. Placing kisses in places I knew would have her squirming.

"Umm hmm," she moaned. "I think we can handle that."

CHAPTER 38

ASIA

September 11, 2002

Gathered at the spot that had been named Ground Zero, I sat through the ceremony marking the one-year anniversary of the day that had been forever burned into the memory of all who were old enough to have a memory. Many had come to share their stories. Most of them sounded the same. We'd all lost a loved one. A friend.

I looked over at Yani and Alex. Nat and Jay were at their side. I looked over to Ray who had become my rock of Gibraltar.

Oh, I know you're wondering what happened with Johnny. True to her word, Amazon bitch called all around town until she was able to contact him. And after all of that he still didn't end up with her. Come to find out he was putting in overtime with the widow of his fallen friend. And he wasn't the only one caught up in the love triangles that had begun to surface. There had been many stories about women who were losing their husbands to a widow of a fallen officer.

I realized I was never cut out to be an officer's wife. The long hours and risks were more than I could handle. The reasons behind the bad dreams I was having.

We're still friends though. I'm not going to say he took the news about me marrying Hayden lightly, but we worked on it and he began to understand. He even came to the christening last month.

Yes, there's been an addition to my branch of the family tree. Haydee is the most precious thing in my life. So, Hayden had left his mark in this world after all.

"Want me to hold her?" Ray asked. I handed over the gurgling bundle of joy.

It had taken some time, but Ray had finally convinced me to take our relationship beyond that of friends. Yes, my friend who became my lover was now my husband. While he knew the baby would carry Hayden's last name, he said he loved me enough to make sure she would be brought into a happy and stable situation. He'd stepped into the role of father with ease. As I once heard someone say, it takes a hell of a man to raise another man's seed. Ray is that and more.

"Ready to go?" I turned to him and asked.

"Whenever you are." He pulled Haydee's bag up on one shoulder as he cradled her in his arm.

"You want to put her back in the stroller while we make our way through the crowd?"

"I'll hold her." He placed his hand around me and guided us out.

I looked back once more at the place where magnificent buildings once stood. Where Hayden's remains—which still hadn't been found and probably never would be—were entombed. The dreams had stopped once I made the decision to be with Hayden. Our love had been real and for that I was grateful.

As we drove uptown to Yani's I thought about how the past year had affected all of our lives.

Brina, who also worked in the south tower, was running late for work that morning. Her alarm clock didn't go off. More than half of the people who worked in her office had been on the list of the missing. It took her over a month to come out of her apartment. Another two to find a new job.

The travel industry was hit hardest and Linda's was one of the many agencies that ended up closing. She'd lived off her savings for the first six months while she worked on a new plan. Part of that plan was her new man, Yohan, who she had been seeing for four months now. He was everything Derrick wasn't, which scored him more cool points with all of us than he could count. Where things would go with them? Time would tell. But right now she was putting her life back together.

Lucia had lost a few of her childhood friends, but it seemed everyone who'd lived in the city had lost someone or knew someone who'd lost someone. She'd gone to more funerals during that time than she'd been to her entire life. Unlike her brother, she talked about leaving every other day. Even went as far as going to North Carolina for two months. But there's nowhere like New York and she found this out and quickly returned.

Ray circled the block looking for a good parking space.

"Right there," I pointed out.

Haydee began to squirm around in her car seat in the back.

"I think someone is getting hungry." My breasts began to throb. It was if she had control over them.

"Everyone should be here by now," I said as I climbed out the car. Ray was already retrieving Haydee, placing the carrier in place on the stroller. I grabbed the baby bag, which doubled as a purse now.

"Ready?" He held out his arm for me.

"Yep." I hooked my arm through his and we strolled up the block and around the corner.

"What would you say to us moving into our own place?"

I glanced over at him. His sight fixed straight ahead.

"I was talking to my father and he told me about a brownstone a friend of his bought, but he's fallen into some financial trouble and now he's trying to unload it. It's in Fort Green. I know you're going to want to see it first and right now it's not in the best condition, but between me and my father, it'll be the best house on the block." He went quiet as I tried to register what he'd just said.

I'd always said I never wanted to leave Brooklyn and Fort Green was definitely a Brooklyn neighborhood.

"Does this house have a yard?"

"It does. And I think it has about five bedrooms, but I was thinking of knocking down a wall or two to make a master bedroom suite."

"A suite?"

"Yep." We came to the entrance of the building. The doorman held open the door for us and smiled. We said our hellos and got on the elevator.

"Maybe we can go see this house later on. When we leave here." I looked over at Ray who had a slight grin on his face.

"I haven't said yes to this yet." I nudged him on the arm. He pulled me to him and kissed me as the doors opened to the floor. "Are you going to tell the Brands we're moving?"

CHAPTER 39

ALEX

"I've got it, Baby. You need to sit down and take it easy." I shooed Yani back into the room where the other guests had gathered. I opened the door and gave Asia a kiss and Ray a pound.

"Is she sleeping?" I peered into the carrier at Haydee, who seemed to be preoccupied with chewing on her fist.

"She's hungry," Asia said as she slipped her jacket off and placed it in my hand.

"You can go into our room for some privacy." I draped the jacket across the sofa with the others and helped Ray put the stroller in the hall closet out of the way.

"Is everyone here yet?" Ray asked as we walked into the room with those who were here.

"Not everyone. We're still waiting on Brina and Linda to get here."

Yani waddled over to us and gave Ray a hug.

"Where's my baby?"

"Asia's in the room feeding her. You know if she doesn't get her hit of tit she'll put those lungs to work."

We all laughed.

"Where is she?" Yani went out the room to search for them.

"She's in our room," I called behind her.

She nodded and continued down the hall.

"How's she doing?"

"She's good, man. We've got less than two months left, so I'm happy about that. We're all happy about it." I laughed.

"I know what you're talking about. Asia was miserable the last two months. All she did was complain about the heat and how much weight she'd gained. How she couldn't wait to get her body back."

"Yani isn't that bad, but the cravings are driving me crazy. I made a run to Brooklyn twice in one week for cheesecake. Down to Veniero's three times for a strawberry shortcake. Let me not forget the countless trips across the street to get her a pretzel or hotdog from her favorite vendor. I'm surprised she hasn't blown up like a blimp." We both laughed.

"Who's a blimp?" Yani asked as she came into the room with Haydee in her arms.

"No one," I said and kissed her on the cheek.

"No one? Okay. Don't think I don't know you were talking about me. I heard you say Veniero's."

I placed my arms around her and rubbed her protruding middle. In two months we'd be the proud parents to what we hoped was going to be a healthy baby. We'd decided to be surprised instead of finding out the baby's sex. I'd been secretly praying for another boy though. But either way was good with me.

"Honey, look at how big she's getting." She held Haydee up and let her bounce up and down on her belly.

"That's your cousin in there. Yes it is," she said as Haydee did what any other three-month-old would do—smile and coo.

"Where's Mama, Yani?" Asia asked as she said hello to the handful of people who were with us.

"She's lying down in the room."

"Hey, Ms. Asia." Carmen came over and gave her a hug. "Let me see this pretty baby," she cooed as she reached down and grabbed Haydee from Yani.

Haydee smiled and cooed as she continued to go from hand to hand. I watched and thought about Hayden not being there to enjoy this. How she would one day grow up and learn the story of her biological father. How he had lost his life the day the world came to a halt.

"You okay, man?" Mike asked as he walked by me.

"I'm good. What about you?"

"I'm good." He nodded his head and blew a kiss to the new love of his life. Yes, Mr. Marriage-Ain't-For-Me had decided to settle down.

I slapped him on the back and went to answer the door.

"Hey, Alex." Linda and Yohan had arrived.

"Hey, lady. Everyone is in there." I took their jackets and placed them with the others.

"Daddy, when are we going to eat?" Jay had come out from a PS2 marathon.

"In a minute. Why don't you go get your sister? I think we're about to get started." He ran off to find her.

The doorbell rang again. This time it was Brina.

"Hey, Alex," she said as she leaned in and hugged me. "Sorry I'm late."

"You're on time in my eyes."

We walked into the room with everyone else.

"Are we ready to get started now?" I asked.

Everyone quieted down and looked at me. I went to the center of the room and took my place.

"I'd like to start by thanking each of you for finding the time to come here with us today. As much as we'd like to forget about the horrible day a year ago that changed our lives forever, I decided to celebrate the lives of the people we loved and lost. I myself lost my best friend. So, in honor of him, his wife, and all the others, I establish this as the first annual day of remembrance." I went to the mantle and lit on of the many candles that had been placed there, one for each person we'd lost. Yani followed behind me and lit her candle for Jen. Asia lit her candle for Hayden and everyone continued until every candle had been lit.

The screen dropped from the ceiling and the movie started playing. I'd gotten together with a few friends and put together a short film documenting the lives of our loved ones. There wasn't a dry eye in the room when the credits rolled up the screen.

"That was so nice, Alex." Everyone came over to congratulate me.

I was proud of everything we had accomplished in the past year. My marriage was good, we had a baby on the way, and my creativity was back strong. Nat and Jay had adjusted very well to the move. Nat had even been able to attend a few classes at NYU Film School that summer. She had even worked on the production of the short film.

As I watched the people mingle and eat I thought about Ed. He would've been proud of me and all I had accomplished.

"I'll never forget," I said and swiped the tear from my eye.

I'll never forget you, man.

CHAPTER 40

YANI

December 31, 2002
11:45 pm

"Y ou really bounced back after this baby. You sure you didn't go to the plastic surgeon for a little help?" Carmen smiled at me as we stood around waiting for the clock to wind down.

"You're funny. This is from a lot of exercising and breast feeding." I placed my hand on my hip and struck a sensuous pose for her.

"What are you ladies talking about?" Alex asked as he slid up behind me.

"I was complimenting your wife on how good she looks. You would never know she'd just had a baby a few weeks ago."

He rocked me from side to side a couple of times and then kissed the back of my neck. "Doesn't she look good?"

"What time is it now?" I asked.

We all looked at the illuminating clock hanging from the ceiling, which had been an added feature in this year's décor.

"I wonder how your mom is making out with lil' Eddie." Carmen smiled.

"She'll be fine. I gave her enough breast milk to last for a week and she has Nat and Jay with her. They compete with each other to see about the baby when we're home."

"Yeah, that's now. Wait until he gets mobile and starts to get into their things and in their way. It'll be a whole different story then."

Alex laughed at us and hugged me tighter.

Edwin Alex Chance was born November 19th at two in the afternoon. It was a known fact that Alex would want to name his son after his friend. And all that time I was thinking Ed was short for Edward.

"Hey everybody!" Bryce said over the music. He handed out the glasses of champagne in his hand to each of us.

I looked at the clock again and saw we had ten minutes to go.

"I think this has been a very good year," Alex said to us as we gathered in a circle.

"Very good," Carmen added.

"Where's Asia and Ray?" I looked out on the dance floor where Alex was pointing.

Ray had proved himself to be above and beyond what a good man was. He was more than Asia could've asked for. He'd stepped up and into places other men would've run from. Taking on another man's child, dead or alive, is not an easy feat, but Ray did it as if Haydee had been his seed. Even Hayden's family loved him.

Asia's life had changed in more ways than we could've imagined also. I'd been afraid of how my sister, who'd been used to only dealing with her own needs and wants, was going to deal with motherhood. But she was a natural.

I was surprised when she took my suggestion to name the baby Haydee. It was the name of one of my good girlfriends and I thought it was perfect.

"Is there a glass for us?" Asia asked as she and Ray joined our circle. We were now down to less than five minutes.

"Here you go," Bryce said and handed her his glass and went off to get two more for him and Ray.

"You two love dancing," I said to Asia and Ray.

"Girl, it's been so long since we've been out we're savoring this lil' bit of freedom."

"You guys are probably going to have to send your mother to a day spa to recoup after tonight."

We all laughed at Ray.

It was now one minute and the countdown was on. Bryce walked up with the champagne and handed a glass to Ray.

"Well, people. As we were saying earlier, this has been a very good year. Two new babies. A new marriage." Alex tilted his head towards Asia and Ray. "I say we toast to friendship and love."

"To friendship and love," everyone said.

"Ten, nine, eight…"

"Well, Baby. Here we are again."

"Yes. In the same room. In the same spot."

"Five, four…"

We stared at each other. Both thinking about the first time we'd kissed three years before.

"One! Happy New Year!" everyone yelled.

I stepped in closer and tipped up so I could reach his lips. "I love you, Alex Chance."

"I love you, Yaniece Chance."

We brought in the New Year with a passionate kiss like we'd done for the past three years.

Everyone around us was singing and cheering as we seemed to be lost in our own world.

"Break it up. Go upstairs and get a room," Asia said.

"Mind your business!" I yelled at Asia over the loud music.

The DJ put on "Let's Dance to the Drummer's Beat" and it was on.

"Soul Train!" someone from the dance floor yelled out.

We all placed our empty glasses on the nearby table and headed out to the dance floor to take our place in line.

Yes, life had been really good to us and would continue to be. As I watched Asia and Ray dance their way down the center of the line, I smiled. You can never predict what your life is going to be like. Or even who you'll spend it with.

As I joined my husband at the opening of the line to dance our way down, I let up a silent prayer of thanks.

Thank you for making all things right in my world. For keeping me in the midst of it all.

ACKNOWLEDGMENTS

It's pretty late and I'm trying to summon my last bit of brain power to complete this book and get it turned in. There are so many people to thank that I'm afraid I'll forget someone. If I happen to, please forgive me. You were lost among the jumble of characters trapped in my head.

As always, I'd like to thank my maker for making me into the woman I am and bestowing me with life, love, and creativity.

My children, Calina and Ramzey, the most precious gifts a mother could ask for. Thank you both for being excited about everything I do. Know that I love you both and I am always in your corners.

My mother, Dorothy Jean Rathwell; my brothers, Lance Rothwell, Brian Rothwell, & Mario Rathwell; and my sister, Sheri Duhart; my nieces and nephews; my sister-in-law, Denise; my aunts & uncles; & all of my cousins; the Rothwells, Harrises, Robinsons, Walkers, Monroes & Cheeks. Thank you to all of you for being the supportive unit you have proven to be time and again.

Michelle V.—Girl, these have been some times. Thank you for helping me to see what it means to be a true Sister-friend. Thank you for your ears when I need a listener, your mind when I need a mental boost, your wit and quirky comebacks when I need some laughter, and your heart when I need a lil' sisterly love. My only prayer for you is that all your hopes and dreams become a reality. You and Cookie have been a Godsend and I love you both dearly.

Zane—for opening doors and for being so patient and understanding with me. You are heaven sent for more reasons than I can say. For giving me the extra push I sometimes need. And for making my dreams a reality. Your friendship is a treasure I keep close to my heart.

Charmaine P.—For being everything and all things needed for Strebor. From editor to publicist. No matter how full your plate is there is always the sound of smile and patience in your voice. Thank you for making this journey as smooth as possible.

Lolita F.—Thank you for planting the seeds of possibilities deep within my being and encouraging me to write no matter how long it takes. For you I am forever grateful.

Pamela C.—For your friendship and advice. Your words are ones I think of often.

My friends—Chiquita Thomas, Sonja Kennedy, Marlina Williams, Della Mayo, Lorraine Gilbert, Camille Jenkins, Onita Sanders, Nikki Jewell, Camille Hartley, Haydee Osario, Robbyne Kaamil, Marvella Nesbitt, Irene Jackson, & Traci Aveni. Thanks for being in my corner and supporting me.

The Gibsons, Duggans, Jacksons, Wests, Bells, Nesbitts, Pooles, Williamses, Ousleys, McKinneys, Cheekes, Try Diggs, Jewells, & Samantha Green & Family. Sistahs-N-Spirit—Betty Dowdell & Kristine Hollis, Shunda Leigh of Booking Matters, I.A.M., Euphoria, Onyx, Sister Chat, Sister Girl, God's Reading Ladies, RAWSISTAZ, Circle of Friends, BookTalk, Nubian Sistas, Pam Marshall and the Crew at Barnes & Noble in Oakwood Plaza, Hollywood, Florida; The Broward County Library System, Romero Review (Alvin), ReadInColor, the ladies of GAAL, and all the readers who took the time to email me. Your encouraging words make this process worth it. Remember, KEEP READING!!

To the writers I have met along the way, Eric Jerome Dickey, Nathan McCall, Leslie Esdaile, Kim Roby, Tonya Oliver, Maryann Reid, Robert Roots, Michael Gainer, Hallema (who I've known forever), Van Whitfield, Jacquelin Thomas, J.D. Mason, Darrien Lee, Daaimah S. Poole, Franklin White, Trista Russell, Kendra Norman-Bellamy, all the writers of Strebor (we have grown in numbers) and the many others who have crossed my life.

Warren—while I may not say it often enough, you are appreciated. Your support in every way is the most important of them all. Thank you for allowing me to lead sometimes. (I know, I know, it's the majority of the time…lol) I love you.

ABOUT THE AUTHOR

Shonda Cheekes is the author of the novel *Another Man's Wife* and two short stories—"Lessons Learned," featured in *Blackgentlemen.com*, and "Silent Suffering," which appeared in *Breaking the Cycle*, all published by Strebor Books. A native of Miami, Florida, she now lives in the Metro Atlanta area with her husband and two children.

SYNOPSIS OF

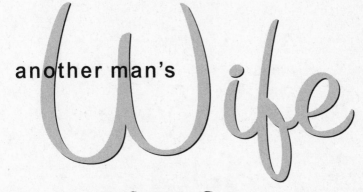

another man's Wife

BY SHONDA CHEEKES

PUBLISHED BY STREBOR BOOKS INTERNATIONAL

When Yaniece Fenton married Jarrin Miller, she thought it would be forever. But without warning, her husband of fifteen years has disappeared without a trace. After five years of hoping and praying for his return, and at the urging of her best friend, Carmen, and her sister Asia, Yani makes the decision to end her miserable existence and start living again.

Alex Chance is a prominent New York businessman who's grown tired of his current girlfriend's love of spending his money. In search of a change, Alex starts to look for that special woman with whom he would like to settle down.

After meeting at a mutual friend's party, their powerful attraction leads to a whirlwind courtship and a fairytale-like wedding. But their happy ending is threatened by the sudden reappearance of Yani's first husband. As Yani learns the whys behind Jarrin's actions, she is forced to deal with overwhelming feelings that she thought were long gone and begins to question her current marital status. Is she in fact *Another Man's Wife*?